Praise for
BLOOD LAW

"Another new voice makes a compelling debut in the urban fantasy genre. . . . Holmes gives every indication of being a promising new talent with a great future ahead!"
—*Romantic Times Book Reviews* (4 stars)

"Fast-paced and full of action, the story never flags, from the discovery of the first body to the exciting [and violent] finale. The characters are fascinating and well developed, but plenty is left for the future: this has excellent potential as a series."
—*Booklist*

"The author maintains a high level of suspense and nonstop action throughout the narrative. . . . Urban fantasy fans will savor this wonderful new addition to the genre, and this reviewer eagerly awaits the sequel, *Blood Secrets*."
—Bitten by Books

"A page-turning debut thriller with a strong female lead—who happens to be a vampire— Jeannie Holmes's *Blood Law* is a unique and compelling paranormal police procedural, spiced with believable relationships, a wholly original vision of the vampire, and a strong statement on crimes of intolerance. Whether you like police procedurals, paranormal thrillers, or just a damn

good read, you'll love *Blood Law*—and develop a blood-craving for the next book in the series."
—KELLI STANLEY,
award-winning author of *Nox Dormienda*
and *City of Dragons*

"The Southern Gothic atmosphere in *Blood Law* seductively pulls you into a sultry world of vampires, ghosts, and bonds that run deeper than death. Holmes's original take on the vampire mythology will leave you hungry for the next book."
—REBECCA CANTRELL,
award-winning author of
A Night of Long Knives

"*Blood Law* shimmers with the mystical, dark energy of the undead—passionate, violent, and sexy as hell."
—LAURA BENEDICT, author of *Isabella Moon*

"Alexandra Sabian, a take-no-crap Enforcer with the Federal Bureau of Preternatural Investigation, battles racist humans, angry vampires, and enigmatic ghosts in her quest to bring a vampire killer to justice in this delightful debut. Scary, funny, and sexy, *Blood Law* is worth sinking your teeth into."
—BEKKA BLACK, author of *iDrakula*

By Jeannie Holmes

Blood Law
Blood Secrets

BLOOD SECRETS

An Alexandra Sabian Novel

JEANNIE HOLMES

BANTAM BOOKS • NEW YORK

A Bantam Books Mass Market Original

Copyright © 2011 by Jeannie Holmes

Published in the United States by Bantam Books, an imprint of The Random House Publishing Group, a division of Random House, Inc., New York.

BANTAM BOOKS and the rooster colophon are registered trademarks of Random House, Inc.

ISBN: 978-0-553-59268-9
eBook ISBN: 978-0-440-42333-1

Cover design: Jae Song
Cover illustration: Kris Keller

Printed in the United States of America

www.bantamdell.com

9 8 7 6 5 4 3 2 1

Bantam Books mass market edition: July 2011

For Mom

acknowledgments

No matter how much we want to delude ourselves into believing writing is a solitary practice, no writer is ever truly alone. Most have at least some form of support system that acts as both a cattle prod and a security blanket as necessary. I am no exception. With that in mind, I would like to thank the host of usual suspects.

Thanks to my fabulous agent, Marian Young, for her enthusiasm, encouragement, and unwavering support. I can't properly convey her awesomeness in this limited space.

A thousand thanks to my editor, Shauna Summers, for her sparkling personality, keen eyes, and boundless patience. Words can't express my gratitude for all your hard work. Many thanks to all the hardworking individuals at Ballantine Bantam Dell who helped make *Blood Secrets* a reality. I may not know all of your names, but I'm humbled by your support and passion.

Extra-special thanks to Vicki Pettersson for being a good sport and letting me immortalize her in the pages of this book.

I've made no secret of the fact that the past year has

been a difficult one, and I can honestly say I wouldn't have survived had it not been for the dedication and love of some very special people. My eternal thanks and love always go to my family and my friends who kept me from completely losing my mind. There are a few special people to whom I would like to pay special thanks because they went above and beyond to help me keep it together and see this book published: Carolyn Haines, Michelle Ladner, Alexis Lampley, Kelli Stanley, Rebecca Cantrell, Ron O'Gorman, Theresa B., Debi, Miki, Raven, Skitty, and Theresa A. All of you saw me at my best and my worst, and you stuck by me. *Mahalo.*

Finally, to my husband, Mark . . . You're still here, and you amaze me. I love you.

BLOOD
SECRETS

prologue

NO MOON SHONE IN THE SKY WHEN HE DUMPED THE
body. He hardly recognized the mangled mess before
him as the vibrant young woman he'd known, even
though their affair had been brief. Hair the color of
darkest flames turned black with dried blood. A dull
silver film encroached on the sparkling blue of her eyes.

Her jaw was marred by a dark smear as he traced its
gentle curve. He pulled back and stuck his thumb in his
mouth, coating his tongue with her blood. An electric
charge jolted his spine. Memories that were not his
own flickered through his consciousness, playing scenes
from her life on the movie screen of his mind, until the
film stopped in a crimson moment of violence.

The rags he'd used to wipe down the trunk and hide
his fingerprints fell from his hand and greedily absorbed the blood pooling beneath the remains. Using
his elbow, he slammed the trunk closed, blotting the
macabre view from sight.

A falling star streaked across the glittering sky. He
closed his eyes and made a wish he'd made a thousand
times before. The vision of his wish coming true filled
his mind.

"Soon." His whisper sliced through the silent night
like a blade. Without a second glance at the trunk-
turned-tomb, he walked away.

one

ALEXANDRA SABIAN SEARCHED THE HALL OF RECORDS for clues that would lead her to a killer. The only problem with her search was that she had no suspects, no witnesses, and the body had been buried for forty-one years.

Her father, Bernard Sabian, had been murdered in the spring of 1968, when she was only five. Someone had left his staked and beheaded body in a cemetery near her childhood home.

Simply because he was a vampire, like her.

At least that was her theory.

In the two weeks since she'd discovered she could access the Hall of Records—a metaphysical storehouse for the memories and experiences of every man, woman, and child who'd walked the face of the earth—she'd been searching through the records, trying to locate her father's. She hoped once she did that she would uncover the clues she needed to find his killer.

It wasn't an easy task she'd set for herself, considering her father was a lost soul, one of the wandering spirits who roamed the neutral zone between the physical and spirit realms. He claimed he'd chosen his fate, had traded his passage to the spirit world in favor of remaining in the Shadowlands. She couldn't—she *wouldn't* accept that her father would willingly condemn himself to an eternity of unrest and was determined to give him the peace he deserved.

And her quest began in the Hall of Records.

Crystals housed in a black granite access terminal projected the large screen before her. Names scrolled by in one column while the adjacent column held a series of numbers showing the location of a door that led to that person's memory.

She hadn't actually tried accessing anyone's memory yet. The thought of viewing a stranger's most intimate recollections made her skin crawl. It was a violation of the worst order. However, if it helped find her father's killer, it was an issue she was willing to work around.

The screen flashed from white to red and bold black letters appeared: ACCESS DENIED.

"Damn it," Alex muttered and dropped her head into her hands. Every time she sought her father's name she met the same result. Varying the combination of search parameters hadn't worked either. Perhaps his records truly were lost.

Sighing, she looked around the Hall. It had transformed since the first time she'd entered as a result of her experiments to manipulate this "reality." What had been a single endless hallway had become a huge ornate multi-level rotunda. Countless doors lay hidden in shadows on each level of the massive round building. Large golden Corinthian-style columns supported each level, and she craned her neck to count ten floors before darkness consumed the topmost levels. Although moonlight streamed through a circular opening in the apex of the rotunda's unseen dome, none of it reached the lower levels. The only light came from the screen in front of her and the softly glowing crystals beside each door.

"All I need are some crickets chirping in the background," she said to no one in particular. She turned her attention back to the screen, ready to try a different approach to her search.

Somewhere in the distant shadows overhead, a door opened and closed.

Alex jerked, reaching for a sidearm she didn't possess. While she'd known others could access the Hall, she'd never been present when it happened. Forcing herself to relax, she waited to see if someone appeared or if she heard footsteps.

No noise broke the silence. No one showed themselves.

"Hello," she called. "Is someone there?"

Only her echoed voice answered.

Frowning, Alex peered into the gloom overhead. Had she imagined it? No. She could feel unseen eyes watching her and sense a presence lurking in the darkness. A feeling of familiarity tickled her mind like a forgotten dream dancing at the edges of awareness.

A persistent, steady beeping sounded from her wrist. She checked her watch and sighed. It was time to leave the Hall behind and return to the real world.

Casting a final glance toward the hidden observer, she rose from her seat and headed for a simple wooden door nestled in a tiny alcove. A series of grinding noises behind her signaled the access terminal's dissolution. It had taken several trips for her to become accustomed to the terminal's disappearance when she was ready to leave. Without looking back, she knew the terminal and chair had dissolved and once more melded with the stone floor, leaving only smooth granite throughout the rotunda. Dim light filled the alcove as she opened the partially concealed door and stepped through.

The moon had reigned over the Hall's interior, but once outside, Alex found a sun low on the horizon and the creeping gloom of twilight. Gravestones stretched to either side in endless rows, casting elongated shadows over soft spring grass. Looking over her shoulder as she walked away, the Hall's door appeared as the entrance to a small mausoleum, what may have been a family name worn away long ago.

"Curiouser and curiouser," she muttered and then smirked at the reference to *Alice in Wonderland*, one of her favorite childhood books. Sometimes she definitely felt like Alice chasing the rabbit.

Parting the Veil, the thin sliver of psychic energy that separated the physical and spiritual planes, required concentration and wasn't a task she'd fully mastered. If she wasn't careful in melding her consciousness with her physical body, a dozen nasty fates awaited her, the least being death.

Her physical body lay in a hotel room in a meditative trance. To an observer, she would appear to be in a really deep sleep. However, waking someone in such a trance could be deadly. Separating the consciousness from the body was a risk, but it was one she was willing to accept if she could find clues to solve her father's murder.

She sighed and closed her eyes, pushing aside the random thoughts that crowded her mind. Once awake, she would be groggy and disoriented, like someone coming out from under anesthesia. In order to shift her consciousness from the Shadowlands and back to the real world, she had to remember details of the room.

Gradually she recalled the feel of the bed beneath her, the coolness of the air, and the hum of machinery from the nearby elevators. The sensation of a pit yawning beneath her made her stomach roll. She'd learned to keep her eyes tightly shut against the kaleidoscopic whirlwind of colors and shadows as she passed through the Veil and returned to the physical plane.

Alex slowly awoke from the dreamlike trance and alarms immediately sounded in her mind. Her skin prickled under the gaze of an unseen watcher.

Darkness cloaked her surroundings. Disoriented, she searched with her senses, probing for signs of life. She steadied and measured her breathing as her eyes adjusted to the gloom. The greenish glow of a security light bathed the window beside the bed on which she lay and cast strange shadows on the wall.

Without turning her head, she looked around the small hotel room, trying to make sense of what she saw. One of the shadows in a far corner shifted and her focus narrowed on it. She eased her hand beneath her pillow, reaching for her loaded Glock G31 .357-caliber pistol.

The shadow detached from the wall and moved toward her.

Alex sat up quickly and aimed her pistol at the shadow as it launched itself onto the bed. Her finger found the trigger.

The shadow landed beside her with an inquisitive warble.

"Damn it, Dweezil," Alex whispered, jerking her finger from the trigger as the large Maine coon cat swished its tail over her bare legs.

Dweezil head-butted her empty hand and purred.

She chuckled and scratched behind his large tufted ears with her free hand. "Don't scare me like that. I almost shot you."

His eyes flashed iridescent green in the light filtering through the window. He winked at her, as if to say, "Gotcha," before moving to her still-warm pillow and curling into a tight ball.

"You sure are jumpy," a voice announced from near the window.

Alex gasped and aimed her Glock at the newly perceived threat.

"It's me, damn it!" A man's silhouette raised his hands and the scent of sandalwood and cinnamon wafted toward her.

Recognition stopped her finger from pulling the trigger. She lowered the pistol, her breath leaving in an explosive puff.

Varik Baudelaire—Director of Special Operations for the Federal Bureau of Preternatural Investigation, her ex-fiancé, former mentor, and current lover—cautiously approached the bed and took the pistol from her. "Fucking-A, baby. What the hell's got you so worked up?"

"Sorry. I'm not used to someone being here when I wake up."

He placed the Glock on the bedside table. "Well, it's little wonder if you make a habit of trying to kill your lovers."

She moved Dweezil from her pillow. "Oh, fuck you," she spat and pulled the covers over her head.

The bed shifted with Varik's added weight and his arms slipped around her. "That sounds like a fabulous idea," he growled and nipped at her ear with his fangs.

Alex giggled and rolled to face him. "Is sex the only thing you think about?"

"No." He kissed her neck. "Sometimes I think of food. Especially whipped cream."

"Whipped cream?"

He pulled back enough that she could see his dark eyes had shifted to the color of molten gold. "It's very versatile and has many uses." His hand slipped beneath her University of Louisville T-shirt to cup her breast. "It's especially good with melons."

She laughed and shoved him away. "You really are a French pig, aren't you?"

He captured her, pulling her close, and brushed his lips against hers as he whispered, "Le oink, le oink."

His mouth covered hers, and his tongue lazily traced the curve of her lips. He rolled her bottom lip between his teeth, teasing her with the possibility of piercing her flesh. A warm tingle blossomed low in her belly when his tongue finally darted between her fangs, exploring and gliding alongside hers.

Alex entwined her fingers in his black hair, reveling in its thickness and the way it slipped over her skin like warm silk. Since taking over as Jefferson's official Enforcer, he'd found having hair to his waist to be impractical and cut it, a decision with which she wholeheartedly agreed.

An upbeat techno song played, and Varik growled when she broke the kiss.

"Your phone is ringing," she muttered.

He kissed the scar along the left side of her neck, making her shiver. "Ignore it."

"It could be important."

"It can wait."

The beat cycled to the beginning, and she sighed. "Varik . . ."

Groaning, he rolled onto his side, reaching for his cell phone. The music died as he answered. "This had better be damn good."

She could hear the distinctive bass rumble of Damian Alberez, Chief Enforcer for the FBPI and boss to both of them. Rather, he was *Varik's* boss. *She* was cooling her heels on the Bureau's shit list because she'd turned rogue a month ago and abandoned her oath to uphold the law.

As a result of her transgression, she'd been placed on administrative suspension and ordered to remain within the city limits until the powers-that-be called her to their headquarters in Louisville, Kentucky. Once summoned, she'd face an official inquiry before the Tribunal, the vampire equivalent of an internal affairs committee, and answer for numerous violations of the Enforcer code of conduct. The most serious charge was one of corruption, which if found guilty carried a mandatory death sentence.

"How long ago was the car found?" Varik asked, swinging his legs over the side of the bed.

Alex stretched and pushed herself into a seated position, back resting against the headboard.

"Are you certain about that?" He glanced at her over his shoulder. "Right. Yeah, I know where it is. I'm bringing Alex along for this one."

She frowned as Damian's voice rose, and Varik was forced to hold the cell phone away from his ear.

"—no way in hell you're bringing her," Damian shouted. "Sabian is suspended until further notice. You know that."

"Yeah, I know that. I also know that if we're going to get anywhere with this investigation, we need all the available *talent* we can get," Varik snarled.

Damian remained silent.

"Varik," Alex whispered. "If he—"

"Fine." Damian's grudging response cut her off. "Bring her along, but you're responsible for her while she's on-scene."

Varik winked at her. "Agreed. We're on our way."

"What—" She gestured to his phone and shook her head. "How do you do that?"

He turned to face her squarely. "How do I do what?"

"Get Damian to agree to whatever you want."

He grinned, showing the full extent of his fangs. "It's part of my French pig charm, *chérie*."

She rolled her eyes. "So what's this scene we're going to?"

"You're familiar with the Mindy Johnson case?"

"The girl who disappeared three days ago."

He nodded. "Someone located her car in front of the women's dorms at Nassau County Community College. Damian and the forensic team are there now."

"Sounds like the scene is under control. Why bring me in?"

Varik rose and pulled her up along with him. "Because you have an ability to see things others don't."

"You want me to use my psychometry to get a vision of what happened to Mindy?" She tried to move away but he held her close. "It doesn't work like that, Varik. I can't control the visions."

"I know."

"There is no guarantee I'll even sense anything."

He kissed her forehead. "Will you at least try?"

Reluctantly, she nodded.

"Thank you."

They took turns in the bathroom, and she was surprised by how easily they fell into a familiar routine. As she washed up, Alex checked her reflection in the age-spotted mirror above the sink. The bruising that had encompassed her ribs, stomach, and the right side of her face had finally disappeared but the fractured cheekbone hadn't fully healed. She could still feel the soreness when she smiled. A bright pink scar ran diagonally over her right biceps, the result of a sniper's bullet grazing her arm.

She secured her shoulder-length auburn hair in a low ponytail. Another scar marred the left side of her neck, a jagged slash starting behind her ear and extending to her collarbone. She fingered the scar, a permanent reminder of a chapter in her life she thought was behind her. Fate, however, had other plans for her.

As if summoned by her thoughts, Varik appeared in the mirror, leaning against the doorjamb. His dark eyes steadily meeting her reflected gaze. "Ready to go?"

She nodded. "I just have to get my sidearm."

He grabbed her arm as she tried to push past him. His thumb traced the blemish on her neck. "I'm sorry I caused you pain," he murmured.

Six years ago, when they'd been engaged to be married, he attacked her, savaging her neck. He'd taken her blood and forged a psychic bond between them. Time and distance had weakened the blood-bond, but a few weeks ago she'd turned the tables and attacked *him*, restrengthening the bond. It hadn't been a conscious thought, unlike when she later slept with him and continued to sleep with him even though a portion of her said she shouldn't.

Her attention flicked to a matching mark on his neck. She followed the jagged edge of the healed wound with her finger. "I know," she whispered. "But now isn't the time to discuss it."

"You always say that."

"We'll discuss it later." She gave him a quick kiss. "I swear."

He released her in silent agreement.

She grabbed her Glock from the side table and paused to give Dweezil's exposed belly a quick rub. "Behave yourself," she told the purring cat. "No barfing on the bed or carpet."

Dweezil yawned and stretched in response.

Varik was shaking his head when she joined him at the door. "Sometimes I think you like that cat more than me."

"Love me, love my cat."

The door automatically locked behind them as they headed for the elevators. "Actually, I'm quite fond of your pus—"

She punched his arm. "Don't you dare complete that sentence, Varik Baudelaire, or I'll kick your ass right here."

He clutched his shoulder, laughing. "Promises, promises."

Alex growled in frustration and hurried ahead, wanting to place some distance between them before she really did hurt him, and pressed the elevator call button. She was still sorting out her feelings for Varik, and even though she cared for him, he often irritated her, especially with his insistence on providing for her.

Her apartment had been damaged in a fire and wasn't ready for her return. She'd been staying with her brother, Stephen, in a studio apartment he rented out over Crimson Swan, Jefferson's only legal blood bar for vampires. However, arsonists led by Harvey Manser, the now former sheriff of Nassau County, had destroyed the bar, leaving her homeless once again.

The hotel room that became her temporary shelter had originally been reserved by Varik when he first arrived in town. Her suspension from the Bureau left Jefferson without an Enforcer so the Bureau had assigned Varik as her provisional replacement and had provided him with a short-term apartment, not that he'd been there often. He gave his hotel room to Alex and had been staying with her most nights. She'd offered to reserve her own room but he'd insisted, claiming that the room was already paid in advance.

She didn't believe his story. However, a check with the hotel's manager had yielded no information of value other than gaining access to the hotel's after-hours gym.

The elevator arrived as Varik joined her, and the doors slid open. He gestured for her to enter first then walked in with a knowing smirk. She ignored him and pushed the button that would take them to the lobby.

As the doors shut, she heard another door open and close somewhere in the distance, bringing to mind her encounter—or lack of an encounter—in the Hall of Records. In the excitement that followed her trip to the Shadowlands, she'd forgotten about it. She was certain someone had been in the Hall. Why had they not shown themselves?

Machinery whirred overhead and while the elevator descended, she was on edge. Dread settled over her like a shroud and she couldn't shake it. Irrational visions of monsters lying in wait in the lobby flittered through her mind. The same sense of a forgotten dream nibbling at the corners of her consciousness made her shudder.

Varik draped an arm over her shoulders. "Are you okay?"

She nodded and stepped away. "Just a little nervous to face Damian," she lied.

His eyes narrowed but he didn't press her.

The elevator reached the first floor, and the doors opened to reveal a well-lit and empty lobby.

Alex silently chided herself as they passed the vacant front desk. She had an opportunity to make up for some of her mistakes and was allowing the events of recent weeks to get to her. She was back in the field, where she wanted to be, and she needed to get her head in the right place.

And yet when she stepped into the rainy dawn, the sense that some unseen menace lay in wait, watching her from the darkness, made her reach for Varik's hand.

He shot her a questioning look, but he never broke stride, and gave her hand a reassuring squeeze.

Once surrounded by the security of his sleek black Corvette and heading into the morning in silence, Alex pushed aside the anxiety that still swirled around her like a palpable cloud, determined not to squander the opportunity she'd been given.

And even more determined to stop jumping at shadows.

Basements weren't possible in southern Mississippi for two reasons: a high water table and a layer of shifting clay within the ground. That was why so many old houses had immense attic space to compensate.

Above- or belowground didn't matter to Peter. All he needed was privacy and the attic offered it. It had taken him nearly a year to perfect the space, tailoring it to his needs. The time had been wisely spent.

A door in the second-floor hall opened to stairs that led to one section of the attic. A very small portion used for actual storage.

The doorway to the remainder was well hidden. He'd made certain it wouldn't be noticed by the casual observer. Not that he had any visitors.

A false panel concealed behind an oversized print of Marcel Duchamp's *Nude Descending a Staircase, No. 2* hid another set of narrow stairs. The Cubist painting depicted both a woman and a staircase consisting of blocks and overlapping angles with little separating the moving nude figure from the irregular background.

The irony was too much. He laughed every time he opened the panel and climbed the hidden stairs, as he did now. Reaching the top step, he entered the wide expanse that was his private heaven.

Shelves containing his most precious collection lined the walls. Bins filled with all the bits needed to create his masterpieces were arranged in a neat row on his workstation. Lamps hung overhead and bathed the table in soft light.

As Peter crossed the time-worn wooden flooring, he felt a rush of power filtering up from the archaic sigils he'd carefully carved into the boards. Each held meaning and purpose, and all were designed to bring him the one thing he most desired.

He pulled a rolling stool from under the table and sat down with a sigh. It felt good to be returning to work. He pushed a button on a remote control and the opening overture for *Carmen* filtered through concealed speakers. His eyes slipped shut. The music surrounded him, caressed him, and lulled his senses into a peaceful calm.

Last night had been a very good night. He'd seen *her*. It had been a brief glimpse only, but it had been enough to rekindle his desire, to assure him that his work was not in vain.

He'd even heard her voice. Her sweet, angelic voice calling to him, seeking him out. He'd wanted to answer, to go to her, but he abstained. She wasn't ready, and he had to be patient. She would come to him soon enough.

Opening his eyes, he removed the protective drape from his current work. It was crude but the subtle features were taking shape in the face. Each doll he created was perfect, an exact copy of his models. However, this one was a replica of a very special model, and like the others, it would be imbued with a vital essence that would bring her to him.

His gaze flickered across the attic to his latest acquisition.

She stared at him, eyes wide and full of wonder. She hadn't struggled in the same manner as her predecessor so the bindings were minimal. Bands across her forehead and throat kept her head immobile. Her arms lay naturally along her sides with black straps holding them securely in place at the elbows and wrists. A special harness crossed over her shoulders and then over her stomach. More straps held her thighs and shins in place.

Her mouth remained uncovered, however, and she said nothing. The drugs kept her pliant.

Peter smiled and picked up the new doll's head from the table.

This one was special.

This was the one that would finally bring Alexandra to him.

This was the one that would make her his.

Forever.

two

LIEUTENANT TASHA LOCKWOOD STARED AT THE LETTER on her kitchen table. Beside it, a teacup sat ignored, the water long since grown cold and murky with over-brewed tea. Instead, she cradled a glass of golden liquid and slowly melting ice cubes.

The letter was printed on heavy linen paper. Balanced scales of justice dominated the neatly printed header for Barnes, Butler, Lockwood, & Associates, the Baton Rouge law firm in which her ex-husband was a partner. Her eyes scanned the letter but her brain still refused to believe the words.

> . . . *presence required in Nassau County Family Court on December 4 to answer the petition for sole physical and legal custody of the minor child, Maya Lockwood* . . .

Ten years after their divorce, Caleb was suing her for sole custody of their daughter.

She hadn't argued when he was granted primary custody and she only received visitation rights. She hadn't even argued when he filed a relocation petition with the court after he was offered the partnership in the law firm. However, she wasn't going to let him take Maya completely away.

She lifted her glass and drained the golden liquid. Its slightly smoky taste was mellowed by the ice, just the way she liked it. Although the bourbon was chilled, it still burned as it slid down her throat. She shuddered and set the glass on the table with a soft *thump*.

Her phone rang and she automatically reached for her cell before she realized it was her personal home line. She frowned. Who would be calling her this early in the morning?

Pushing herself up from the table, Tasha picked up the cordless receiver. "Hello?"

"Judging from the angry message you left in my voice mail, I'm assuming you got my letter."

"What the hell is going on, Caleb?" She backed against the wall for support. "Is something wrong with Maya?"

"Nothing's wrong with Maya."

"Then why are you trying to change the custody agreement?"

Caleb sighed and the familiar *squeak-pop* of his favorite reclining chair sounded over the line. "Maya doesn't want to come to Jefferson anymore, Tasha. She says she's happy here with her friends, me, and Shantee, and doesn't want to leave anymore."

A knife lodged in Tasha's stomach, cold, hard, and painful. "I don't believe that, and who the hell is Shantee?"

"Believe what you want, but I'm telling you exactly what Maya's told me." He cleared his throat before continuing. "Shantee is my wife."

The knife in Tasha's stomach slowly twisted. "Your wife? You got remarried and didn't tell me?"

"I sent you an invitation."

"I didn't get it."

"Not my problem."

"You could've at least called."

"I did." His voice adopted an irritated edge. "If you weren't so busy playing a vampire's bitch—"

"I am *not* a vampire's bitch! I'm the fucking liaison officer for Jefferson PD, Nassau County Sheriff's Department, and the FBPI. It's my *job* to work with vampires."

"And given your fear of them, how's that working out for you?"

"Don't be a dick, Caleb, and stop trying to change the subject." She moved to the table and poured another round of bourbon. "I'm not going to let you take Maya."

"I'm not taking her, Tasha. I've already got her. This is her decision. I'm just trying to do what's best for her."

"What's best is for her to spend time with her mother." She gulped down the bourbon. "Not some wannabe stepmother floozy she barely knows."

Silence consumed the line, and Tasha quietly cursed herself. "I'm sorry," she whispered. "I shouldn't have—"

"I have to get ready for work," he interjected.

"Caleb—"

"Good-bye, Tasha."

The line clicked closed before she could respond. She returned the cordless handset to its cradle and sucked in a deep breath.

Caleb had been her first love. She was a high-school junior and he was a college freshman. After dating for three years, they married, and she joined the Jefferson Police Department while he worked full-time on his law degree. She enrolled in night classes and studied criminal justice. Maya was born a few years later. Life had been hard but good.

For a while.

Tasha first began drinking to relax from the rigors of working as a patrol officer. It was no big deal to have a few beers with her fellow officers after a shift. However, Tasha soon found herself sneaking shots before her shifts and then during. She told herself it wasn't a problem, that everyone had their ways of coping. She rationalized it by saying she risked her life and deserved a little liquid compensation once in a while. No harm and no foul so long as no one saw her and the bad guys were going to jail.

Then Tasha's drinking caught up with her a few months after she earned her detective's badge. She failed to report for an important court date. The police chief wanted her fired on the spot. Caleb convinced the chief to place her on administrative leave, and she entered a treatment program.

When she returned from rehab, Caleb and three-year-old Maya were gone and divorce papers left in their stead. Tasha was devastated but didn't fight Caleb's demands for primary custody of their daughter. She was newly out of treatment, struggling to deal with her addiction and still maintain her job as a police officer. Maya was happy and well cared for with Caleb. The court awarded Tasha visitations once a month, every other major holiday, and four weeks during the summer.

That was ten years ago. Why was Caleb now seeking sole custody? Tasha glanced at the empty bourbon glass on the table. Did he know about her relapse? About her violating the chain of evidence?

The phone rang again and she jumped. She picked up the receiver.

"Listen very carefully," a familiar distorted electronic voice droned. "We will say this only once."

"Who is this?"

"We know you are in danger of losing your daughter."

Tasha glanced at the cordless phone base and then to the narrow window overlooking a small backyard. "How do you know that?"

"That is unimportant. We can assist you."

"Help me? How? Why?"

"Again, that is unimportant. If you want to see your daughter, you will follow our instructions."

She hesitated and then sighed, slumping against the kitchen wall. "What do you want from me?"

"You are assisting the vampires in their search for Mindy Johnson."

"I'm assigned to the task force, yes."

"You will gather information on the one called Sabian."

"Alex? But she's on suspension."

"Vampire Sabian was reinstated to full active duty status as of oh-six-twenty-seven this morning."

Tasha's head spun. "You want me to spy on a federal agent?"

"You will gather information on Sabian. Observe her behavior. Make a record of what she says and does."

"I don't understand why—"

"Understanding is not required. You will also retrieve Mindy Johnson's journal and keep it safe until further notice."

"Why do you want Mindy's journal?"

"We will be in touch."

"Wait!"

The line clicked three times and then switched to the monotone hum of a dial tone.

"Damn it!" Tasha jammed the handset into the cradle and it beeped in annoyance. She knew better than to check the caller ID logs. It would only show an unnamed caller and no number.

The same was true of trying to trace the call. She'd had similar calls during the Darryl Black investigation, including one instructing her to compromise the chain of evidence. Her conscience had eventually gotten the better of her, and she'd confessed her transgression to Varik. She could still hear his threat in her mind as clear as if he stood in the room with her.

If anything happens to Alex as a result of your actions, there will be nowhere on this earth you can hide from me.

Tasha believed if anyone could make good on a threat, it was Varik Baudelaire. She'd been checking into his past, and the little information she was able to unearth frightened her. Born in 1833, the only son of an aristocratic Parisian family, Varik had turned his back on his family's wealth at the age of twenty-three. She found no mention of him after he walked away from the Baudelaire fortune until he surfaced in Louisville, Kentucky, in 1968, immediately following Bernard Sabian's murder. She could only imagine what he may have been doing in that missing century.

Her gaze fell to Caleb's letter and then shifted to the half-empty bourbon bottle. Hate and anger, fear and self-loathing warred for control of her emotions. She picked up the bottle and tossed it in the trash.

"I will *not* be intimidated," she said to the last vestiges of night outside her window. "I will *not* succumb to my fears."

Spinning on her heel, Tasha grabbed her cell phone and headed for her bedroom to dress for the long day of work ahead of her.

A nagging little voice in her mind laughed at her and made her pause in the threshold between the kitchen and hallway. *Caleb's right. They own you,* the voice whispered. *You fucked up. The vamps covered it up.*

After confessing to Varik that she'd broken the chain of evidence, he and Alex had omitted Tasha's violation from their official reports. If she was discovered tampering with evidence again, she felt certain neither vampire would be so forgiving.

Now they own you, her inner tormentor teased. *They're never going to let you go.*

Fear overwhelmed Tasha and rooted her to the floor.

If Caleb finds out what you're doing, you'll never see Maya again.

She couldn't let that happen. She couldn't lose her daughter. Not again.

You're weak. You know you can't fight the vamps and Caleb. Not without me.

Tasha groaned and crossed the room. Her hands shook as she extracted the bourbon from the trash while her inner voice cackled in triumph.

Emily Sabian had always been an early riser, greeting the sun with a cup of coffee and usually one or two hours of work already behind her. Today was no different. She'd already cleaned the living and dining rooms, scrubbed the guest's bathroom, and straightened her bedroom. The clothes dryer quietly spun in the laundry room off the kitchen.

Sitting at the island breakfast bar, she waited for the other two occupants of the house to rise while she looked around at the purple walls, white cabinets, and tan-colored granite countertops. It wasn't her style, but then again, she was simply a guest.

Emily sipped her black coffee and pretended she didn't hear the whispers filtering from beneath the closed door down the hallway. She pretended she didn't hear the steady rhythmic creaking of a headboard or the low moans of pleasure. What her son and his human girlfriend did in their own home was none of her business.

She checked the clock display on the microwave and set her coffee aside. Emily moved to the refrigerator and took out a small test tube filled with thick crimson liquid. Unlike her children, Stephen and Alex, she no longer had her fangs and therefore couldn't bite a donor. Like many vampires over the age of two hundred, Emily's fangs had been filed down and capped in order to achieve a more human appearance. Blood was obtained through needles and stored in test tubes. At least she no longer had to hide the tubes.

In the time before vampires revealed themselves to humanity, blood was hidden in a variety of ways, wine bottles being the most popular. When Stephen and Alex were children, one of the more clever methods Emily had devised was mixing the blood with cherry Jell-O. The kids had loved it.

She placed the cold tube in a shallow bowl and reached for the teakettle warming on the stove. The water would gently warm the blood to the perfect temperature for consumption. She poured a stream of steaming water into the bowl, being careful not to spill.

A joyful shout from the master bedroom startled her. Hot water splashed on her hand. Crying out in pain, Emily dropped the kettle. It hit the stone counter and clanged to the tile floor.

"Mom!" Stephen called from down the hall. Rapid footsteps announced his approach a moment before he entered the kitchen, naked with blood dripping from his chin. "What is it? What happened?"

Emily quickly averted her eyes, grabbing for a dish towel. She wrapped it around her hand to hide the spreading blister. "I'm all right, Stephen."

"You burned yourself," he said. He reached for her hand. "Let me see."

She pulled away. "I'm fine. I was warming some blood, and I dropped the kettle. That's all."

"You could've put it in the microwave for a few seconds." He bent over, picked up the now-empty kettle, and set it back on the stovetop.

Emily kept her eyes locked on the sink in front of her. "I don't like the way it makes the blood taste, and I'm not entirely comfortable discussing this with you while you're naked."

Stephen laughed and shook his bare butt at her. "Why? It's not like you haven't seen my ass before."

Movement from the doorway captured her attention. Janet Klein, Stephen's girlfriend, entered the kitchen wearing one of his T-shirts and holding a tissue to her neck. She passed a pair of faded jeans and a cell phone to him.

Emily's gaze met her son's. "You were much younger then and not so—"

"Impressive?" He smiled as he stepped behind the island so she only saw him from the waist up as he dressed.

Heat rose in her face. "I was going to say 'healthy.' "

Janet tapped his chin as she yawned and then staggered to the nearby bathroom. Stephen wiped away the thin trickle of blood with a finger and promptly stuck it in his mouth. A shudder passed over him and his sky blue eyes began to bleed over to dark amber.

Emily checked the burn on her hand. It wasn't as bad as she'd feared. The skin around her thumb and index finger was bright red and throbbed with every beat of her heart. She'd suffered much worse though, and knew from experience that the burn would heal completely within a day or two.

"Got a text message from Alex," Stephen said, drawing her focus to him. He leaned against the island, elbows supporting his upper body as he read from the small screen. "Varik pulled some strings and convinced Damian to reinstate Alex. They're on their way to a crime scene."

"What kind of case is it?"

"You heard about that missing girl?"

"Yes."

"That's it."

"Oh, good. The sooner Alex can focus on something besides this inquiry, the better." Emily realized how callous her statement sounded and rushed to correct herself. "I don't mean it's good a girl is missing, but that she'll have something else to think about for a while."

"I know what you meant, Mom." He laid his cell phone to the side and ran a hand through his disheveled golden curls. "I just wish she wasn't determined to shack up with Varik at the same time."

"Don't start, Stephen."

"I can't help it. I don't trust the guy. Besides, Alex wouldn't have to worry about an inquiry if Varik hadn't shown his ass up here in the first place."

The loathing Stephen had for Varik wasn't news to Emily. He delighted in complaining about his sister's relationship at every turn.

Sighing, she used her unburned hand to check the temp of the test tube still soaking in water. "I really wish you would give Varik a chance."

"Why should I? The bastard nearly killed Alex—twice—and bound her to him against her will."

"It wasn't like that and you know it."

"You didn't see what he did to her, Mom. He practically tore her throat out and left her lying on the floor to die. She would've if I hadn't shown up when I did."

"It wasn't his fault. He was injured and the blood-hunger was too much."

"He's a killer!"

"That was a long time ago and he was just doing his job."

"I don't understand why you keep defending him," Stephen growled.

Janet returned and stopped short when the vampires ceased their conversation. She nervously covered the bite on her neck with her hand. "I, uh, I'll come back for coffee."

Emily removed the test tube from the water and watched Stephen's eyes track his girlfriend down the hall to the master bedroom they shared. Once the door closed, she said, "I defend Varik because Alex is in love with him and needs him, especially now. I would do the same for you if Janet's family ever turned on you."

"Janet doesn't have a family. Her parents are dead and she's an only child."

Sympathy for the girl stabbed Emily's chest. "I didn't know." She ripped the stopper from the test tube and upended it, draining the blood.

Memories from the unknown donor's life darted through her mind like phantoms. Fragments presented themselves for her review but were not retained. A rush of psychic energy surged through Emily's body, revitalizing her.

"There's a lot you don't know, Mom," Stephen said quietly once she'd thrown away the tube. He pushed himself up from the counter. "Especially about Varik."

Emily watched him follow Janet's path to the bedroom. She pulled on the silver chain at her neck and cradled the small silver four-leaf clover charm in the palm of her hand.

Thoughts of her husband, Bernard, crowded her mind. The charm had been his, a symbol of a secret she would do anything to protect. "I know enough, Stephen," she whispered. "I know enough."

She returned the chain to its place beneath her blouse and leaned against the sink. Staring out the window at the brightening eastern sky, she hoped the sun would burn away the darkness that continued to prey on her family.

three

RAIN ALWAYS MADE EVIDENCE COLLECTION AT OUTDOOR crime scenes difficult. Water either washed it away or destroyed it altogether. Although the thunderstorm had moved on, water continued to flow through the center of the parking lot in front of Nassau County Community College's women's dormitory. Varik studied the makeshift stream and wondered how much had already been lost.

By the time he and Alex arrived, a protective canopy had been erected over Mindy Johnson's abandoned car to minimize the amount of evidence lost. Freddy Haver and Reyes Cott, the two forensic analysts on loan from the FBPI's headquarters in Louisville, were already processing the vehicle. Other Enforcers and uniformed humans from the Jefferson police and Nassau County Sheriff's Department canvassed the area, interviewing anyone who may have seen something. Their efforts would most likely prove fruitless due to the early morning hour, but they had to be thorough, especially if his own suspicions were correct.

He shifted his attention from the storm runoff to Alex, who stood with Chief Enforcer Damian Alberez near Varik's Corvette. Damian had greeted them and pulled Alex aside as soon as her feet hit the pavement. Even though Varik couldn't hear their conversation, he sensed Alex's rising impatience and anger through the blood-bond.

Varik sighed and shoved his hands into the pockets of his jeans. He loved Alex and her fiery spirit, but a pissed-off Alex could complicate an already challenging investigation.

Alex broke away from Damian and headed toward the yellow tape marking the boundary between public area and crime scene.

"What did he say?" Varik asked, moving to intercept her.

"Not much, just that I'm completely fucked."

He blocked her path. "What do you mean?"

She crossed her arms in front of her, eyes downcast. "Chief Magistrate Woody Phelps has taken a personal interest in my inquiry."

"Phelps? Why would he—"

She shrugged. "Damian doesn't know. All he knows is a special investigator for the Tribunal will be here in a few hours to grill my ass, and the SI is to report directly to Phelps."

"Oh, baby," he murmured and laid a reassuring hand on her shoulder. "I'm sorry."

She brushed his hand away and sidestepped around him. "I don't want your sympathy, Varik. I just want to get through this shit. Alive."

He watched as she ducked under the tape barrier and signed in with the officer tracking who came and went from the scene. He understood her frustration. He'd faced his own inquiry long ago.

In the years before the Bureau's formation and the inception of Enforcers, he'd been a Hunter, one of a select group who ensured the vampire community remained hidden from humans. Vampires had few laws, but punishment for breaking them was swift, with the only penalty being death. Generations of vampires lived in fear of the Hunters, but even the Hunters weren't above the law they maintained.

For over a century, Varik specialized in tracking down and disposing of other Hunters who broke vampiric law. His assignments took him across the globe, and he prided himself in his efficiency. However, one assignment turned into a nightmare when faulty information resulted in the death of an innocent teenaged vampire.

The incident led to an official inquiry by the Tribunal, the Hunters' governing body. His name was cleared but he hadn't been the same and swore never to kill again, a vow he'd kept for over fifty years.

Movement behind him drew his attention and he turned to find his oldest and best friend glowering in Alex's direction.

"I don't like this one bit," Damian grumbled. "I don't like her being on this case."

Varik glanced over his shoulder at Alex, who'd joined Reyes and Freddy beside Mindy Johnson's car. "We need her. You know we won't catch this guy without a Talent, and Alex is the closest thing we've got to one."

Damian frowned and shifted his weight from one foot to the other. Standing nearly seven feet tall with muscles to rival a young Arnold Schwarzenegger and polished ebony skin, he was an impressive figure before he ever flashed his fangs. "She hasn't been properly tested. You have no real proof she's a Talent."

Talents—vampires who displayed any form of psychic ability—were rare and highly prized in many fields, especially law enforcement.

"The fact she's been an Enforcer for over twenty years and hasn't been tested is odd," Damian continued. "Don't you think? Especially given that she's Bernard's daughter."

Alex's father had been the undisputed leader of the Talents in the pre-FBPI era. As the top-performing Hunter, Varik had been partnered with Bernard for many years, long before Alex was born. A secret he worked daily to keep hidden from Alex.

Varik shrugged and faced the crime scene, watching his former trainee as she worked with the forensic analysts. "It's a little strange, I suppose, but I'm not the one who decides which recruits are tested and which aren't."

"Yeah, but you do have a knack for pulling strings."

"I learned from the best."

Damian grunted.

"I've been inside Alex's head. Yes, she lacks the training and discipline, but I've seen the things Alex can do. Trust me. She's one of the best Talents I've seen in a long time."

"For your sake, you'd better be right about her abilities. I had to do some serious maneuvering to get her reinstated. If she can't deliver, I'm going to make your life hell."

Varik scoffed. "You've been doing that ever since you pulled my ass out of retirement."

"A decision I'll be regretting for a long time, I can assure you."

Varik gestured for Damian to move toward the tape barrier and fell into step beside him. "Did you have a chance to examine the doll?" he asked, changing the subject to one of a more immediate concern.

Damian nodded. "Yeah. It definitely looks like the Dollmaker's handiwork."

"Shit. I was really hoping you wouldn't say that."

"I'm not happy about it either. Hell, you tried to catch this son of a bitch for years with no luck. He drops out of sight and now suddenly he shows up in Jefferson, of all places. Why?"

"How the hell should I know? As you pointed out, I had no luck catching the bastard."

"Don't be a smart-ass. There's still the possibility of a copycat."

"Damian, you know as well as I do that we made certain to keep his signature under wraps to *prevent* copycats. It *has* to be him."

They stopped beside the temporary yellow barricade and both focused on Alex as she leaned over a kneeling Freddy Haver to examine something the forensic analyst pointed to on the car's open door.

The omnipresent low hum of the blood-bond in the back of Varik's mind grew louder as Alex seemed to sense their focus. She righted herself and when her eyes found his, Varik's heart jumped with a surge of adrenaline. The bond crackled between them and made his flesh prickle. He couldn't prevent the smile that sprouted on his face.

She gave him a half-smile in return and refocused her attention on Freddy.

Damian clamped a hand on Varik's shoulder. "Keep it in your pants, Baudelaire," he muttered.

Varik's glare earned a throaty chuckle in response.

"Just remember one thing," Damian said as Varik ducked under the barrier. "While you're watching her ass, the Tribunal will also be watching it, and yours."

Varik recoiled in mock horror. "Kinky bastards."

"I'll be sure to tell the Special Investigator you said that."

Varik laughed as he added his name and badge number to the communication officer's log and then pulled a pair of latex gloves from the box offered by the officer. "Don't you have some paperwork to file or something?" he asked Damian as he snapped the gloves in place.

"Just watch your step." Damian spun and backtracked toward the women's dorm. "Keep me posted on your progress," he shot over his shoulder.

Varik let the comment go without response and joined Alex beside the car.

"What's up with Damian?" Alex asked as he approached. "He looked pissed as hell just now."

"He always looks that way."

"True, but I know that look, and it said 'I'm going to kill Varik.' What did you say to him?"

"I told him the office was out of creamer for the coffee." He circled the car and ignored her scowl. "Have Freddy and Reyes finished processing the interior? Taken photos?"

"All done. It's all ours until it's moved to the impound lot."

He nodded. "Who found the car?"

"According to Reyes, a security guard making his usual rounds. He noticed the driver's-side door was left open, and investigated. Found a backpack and purse on the backseat. Identification in the purse and a check on the car's registration all point to Mindy Johnson."

"No sign of the driver?"

"None."

"Have her parents been notified?"

"I called Tasha. She's going to talk to them." Alex picked up a clear plastic evidence bag from a bin next to her feet. "The security guard also found a BlackBerry shattered on the ground beside the car."

Varik took the bag from her and flipped it over. The contents shifted and clanked against one another. "Do we know if it belongs to Mindy?"

"No. Freddy says he may be able to pull something usable from the SIM card, but he doesn't hold out much hope."

He handed the bag to her, and she replaced it in the bin. "Anything else?"

She nodded and knelt beside the open driver's-side door. "Freddy and Reyes found a few fingerprints on the steering wheel and door handle. They also found blood spatter on the passenger seat."

Varik poked his head into the open door, brushing against Alex as he leaned forward.

She shifted her weight to create space between them. "Reyes ran a field test and determined the blood isn't vampire. He'll have to wait until he gets back to the lab to run more tests, but he's pretty certain it's human."

Forensics had progressed greatly over the last few years while Varik enjoyed his retirement. Before he'd left the Bureau, the only way to determine if blood at a scene was vampire or human required lengthy lab processes. Now field tests to determine the origin were relatively simple. All analysts needed were cotton swabs and a few drops of a special chemical that reacted with the high iron content of vampire blood. If a reaction occurred, the sample was deemed vampire. No reaction meant it was most likely human blood.

Alex continued to tell him of Freddy's and Reyes's discoveries, but her natural scent of jasmine and vanilla called to Varik and his focus shifted from her words to her body.

The car's dome light set her auburn hair aflame and made her pale skin glow. Her eyes had returned to their normal color and reminded him of emeralds rimmed in gold. Her soft curves belied the strength she possessed and rose-colored lips hid the delicate ivory points of her fangs.

His hand slipped to his chest and fingered the two-carat pink diamond ring he wore on a chain beneath his clothing. The ring had been hers. He'd slipped it on her finger while she slept six years ago—his way of proposing. She'd accepted but a few months later everything ended when he lost control of his blood-hunger and attacked her.

Now she'd consented to having him back in her life,

and he wasn't going to squander his chance to make things right.

"Hey," Alex said, snapping her fingers in front of his face. "Earth to Varik."

He thrust aside the memories he'd been indulging. "What?"

She smirked. "You were a thousand miles away. What were you thinking about?"

"You," he answered truthfully. "Us."

She sighed and stood, forcing him to take a few steps back. "Varik, now isn't—"

"I know," he snapped. "Now isn't the time. You're here to work so let's work. What were you saying?"

She stared at him. Hurt swam in her eyes but was quickly captured and locked away. "I was asking you if we knew Mindy's height."

"Five feet, three inches."

"Something's not right." She motioned to the driver's seat. "Notice anything unusual?"

He looked to where she pointed and shook his head. "No."

"The seat is too far back. Look at the distance between the steering wheel, the foot pedals, and the seat. I'm five feet seven, and the distance is too far even for me. It's set for someone closer to your height."

"So whoever drove it last must be at least six feet."

"Exactly, and they forgot to adjust the seat or simply didn't bother." She looked toward the dormitory. "The driver also parked in plain view of the dorm's front door. Whoever he is, he's got a set of brass balls."

"Does the building have security cameras?"

Alex nodded. "Reyes already collected the tapes and talked to the security guard working the front desk, who claims he didn't see anything suspicious." She thrust her chin toward the back of the car. "And then we have that thing."

A sense of dread crept over Varik as he moved closer to the car so he could view the small doll lying on the backseat.

It was dressed in a pristine white gown with sleek black hair styled in a bob, and large dark brown eyes that seemed to follow him when he moved. The effect was not only disturbing but familiar. Recognition kicked his pulse into overdrive. Memories of similar dolls paraded through his mind.

Alex touched his arm. "Are you okay?"

"Yeah," he croaked. "I'm fine."

"Bullshit. You recognize it, don't you?"

He paused, debating how much information to give her. On the one hand, he didn't want her unduly influenced by his prior knowledge. However, on the other, she needed to know enough to appreciate the severity of the danger they faced. Caution finally won. "When you were at the FBPI Academy, did you ever study or hear of an unsolved case known as the Dollmaker Murders?"

"I remember reading about it. The murders began in the Chicago area back in the 1920s. A dozen or so young girls went missing. Their bodies were found two or three weeks after their disappearance was reported. Each one had a handmade doll tied to the body, and the dolls supposedly resembled the girl in some way."

He met her steady gaze. "I worked that case."

Her brows rose and she glanced at the doll. "Copycat?"

"I don't think so. The last Chicago murders were in 1924 and the trail went cold. Another series of murders started in southern Nevada in 1938, and again in 1943 in Rhode Island."

"Why haven't I heard of these other murders?"

"The Bureau didn't exist yet, at least not in its current incarnation. There were no Enforcers or central headquarters. Hunters worked out of regional bases of operations across the globe. Communications weren't great, and information, when we could get it, was sometimes days or weeks old. By the time I heard about some of the killings, too much time had passed for me to be certain they were connected to the Dollmaker."

"But you checked into them anyway?"

He nodded. "I broke in to coroners' offices, police stations, courthouses, anywhere I had to in order to get the information."

"You broke in?"

"Don't look at me like that. I did what was necessary. You have to remember vampires were still hiding from humans back then. I couldn't exactly walk into the coroner's office, flash a badge, and ask to see the bodies."

"Please tell me you never robbed a grave."

"Define 'robbed.' "

Alex threw her hands up and turned back to the car. "Never mind. I don't want to know."

Varik chuckled. "You asked."

She opened the car's back door, squatted to examine the doll more closely, and changed the subject with her question. "If this really is the work of the Dollmaker and not some whacked-out copycat, what's he doing in Jefferson of all places?"

"That's what we need to find out."

"When was the last report you had of his activity?"

He shuffled his feet. Apprehension sliced through him and he strengthened the mental barriers separating his mind from hers. "March 14, 1968."

Alex stilled. Her voice was low and steady when she spoke. "Where?"

"Louisville, Kentucky."

Silence reigned beneath the protective canopy and between them.

Varik could feel her mind pressing against his mental

barriers, seeking entry. He sensed the deeply rooted desire to know more pulsing over the blood-bond. "Alex—"

"Two days," she whispered.

Varik waited for her to continue.

"The last murders were two days before my father's?"

"Yes."

She rose and faced him, a question embedded within her emerald eyes.

"No," he answered before she gave it a voice. "I don't think there is a connection between the Dollmaker and Bernard's death."

Alex's eyes narrowed. "I don't believe you."

"Believe me or not, but I'm telling you what I know."

Her barely controlled anger vibrated the bond and made his head pound. "You know more than you're telling me."

His own anger heated his words. "You're reading too much into things and jumping to conclusions. Why can't you just trust me and leave it at that?"

"Because I know you, Varik. You always have an ulterior motive. You convinced Damian to reverse my suspension. You dragged me out here. You asked for my help. Why?"

"I want your help to catch this freak." He pointed to the doll lying on the seat. "Before another girl goes missing."

"Why was the Dollmaker in Louisville?"

"I don't fucking know but I'll be sure to ask him as soon as I catch his ass."

She folded her arms in front of her and looked away.

"Damn it, Alex, I don't want to fight with you. I need your help with *this* investigation. Not something that happened forty goddamn years ago! If you can't do that, then you can go back on suspension."

"You want my help? You've got it." Alex ripped away one of her protective gloves.

"Wait—"

She seized the doll. Her body went rigid, and her head snapped back, eyes wide and staring.

"Alex?" Varik reached for her and stopped, uncertain.

She began to shake.

"Baby, can you hear me?"

She screamed.

"Fuck," Varik hissed and batted the doll out of her hands.

The doll landed on the car's seat. Alex collapsed into his arms, clawing at her eyes. She continued to cry out in pain as Damian and other Enforcers converged on the scene.

"Alex!" Varik seized her wrists in an effort to keep her from damaging her eyes.

"Get off!" She fought against him and whatever vision she'd seen.

"Stop!" Varik tightened his grip and pulled her closer to him. "You're safe, baby. Nothing can hurt you."

She screamed again, arched her back, and convulsed.

"Alexandra!"

Finally, she fell limp in his arms, motionless, eyes closed, but breathing rapidly.

"Alex?" He shook her gently. "Talk to me."

She remained unresponsive.

He dropped the mental shields that kept his mind separate from hers and opened the bond. The familiar warmth of her mind washed over him, but it seemed to come from a great distance. She was alive but lost in whatever vision she'd tapped into by touching the doll.

Damian knelt across from him, careful not to touch either him or Alex. "Damn."

Varik held her close and glanced at Damian over her shoulder. "So you believe me now?"

He nodded slowly.

It was little consolation to Varik. He brushed the hair from her face, reaching out to her over the bond. *Come back to me, baby.*

Minutes passed before she groaned. Her lids parted into thin slits. "Varik?"

Relief washed over him. "It's okay. I'm right here."

She reached for him and he caught her hand. Fear, pain, and anger surged through the blood-bond. Tears slipped over her temples to mingle with the murky puddle beneath her. Her arms slipped around his neck and she clung to him as she sobbed.

"You're safe, baby," Varik murmured in her ear. "What did you see? Tell me."

"Death," Alex whispered between sobs. "I saw death."

The FBPI's mobile lab was a forty-foot-long converted recreational vehicle. Tasha kept her eyes on the smoked windows as she approached it.

Alex had called her earlier to tell her to inform Mindy Johnson's parents that the Enforcers had recovered their daughter's car and to ask the Johnsons some follow-up questions. Tasha asked if a forensics team was present—a natural enough question—and was told both Freddy and Reyes were processing the car on-scene.

While she suspected someone might be on hand to guard the lab, it was an opportunity to retrieve the journal she couldn't let pass. The Johnsons lived only a few blocks from the Nassau County Municipal Center, where the mobile lab was parked. She could easily stop at the lab, grab the journal, and be on her way with no one being the wiser.

In theory. She just hoped her suspicions about guards and security systems were wrong.

As she drew closer, the RV remained a silent fixture in a little-used corner of the Center's parking lot.

She reached the door and glanced around, expecting someone to appear and question her presence. When no one confronted her, she pulled on the flipper-style door handle.

The lock clicked and the door quietly swung open.

"This is too fucking easy," Tasha muttered and mounted the steps.

The lab's interior was cool and eerily still. Again, no one confronted her or challenged her right to be there. Her heart raced inside its bony cage as she moved around the various equipment and stations to the back.

Dozens of bins filled with evidence bags of different sizes and shapes had been crammed into the small lounge area at the rear of the RV. Looking over the ordered chaos, she discovered a small binder cataloging the contents of each bin. She flipped through the pages, scanning for the one item she sought.

Once she located the correct bin, Tasha rifled through the various containers until she found a small brown paper bag sealed with red tape with blocky letters reading EVIDENCE printed diagonally across the tape's surface. She checked the chain of possession grid printed on the front of the bag.

CASE NO. 200911-23-NC   ITEM NO. 14
DATE COLLECTED: 11-14-2009   TIME COLLECTED: 13:24
COLLECTED BY: F. HAVER   BADGE NO. 9851
DESCRIPTION OF ITEM: small journal, embossed pink leather
LOCATION WHERE FOUND: right bedside table, Mindy
Johnson's dormitory room, RM# 2-16

This was the journal she'd been instructed to retrieve. However, now that she had it, what was she to do with it? For that matter, why did her mystery caller want it?

She hesitated to pick it up. If she took the journal, she would be starting down a path she knew could end her career. If she didn't, she risked losing something even more precious.

"It's for Maya," she whispered. "Think of Maya."

Her hands closed around the brown bag and freed it from the bin. Stuffing it in an inner pocket of her jacket, she replaced the boxes and catalog and hurried outside, making sure to close the lab's door behind her.

As she turned to leave, she thought she heard a soft double click. She frowned, fearing she'd triggered some hidden security system, and pulled on the door's handle.

The door refused to open. She tried again and realized the door was now locked.

"What the hell?"

Her cell phone clipped to her belt beeped with an incoming text message.

EXCELLENT WORK. WE'LL BE IN TOUCH.

Fear lanced her spine. She scanned the lab's exterior, searching for hidden cameras, but found none. How could anyone know what she'd done, so quickly?

Did it matter as long as the deed kept her from losing Maya?

Her thoughts leapt to the Johnsons, tucked in their home, jumping whenever the phone or doorbell rang, anxious to learn of their daughter's fate. For ten years, she'd experienced a milder form of their anxiety, separated from Maya by her own inability to stand up to Caleb.

She wouldn't allow Maya to completely slip away.

Tasha returned her phone to its holder and inhaled the damp and chill November air. Squaring her shoulders, she marched across the parking lot to her car.

If the cost of keeping her daughter in her life was betraying a few vampires, then so be it.

four

KIRK BELJEAN GREEDILY LAPPED AT THE BLOOD SEEP-
ing from the girl's neck. She moaned as he rhythmically
thrust his hips. He loved entering her from behind. The
position gave him full control of her movements and he
could watch as he slipped in and out.

It also meant he didn't have to see her face. She was
pretty enough but the expressions she made during sex
were comical. He couldn't fuck her face-to-face unless
she was drunk or high, and then she usually passed out
before he finished. It didn't stop him, of course. In fact,
he preferred her that way. That was when he had the
most fun.

Of all the blood bunnies in his stable, Piper was his
favorite. Not because she was willing to do anything he
wanted in bed. Not because her blood tasted sweeter
than the others. She was his favorite because she was
pliable, easily manipulated. All he had to do was suggest that he wanted something and she would see that it
was done.

The stupid bitch even believed he loved her.

It hadn't taken much. He gave her the attention she'd
never gotten from human guys. Made her feel as
though she was special to him and in return she gave
herself over to his will.

Thinking of how easily he'd twisted her into his personal suck and fuck threw off his concentration. The
flood he'd been holding back broke free. He roughly

grabbed her hips, his fingers digging into her flesh, and held her tightly against him.

"Not yet, Kirk," Piper pleaded. "I'm not close. Just a little—"

A primal roar burst from his throat as he ignored her pleas to wait for her to climax with him. He bent her forward, burying her face into the pillows, and rammed himself into her.

Piper's muffled squeals and violent thrashes spurred his blood-hunger as well as his lust.

Kirk grabbed her long blond hair and pulled her head out of the pillows.

She gulped for air as he sank his fangs into her neck. Blood spurted, hot and sweet, into his mouth. The rush of memories from her life forcing themselves into his mind proved too much for him. He buried himself within her, riding the waves of his climax until his pleasure fully drained from him. Shaking, he withdrew and collapsed next to her on the blood- and semen-stained bed.

Breathing heavily, she rolled onto her side and draped her arm over his chest. "That . . . was a-fucking-mazing."

"I wasn't asking for your approval." He shoved her away and reached for the pack of cigarettes on the nightstand.

The hurt from his rejection passed quickly and she smiled, drunkenly. "So what's got you in such a good mood, sweetie?"

"None of your damn business," he grumbled, blowing smoke in her face. He stretched while she coughed.

"Can't you give me a teensy weensy hint?"

Muttering obscenities under his breath, he grabbed his wallet from beside the bed and opened it. He pulled out a wad of cash and tossed it at her. The stack of hundreds and fifties bounced off her chest to scatter over the rumbled sheets.

Piper blinked and then the sight seemed to finally register and she shrieked in delight. "Where did you get all of this?"

"New client." He took a draw off his cigarette and blew the smoke out his nose like a dragon. "He has a very specific taste and is willing to pay out the wazoo to satisfy it."

She gathered the bills and laid them on top of her naked form, creating a sort of money blanket. "What does he like?"

"Redheads."

Piper's expression froze. "When did he pay you?"

He didn't answer.

She looked at the money and then at him. "Did you send Mindy to him?"

He thumped her forehead and made her flinch. "What have I told you about asking too many questions?"

"I'm sorry," she whimpered.

He stabbed out his cigarette on the edge of the nightstand. "Mindy was scheduled to meet him but that dumbass cousin of yours flaked out and didn't show. Now I'm going to need you to find me a new redhead."

"Where am I supposed to do that?"

"I don't care, just find one, by tomorrow night."

"Tomorrow?" She sat up, spilling money across the bed and floor. "Why so soon?"

Kirk yawned and stretched again. "I'll have to break her in before I can send her out to clients."

Piper's eyes flashed angrily. "Why?"

"Why what?"

"Why do you have to break in every girl?" She pouted. "Aren't I enough for you?"

He laughed and pulled her on top of him. "Darlin',

I'm not gonna fuck her. Those bunnies are just the warm-up for the main event. You know that."

She straddled him and wiggled her sex against his growing erection. "And I'm the main event, right?"

"Damn right."

"Prove it."

His arms snaked around her, crushing her to him as he kissed her. He rolled her over onto her back, hundred dollar bills crunching beneath them, and gave her the proof her body craved.

Allen and Leah Johnson lived in a Victorian manor in the heart of Jefferson's Old Towne district. Tasha had always loved the eclectic mixture of elegant antebellum mansions, brightly painted Victorians, and earthy mid-century bungalows. She'd even dreamed of the day she, Caleb, and Maya would own a home in the coveted neighborhood.

It was a dream that would never come to fruition now, and she found herself settling for a rented cottage in one of the fringe areas surrounding Old Towne.

As she guided her unmarked police cruiser into the driveway beside the Johnsons' stately home, she couldn't help feeling a twinge of jealousy. She pushed aside the resentment and made her way up the front walk while the various possibilities behind their daughter Mindy's disappearance ran through her mind, a new one forming with each step.

Kidnapping for money had been ruled out. More than forty-eight hours had passed without a single ransom demand made. Of course, money wasn't the only reason people were abducted. Even though Mindy's car had been found the possibility she'd left town of her own volition couldn't be ruled out. However, as the days fell away without the girl contacting her family, it seemed unlikely.

The most likely scenario involved foul play. Tasha started her law enforcement career as a street cop a few years after high school and worked her way up through the ranks. Over the years she'd honed her investigative instincts and her gut told her Mindy wasn't being held. It told her the girl was most likely already dead but she couldn't voice that opinion. To give it voice would ripple through the cosmos and make it reality.

Leah Johnson answered the door before the final chime of the bell had faded. "Lieutenant Lockwood," she said, brushing a strand of coppery hair from her face. "Has there been any word on Mindy?"

"I have some news." Tasha avoided directly answering the woman's question. "Is Allen home?"

"Yes, he's home." She stepped back, opening the door wide to admit Tasha. "Please, come in."

Tasha entered the home's small foyer and then a cozy room to the right as indicated by Leah.

"What's the news? Did you find Mindy? Is she all right?" Leah's questions came rapid-fire, burning with the same strained hope that filled her jade-like eyes.

"I think it's best if I tell you and Allen together."

A shaking hand fluttered up to cover Leah's mouth. "Oh, sweet Jesus. She's dead. Isn't she?"

Tasha realized how her previous statement could've been misconstrued and moved quickly to correct her mistake. "No, Leah. We don't know that. We're still looking for her, but we *did* find her car."

Leah made a sound somewhere between a relieved sigh and a mournful sob.

"I have some follow-up questions for you and Allen, if you're up to it."

"Yes," Leah said, nodding. "Of course. I'll let Allen know you're here."

Tasha took a deep breath and released it slowly while Leah made her way up the stairs lining the left side of the foyer. The Johnsons' living room sported high ceilings, denim blue walls, comfortable furniture perfect for watching movies on the big screen plasma television, and dozens of family photos. She paused to look at a framed portrait of Mindy in her high school graduation cap and gown.

The smiling girl in the photo was a younger version of her mother. Coppery red hair curled around a peaches and cream face. Jade green eyes twinkled with excitement and the promise of the life that lay ahead of her.

Tasha had seen that same excitement in Maya's eyes in the last photo she'd received. She was twelve in the photo, but had turned thirteen a few days after it was taken. Looking at the proud display the Johnsons had created for Mindy, Tasha felt a pang of guilt. She didn't display Maya's photo at home or on her desk. She kept it tucked away with her badge, her secret guardian angel and a reminder of why she risked her life to make the world a safer place.

Another picture of the entire Johnson family caught Tasha's eye. It was a snapshot from what appeared to be a vacation at the beach. Leah and Mindy knelt on sandy towels, hugging and laughing. Allen sat on an ice chest nearby, smiling and watching mother and daughter as they mugged for the camera. The perfect example of a familial happiness Tasha had never known.

"Lieutenant," a man's voice called from the foyer.

Tasha looked up from the photo and was greeted by an identical smile plastered on the living face of Allen Johnson.

"I'm sorry to keep you waiting. Leah says you found Mindy's car." He directed her to an overstuffed and oversized armchair while he and his wife took positions on the opposite sofa.

"It was left in front of the women's dorm at the community college."

As they sat, Tasha scrutinized the couple. The Johnsons were a study in contrasts. Leah was petite, fair-skinned with equally pale red hair and green eyes, and a youthful glow that made her age difficult to determine based solely on appearance. Thick muscles rippled under Allen's mahogany skin, creating a solid girth to match his height. Naturally wiry hair had been tamed, cut close to the scalp but retaining the salt-and-pepper characteristic of a man in his late forties. His eyes were a light golden brown, sharp and piercing in their intensity.

"Is there any indication that she's the one who left it there?" Allen asked.

"No, but forensic analysts from the FBPI will be examining the car. If there is any evidence to be found, they'll find it."

"No one saw anything?" Leah asked.

"No one has come forward yet."

"How can someone leave a car in plain sight and no one see the driver?" Leah's voice took a hysterical edge. "It doesn't make sense!"

Allen wrapped his arm around his wife's shoulder. "The police are doing everything they can, sweetheart."

Tasha nodded. "It's true. We have officers canvassing the campus and surrounding areas with Mindy's picture and a description of the car. Unfortunately, these cases can take time to crack. But someone, somewhere, holds the key bit of information we need. We just have to find them."

Leah dropped her gaze, and Allen cleared his throat before asking, "You said you had some questions for us?"

Tasha pulled from her pocket a pen and small note-book containing a few hastily scribbled notes she'd made during a brief phone conversation with Alex. "One of the Enforcers found a couple of items in Mindy's car that perhaps you could help put into context and give us a better understanding of how they fit in with Mindy's life."

"Of course," Leah said, wiping at her eyes as she looked at Tasha. "Anything we can do to help bring Mindy home."

"The Enforcers found a large amount of cash in her backpack. Was it customary for Mindy to carry around a lot of money?"

"No, but how much is 'a large amount'?" Allen asked.

"Almost one thousand dollars."

"Where would she get that kind of money?" Allen looked at his wife, who shook her head.

Tasha scribbled in her notepad. "Did she have a job?"

"No, we paid all her expenses."

"They also found a donor card bearing Mindy's name. Were you aware of Mindy's status as a registered vampire blood donor?"

"Yes," Allen answered quickly, removing his arm from Leah's shoulders. "She told us a couple of months ago but she said she wasn't working anywhere yet be-cause of her class schedule."

Vampires required small amounts of blood for sur-vival. However, they weren't allowed to pick random human victims. All blood transactions were closely reg-ulated by a joint effort between the Centers for Disease Control and the FBPI. Humans wanting to give their blood to vampires—and there wasn't a shortage of will-ing donors—were required to pass a battery of physical and psychological tests. Once they were deemed fit, their name and information were entered into the Central Donor Registry. They were then required to show a valid donor card to any vampire wanting to hire them as a donor.

It was a practice, regardless of the safeguards that had been implemented over the years, that Tasha simply didn't understand. She'd heard some donors speak of the rush they got from donating to a vampire. The way they talked it was as though they were addicted to it.

You know something about addiction, don't you? the nagging voice in her head taunted. *You chose me over your husband, your child, even your job. Now look at you. Nothing but a couple of vampires' lapdog.*

She massaged her temple, trying to rub out the voice's source as she asked, "Did Mindy say who her private recipient was?"

Allen sighed heavily and interlaced his fingers with those of Leah's free hand.

"I'm not certain I understand your question. Private recipient?" Leah asked.

"Most donors work in blood bars, but there are a few who apply for private donor status, reserving their blood for one vampire only. Mindy's application carried a private donation waiver."

Leah gasped and covered her mouth with her hand. "Allen—"

His hand closed around Leah's, cutting off her question. "Are you certain it's *our* Mindy?"

Tasha nodded, carefully watching the couple's interactions. "We confirmed all the information with the Central Donor Registry. Unfortunately, her private recipient wasn't listed."

"How can they not have that information on record?" Allen asked.

"The Enforcers are looking into it now."

"It can't be true," Leah said, her voice shaky. "It can't be."

"Sometimes when kids leave home for the first time, they do impulsive things," Tasha offered. "Maybe Mindy—"

"No." Leah shook her head. "Not Mindy. She isn't like that!"

"She registered without telling us first," Allen said quietly. He cleared his throat when Leah stared at him. "Why should a private donor be any great shock?"

Leah continued to stare at him in silence.

"Is there anyone you can think of she would've told about her private donor, Mr. Johnson?" Tasha asked.

"Her cousin, Piper. She and Mindy are very close. When I saw the two of them a few days before Mindy disappeared, I had the feeling there was something going on, but I didn't press the issue. I thought Mindy would come to us when she was ready."

"You saw her?" Leah whispered.

He nodded.

"And you didn't tell me?"

Allen enclosed her hand in both of his. "I didn't want to upset you. It was in passing. They were sitting in a coffee shop. I was running late for a meeting but I waved. They must not have seen me because—"

"How can you be so calm about all of this?" Leah demanded. "My baby is missing and you're prattling on like it's the most common thing!"

"I don't believe hysterics are going to help bring Mindy home."

"You bastard." Leah pulled her hand away from his and stood.

Tasha jerked in her seat with the surprise force of Leah's hand connecting with her husband's face. Sobbing, Leah fled the room and up the stairs. The glass panes in the window behind Tasha rattled when a door slammed somewhere on the second floor.

Allen stared at the ceiling for a moment before turning his attention to Tasha. "I'm sorry, Lieutenant. Leah can be overly emotional at times. Mindy's our only child, and the stress of the last few days is starting to really take its toll."

"I understand completely. I have a daughter of my own."

"How old?"

"She's thirteen."

He smiled wanly. "That's a great but difficult age."

Tasha sighed, suddenly uncomfortable with the turn in the conversation. She flipped through her notes. "Mindy's your stepdaughter, isn't she?"

"I'm not her biological father, no, but I did legally adopt her a few years after Leah and I married. Mindy was three or four at the time."

"Where's her biological father? If we could talk to him, he—"

"You're wasting your time, Lieutenant. Connor, Leah's first husband, died when Mindy was only a few months old. Hunting accident. He fell out of a tree stand and his gun accidentally discharged."

Tasha winced and her inhaled breath whistled as it passed through her clenched teeth.

"After Leah and I married, it just seemed easier to adopt Mindy than have her grow up with a different last name. Oh, I know it's common now for kids and parents to have different last names, but I think it's confusing for the kids and can be frustrating for the parents. I wanted to save Mindy and Leah from having to go through that."

Tasha nodded her understanding. She made a few notes in her notepad and redirected the conversation. "Where did you see Mindy?"

"The coffee shop on Jefferson Boulevard—Mug Shots."

"And you don't know what she and her cousin were talking about?"

"No, and there was someone with them. A boy. As I said, I was running late for a meeting. I ran in, grabbed a cup of coffee, saw Mindy and Piper sitting in the back, and waved. They must not have seen me because they kept talking."

"If you didn't hear the conversation, what makes you think there was anything wrong?"

"Mindy looked as though she'd been crying."

"Did you recognize the boy with them?" Tasha asked as she quickly scribbled notes.

"No, but I think he may have been Piper's boyfriend. The two of them were sitting beside each other, and he had his arm draped over her shoulders."

"Can you describe him?"

Allen took a deep breath and tilted his head, staring out the window behind her. "I only saw his profile, but he had sort of longish brown hair, wore one of those knit caps with the brim, flannel shirt over a white T-shirt, jeans. There was a denim jacket hanging on the back of his chair."

"And you'd never seen him with either Mindy or Piper before that day?"

He shook his head.

The cell phone clipped to the waistband of her slacks vibrated, and Tasha checked the text message that showed up on the screen.

SUSPICIOUS VEHICLE AT COONE'S AUTO SALVAGE. PROPERTY OWNER REPORTS STRANGE ODOR EMANATING FROM TRUNK.

Tasha added the last of the description that Allen had provided to her notebook and rose. "I'm sorry to cut this short but I have an urgent call. I have to go."

Allen stood with her and shook her hand. "You'll let us know the moment you hear something, won't you?"

"Of course."

He escorted her to the entrance and thanked her for stopping by.

Tasha heard the door close behind her as she hurried to her car. Backing out of the drive, she thought she saw Leah staring out from one of the second-story windows. The vision was gone almost as soon as she spotted it, leaving only shadows backing the windows, and she couldn't help but wonder if those windows reflected a darkness growing within.

five

ALEX LEANED AGAINST THE TRUNK OF VARIK'S CORVETTE and hugged herself as she watched the flatbed tow truck winch Mindy Johnson's car into place. It was being transported to Jefferson Police Department's impound yard and its contents would go with Freddy and Reyes for further forensic processing.

Other Enforcers and uniformed Jefferson police were dispersing in separate vehicles, returning to patrols and assignments. She envied them. Less than two hours back on the job and she was already feeling the pressure of Damian's scrutiny.

"Tell me again about this vision," he said, shifting his stance to block her view of the tow truck.

The vision she'd received when she picked up the doll flickered through her mind and she shuddered. "We've been through this once. Do we really need to go over it a second time?"

"We'll discuss it as many times as I think necessary. Now start talking."

She sighed and jammed her hands in her jacket pockets. "I saw a room lit by candles. There was a circle drawn on the floor with some kind of weird writing around it."

"Would you recognize the writing if you saw it again?"

"I don't know. I didn't really get a good look at it because that's when I saw the girl." Alex glanced at Varik as he joined Damian. "She was lying in the center of the circle. Her throat was slit."

"Describe her."

"Dark hair and eyes, about my height."

"Did she look like the doll?"

"Yes," she hissed. Annoyance gave her words a sharp edge. "Aside from being naked and dead, she looked *exactly* like the damn doll."

Damian growled a warning.

Varik's mind brushed hers. *Behave yourself.*

She met his stern gaze and dropped hers, sighing. "Yes, the girl looked like the doll. No, I don't know a name or a location, but I saw someone moving in the shadows beyond the candlelight."

"Could you see who it was?" Varik asked.

"I never saw his face."

"But you're certain the person was male?" Damian asked.

"I could hear him chanting. I think it was Latin, but I couldn't understand it." The memory of the scene that played out before her turned her stomach. Her eyes closed in a futile attempt to block it.

An arm snaked around her shoulders, and Varik's natural scent filled her senses, giving her a renewed feeling of security.

"The chanting got louder." Alex forced her voice to remain level. "Then it was as though I was no longer watching this . . . ritual from across the room. It was like I *became* the girl in the circle." She opened her eyes to stare up at Damian's impassive face. "I felt like my soul was trapped in that girl's body."

Varik gave her shoulder a reassuring squeeze.

"This is the part where it gets really fucked up. I couldn't see the room anymore but I could still hear the chanting. I tasted blood, *lots* of blood. Then it felt like someone was pulling me up." A lingering cold chilled her blood, turning it to an icy sludge, and she shivered.

"Take your time," Varik said softly.

"I felt pressure, like someone was sitting on my chest, and then pain." Tears slipped down her cheeks. "I can only describe it as being ripped into a thousand tiny pieces. All I could see was darkness. All I heard was that fucking chanting."

Varik pulled her closer to him.

Damian cleared his throat before speaking. "Is there anything else you can tell us about this unseen person? The room? The girl?"

Alex swiped at her tears with shaking hands. "Only that before the vision changed, when I was still observing from across the room, I felt . . ." She hesitated and felt heat coloring her cheeks. "Incredibly aroused," she murmured.

Varik shifted next to her so she could see his face. "Aroused? You mean—"

"Yes, sexually." The heat in her cheeks spread to her entire face. She sucked in a deep breath and released it in a huff. "Whoever this guy is and whatever he's doing to these girls, he *really* gets off on it." She crossed her arms in front of her. "And I hope I never experience anything like that again."

"Baudelaire," Damian said as he turned and indicated for Varik to follow him.

Varik gave her a sideways hug and kissed the top of her head. "I'll be back in a minute."

Alex watched them walk several feet away and stop when they were certain she was out of hearing range. Even though the sun was now above the trees and gradually bathing the parking lot in its light, it did little to chase away the shadows in her mind. The vision had drained her emotionally and physically, leaving her feeling cold and numb.

She pried at a protruding rock in the pavement with the toe of her boot. She'd inherited her powers of psychometry—the ability to have visions and gain information from objects as well as her gift to part the Veil and access the Hall of Records—from her father. Unfortunately he'd been killed before he could teach her how to control either of them. Support groups for vampires with psychic abilities didn't exist so most of the control she possessed was from years of trial and error.

"How are you holding up?" Varik asked as he rejoined her.

"I can't get that vision out of my head." The pavement cracked around the rock she was pushing with her foot.

"It was just a vision. It can't hurt you."

"I know but . . ." She tapped the rock back into place.

His hand slipped beneath her chin, gently encouraging her to raise her head and look him in the eye. "But what?"

"There's something I didn't tell Damian about the vision."

"You withheld information?"

She nodded.

"Damn it, Alex." Varik raked a hand through his hair. "You can't keep secrets from Damian—"

"You don't understand. There was someone—"

"—not when you're facing a Tribunal inquiry."

"He tried to force himself into my mind!"

Varik quieted and they stared at each other for a moment. Finally, he broke the silence. "What do you mean?"

"When everything was black and it seemed like I was being ripped apart, it felt as though someone was trying to force his way into my mind. It only lasted a few seconds, but I definitely felt it."

He clasped her shoulders, bending slightly to ensure eye contact. "You're absolutely certain the connection was with a male?"

She nodded.

Under vampiric law, forcing one's way into another's mind was tantamount to rape. The invasion and fear she'd experienced had left her shaken.

"Listen to me." Varik gently placed both hands to the sides of her face. Tightly controlled anger made his body vibrate against hers and the blood-bond buzzed in the back of her mind like a swarm of angry bees. "I will find the son of a bitch who did this, and I'll rip his fucking head off."

"There's more."

"Tell me."

"I'm not even sure it's part of the vision. It doesn't make sense, but just before I woke up, I saw my father."

"You saw Bernard?"

"Yes." Alex took a deep breath before continuing. "He was with a woman and they were kissing. I couldn't see her face but it was definitely *not* my mother."

Varik released her but remained silent.

"Like I said, it doesn't make sense."

He wrapped her in his arms and held her. "No, it doesn't, but we'll figure it out."

She nodded against his chest, unable to speak past the maelstrom of emotions that swirled within her.

He pulled back and his lips found hers while his voice whispered in her mind. *I love you, and I won't let anything happen to you.*

She broke the kiss and stroked his cheek with her hand. "I know," she murmured. "But you shouldn't promise something you can't deliver."

"Alex—"

"We should follow Freddy and Reyes to the lab." She

moved away. "We have a lot of work to do if we're going to catch this Dollmaker of yours."

Varik looked for a moment as if he would protest, and then simply nodded and pressed the button on his key ring to unlock the Corvette's doors.

Alex sank into the cool interior and was grateful when he started the engine and turned on the heater. Her thoughts ran in circles—recalling images of the dead girl, bits of the strange chants she'd heard, and the sensation of being pulled apart.

Anxiety gnawed at her spine. But was the source of her anxiety what she'd experienced or the brief glimpse of her father kissing another woman?

As Varik sped down the highway and into the heart of Jefferson, Alex watched trees give way to houses and single-story commercial buildings and realized she didn't know.

Tasha eased her sedan through the minefield of dry potholes and ruts that comprised the driveway of Coone's Pull-n-Go Salvage Yard. A chain-link fence topped with rows of barbed wire enclosed the yard but didn't hide away the hundreds of derelict cars, trucks, motorcycles, and farm equipment scattered across what had once been several acres of pastureland. She parked beside a small single-wide mobile home that had seen better days and tried not to twist her ankle among the many ruts when she stepped from the vehicle.

"You the police?" an older man with a bushy gray beard asked from the mobile home's porch. He adjusted the band on a grease-stained cap before using it to cover an equally unruly patch of matching hair on his head.

She flashed her badge as she rounded the front of her sedan. "Lieutenant Tasha Lockwood." The edge of a deep pothole gave way and she had to catch herself on the hood of her car to keep from falling.

"Watch your step there," the man said. "Some of them holes could break a leg if you fell right."

"You should do something about that."

The man shrugged. "Don't do no good. First gulley washer that comes through and they're back."

Tasha reached the porch's steps and stood on the lowest, still looking up at him. "Are you Mr. Coone?"

"Last time I checked."

"Are you the one who called in to report a suspicious vehicle?"

"Nope. That was my son, Buddy."

"Is he here?"

The elder Coone pointed toward the yard and the sound of an approaching vehicle.

Tasha turned to see an all-terrain version of a golf cart speeding in their direction. The cart bounced over holes and kicked up a plume of reddish dust behind it. The morning's rain hadn't affected this part of the county and the dust cloud overtook the vehicle. The driver stopped beside the porch and dust settled on everything in its path: the sparse brown grass, the weather-roughened wooden steps, the hood of Tasha's car, and Tasha herself.

The driver hopped from the cart and retrieved a tool-box and cylinder-shaped car part from the rear flatbed. He nodded to Tasha as he set the box and part on the edge of the porch. "Are you here for the alternator?"

Before she could answer, the elder Coone spoke. "She's police. Here about the car."

Tasha showed her badge and introduced herself. "You made the call, Mr. Coone?" she asked the younger man.

"Yes, ma'am. Found it sitting in the back this morning when I went to pull a radiator. It's definitely not one of ours."

"Please don't take this the wrong way, but how can you tell?" she asked, glancing over the rows of rusting shells and partially stripped hulks.

The older man snorted and the younger chuckled. "We keep track of all vehicle identification numbers. When a new one comes in, we log the number into our computer system. Anytime we pull a part we enter the part into the system and which VIN number it came from. Saves us a lot of time searching for viable parts."

"That's how you knew this vehicle wasn't one of yours."

Buddy Coone nodded. "Plus this car stinks to high heaven. Smells like something big crawled up in it and died."

"Did you open the car?"

"I didn't touch it except to check the VIN number through the windshield. Couldn't stand being that close to it." He gestured to the cart. "We can take a ride out there in the Mule and you can see for yourself."

Tasha joined him in the cart and winced as they bounced over the poorly maintained pathways of the salvage yard.

Buddy pointed to a sturdy grab bar attached to the cart's metal frame near her head. "You may want to hold on to that 'oh shit' bar. This is going to get a little rough."

She barely had time to catch the bar before he guided the Mule into a shallow gully. Muddy water splashed up from the wheels, spattering her pants with brown and orange.

He gunned the engine and spurred the vehicle up the opposite side and back onto an overgrown path. They slowed as a chain-link fence and a row of metal frames that had once been cars came into view.

Buddy stopped beside a section of the fence sporting bright red stakes woven through the links and driven into the ground. He pointed to the stakes as he and Tasha stepped from the cart. "Before I found the car, I noticed the fence here had been cut and pulled back. See these tracks?" He waved his hand over the ground in front of them.

Tasha noted the wide swath of grass and weeds that appeared to have been crushed. "Looks like something big was pulled through the fence."

"My guess is whoever dumped the car here cut the fence and either pushed or dragged it in."

"And the stakes in the fence?"

"Temporary repair. I'm going to have to replace this entire section here but at least this keeps the deer from wandering through."

"Who owns the property on the other side?"

"That's part of the old Cottonwood Plantation. It used to belong to Benjamin Corman but he passed away a few years ago. I'm not sure who owns it now."

Tasha nodded, making a mental note to visit the plantation.

Buddy motioned for her to follow him. "After I saw the fence, I followed the tracks and found the car over here."

As they approached a battered dark blue Ford Focus, the slight wind that had been rustling the dried leaves of a nearby sweet gum tree picked up, carrying with it the unmistakable odor of decay.

Tasha grabbed Buddy's arm, halting him. "I need you to stay back here."

He covered his nose with his hand and nodded, his face pale.

A gnawing sense of dread ate at her brain. She drew her sidearm, startling the salvage yard owner. Tasha picked her way through the tall grass toward the Ford, keeping her nine-millimeter Beretta pointed toward the ground but poised to swing into a firing position at any moment.

She studied the vehicle as she carefully approached from the side. It sported heavy dents in the sides, roof, and hood. The windshield had been shattered from what appeared to be multiple impacts. A quick glance showed glass shards on the floor and backseat as well as dark stains on both front bucket seats.

She moved to the trunk, and the stench of rot worsened, forcing her to fight against her natural reaction to gag. A breeze blew over the car, swaying the partially open trunk and driving another wave of putrid odor into Tasha's face.

She searched the ground for something to open the trunk without contaminating the scene with her fingerprints. She found a length of a broken oak branch, and holding it in one hand while readying her Beretta in the other, she wedged the branch into the gap between the trunk and tailgate and levered it open.

It took her mind several seconds to piece together what she saw lying in the dark well of the trunk. Once the mosaic clicked into place, forming a complete picture, Tasha stumbled away and retched into a patch of weeds.

"You okay, ma'am?" Buddy called to her.

Tasha held up her hand to signal she was fine and for him to stay back. She used a spare tissue she found in her pocket to wipe her mouth and then pulled out her cell phone. She hit a button and the phone dialed a preset number.

"Jefferson Police Department," a woman's voice answered. "How may I direct your call?"

"This is Lieutenant Tasha Lockwood. I need a forensics team, a flatbed tow truck, and the coroner to come to Coone's Pull-n-Go Salvage Yard right away. I think I just located Mindy Johnson."

Ecstasy encased Peter's mind. His body shivered with the remembered thrill of feeling her so close.

"Alexandra," he whispered her name, reveling in the memory of their encounter.

It was the briefest of caresses, but for a moment her warmth had flowed through his body and his through hers. He'd pressed forward, excited that she had come to him in such an intimate way.

She'd been shy, shrinking from his advances.

And then she was gone. Ripped away by *him*.

Rage over his denial burned through Peter's body. The Dark One continued to stand between them, an obstacle to be eliminated. It wouldn't be easy. The Dark One was strong, far stronger than he.

But Peter was smarter. He knew the Dark One's weakness and he would exploit it. He would crush the Dark One's spirit, break him, and destroy him.

And then Alexandra would finally be his.

six

IN THE CONVERTED RECREATIONAL VEHICLE THAT WAS one of the FBPI's three mobile forensics labs, Alex sat at a small table in the rear section that served as a tiny lounge and sleeping area. Other sections of the forty-foot RV housed an on-site command center with satellite links to the Bureau's main lab in Louisville. Separate areas for processing firearms, narcotics, fingerprints, audio/visual, and questionable documents completed the mobile lab's complement of workstations.

Alex brushed a lock of hair behind her ear and glanced at the stacks of boxes crammed into the tiny space. Plastic bins containing bags of items from Mindy Johnson's car and dorm room surrounded her while she sifted through reports, transcripts of conversations, and evidence documentation. She'd been poring over the information for hours, trying to absorb as much of it as possible, but the memory of her early morning vision continued to intrude upon her thoughts.

She focused on the preliminary report of the bloodstains found on Mindy's passenger seat, but her gaze drifted to the large brown paper bag containing the doll. Forcing herself to look away, she sighed and used her hand to both prop up her head and shield the bag from view.

The report showed the blood was definitely human. The type matched that on file for Mindy with the Central Donor Registry, but it would take much longer to run a complete profile comparison. For now, they were working on the assumption that the blood was Mindy's.

She skimmed through the list of items taken from the girl's dorm room: syringes, flexible latex tubing, alcohol swabs, an open pack of condoms, a date book, and a journal. Other items were listed as well, but the date book and journal piqued her curiosity. She rummaged through the plastic bins spread over the table to locate them. She found the date book but the journal wasn't there.

Alex glanced around the lab and spotted Freddy hunched over a microscope. "Hey, Freddy."

"Yeah, boss?" he asked, his eyes still trained on whatever he had under the scope.

"Any idea where this journal, Item Fourteen, is?"

He looked up and frowned. "It's not in the bins?"

"No."

"It should be there." He joined her, pulling off his latex gloves and tossing them into a large trash can. He poked around in the same boxes she'd searched, and scratched his head. "No one's touched these since yesterday except to add what we picked up from the car this morning."

"It's not here."

"Reyes," Freddy called to his lab partner. "Do you have Item Fourteen?"

"Nope," Reyes responded without taking his eyes off the computer screen in front of him.

"Could someone have checked it out?" Alex asked.

"If they did, they would've signed it out in the catalog." He pulled out a small binder and flipped through the pages, shaking his head. "No one signed for it. Maybe Varik took it with him and forgot to sign."

Alex shook her head. "Why would he take evidence with him on a coffee run?"

"Good point." Freddy sighed. "Well, it has to be here somewhere." He began searching through more bins.

She glanced at her watch as she stood up to help. Varik had left nearly an hour ago on a mission to get what he considered "proper coffee" for the lab. The generic store brand Freddy and Reyes consumed by the pot wasn't good enough for him. Even when they were engaged, he'd insisted on buying whole beans and grinding them himself.

Alex smiled with the memory. She wasn't picky about her caffeine source, but even with Varik's snobbishness, it shouldn't take an hour to buy coffee, not in a town as small as Jefferson.

Beethoven's Fifth Symphony sounded from her pocket. She pulled her cell phone free and checked the caller ID before answering. "Sabian."

"Where the hell are you?" Tasha asked without pre-amble. "The coroner is here as well as the tow truck. Tony is already processing the car. What is taking you so long?"

"I'm at the mobile lab, and what the hell are you talking about? What car?"

"One of the owners at Coone's Pull-n-Go called in a report of a suspicious vehicle this morning. I came out to follow up after leaving the Johnsons', checked the car, and found a body in the trunk. I think it may be Mindy."

"Ah, shit." Alex surged past a startled Freddy and headed for the exit. "I'm on my way."

"Enforcer Sabian!"

She whirled to face Freddy as she ended the call with Tasha.

"What should I do about the journal?"

"Find it." She bounded down the steps and hit the pavement running. Rounding the front of the RV, she slammed into a very large warm body. "Fucking hell!"

"Nice to see you, too, Enforcer Sabian," Damian Alberez rumbled.

Alex dropped back a few paces. "Sorry. I didn't see you." She glanced at the woman standing beside Damian. "Sir."

"Going somewhere?" Damian asked.

"A body's been discovered. I'm on my way to—" She remembered her Jeep was still parked in front of her temporary hotel home and inwardly groaned. "—call Enforcer Baudelaire."

The woman stepped closer to Damian. "Is the scene secure?"

"Yes, but—"

"If the situation is under control, and since you can't *possibly* be the primary investigator, I'm certain it can wait a few moments," the woman murmured.

Alex's temper flared. "And just who the hell are you?"

"Enforcer Alexandra Sabian, meet Morgan Dreyer, Special Investigator to the Tribunal," Damian said.

Morgan smiled, revealing sharp white fangs, and Alex's anger withered.

"Where's the scene?" Damian asked.

"Coone's Pull-n-Go Salvage. The body could be Mindy Johnson."

"Who made the discovery?" Morgan asked.

"Lieutenant Tasha Lockwood of the Jefferson police, but she hasn't been able to reach Varik and—"

"That would be Varik Baudelaire, Director of Special Operations?"

The way Morgan almost purred when she said Varik's name caused a rush of possessiveness to sweep over Alex. She fought the urge to grab the dark brunette braid that snaked around the other woman's shoulder and ram her head into the front of the mobile lab. Physically assaulting the Tribunal's Special Investigator wouldn't help Alex's corruption case nor would it help her get to the salvage yard. She managed to keep her emotions in check, but unable to trust herself to speak, she simply nodded.

"Chief Alberez."

Damian swiveled to face Morgan with a carefully maintained façade of neutrality.

"I believe this would be an excellent opportunity for me to observe Enforcer Sabian in the field."

"What?" Alex scoffed.

"As part of my investigation, I'm required to monitor you in the field," Morgan said. "My observations of how well you follow proper procedure are reported to the Tribunal and will be used in their accounting of your guilt or innocence."

Alex looked to Damian. "Please tell me she's not serious."

He glared at her.

"This is the biggest crock of shit—"

Damian clamped his hand on her shoulder and spun her, herding her around the side of the mobile lab. "Excuse us," he grumbled to Morgan. "I need a word with Enforcer Sabian *in private*."

Alex tried to keep in step with him but found it hard when his tight grip on the collar of her jacket kept threatening to lift her feet from the ground.

They moved past the midway point of the forty-foot-long RV and he finally released her, shoving her back against the cold metal siding. "What the hell do you think you're doing?"

"At the moment I figure I'm getting my ass chewed."

"Don't get cute." He folded his arms in front of him and gave her his best impression of a pissed-off boulder. "I swear you sound more like Varik every fucking day."

"Excuse me?"

"*You* know better than to provoke someone like Morgan."

Alex readjusted her jacket and checked the position of the silver badge clipped to her jeans's waistband. "Does she really have to shadow me in the field? I thought the Tribunal was only interested in my past cases."

"They were, until you were reinstated. They're not going to pass up the opportunity to have firsthand observation of your methods. You can thank Baudelaire for screwing you on that."

"I will." She cracked her knuckles. "Trust me."

"Where is he?"

She shrugged. "He left over an hour ago to get coffee. Tasha said she called him but he isn't answering his phone. I was going to try reaching him through the bond."

"He hasn't checked in?"

"No, but that's not unusual. If something were seriously wrong, I would've sensed it. He's just ignoring Tasha for some reason."

"Find out what the hell he's doing and then the two of you get your asses out to that salvage yard."

"Anything else?"

"Just remember Varik is primary. Work clean. Follow his directions. I'll put my foot up your ass if you screw up this inquiry and get yourself killed."

"Gee, I didn't know you cared."

"Cut the attitude," he said softly. "And don't antagonize Morgan like you do Varik."

"I do *not* antagonize Varik! He bugs the crap out of *me*!"

"He bugs the crap out of everyone." He sighed and placed a hand on her shoulder. "Take care of yourself. I don't want to be the one to bear bad news to Emily again."

Alex watched him leave. She wasn't sure what to

make of his parting remark. Again? When had he delivered bad news to her mother in the past? Alex had been the one to find her father's staked and decapitated body in the cemetery near their home, so Damian couldn't have meant that.

She checked her watch. Where the hell was Varik?

As she dropped the shields protecting her mind from Varik's, Morgan rounded the corner of the lab. "Enforcer Sabian, a moment, please."

Alex swallowed the smart-ass retort that was her first instinct and recovered her mental barriers. "Of course."

"I want it to be perfectly clear that I'm here at the request of the Tribunal. I could care less about who your father was and I'm not here to be friends."

"Damn, and I was hoping we could go shopping later." She knew the statement was a mistake as soon as Morgan's hazel eyes narrowed.

"This sort of flippant attitude makes me wonder if you're capable of being an effective Enforcer."

"You have no idea what I'm capable of."

"You turned rogue. That speaks volumes."

"Let's get something straight right now." Alex stepped close, her words a low hiss. "I don't like you, and I don't give a shit what you, or the Tribunal, think about me. Right now, my concern is Mindy Johnson and giving her family some closure. If I clear my name in the process, so be it, but the girl comes first."

Morgan held her ground. "We'll see if you still feel that way once the Tribunal convenes next month."

Alex stalked away, no longer caring if Morgan shadowed her. It was common for Internal Affairs Special Investigators to goad the object of their scrutiny to elicit a reaction, to provoke them into showing a weakness. She'd shown she had a temper. If she wasn't careful, Morgan could easily paint her as a loose cannon to the Tribunal and that would be all the justification they needed to retire her.

Permanently.

Varik sat in a back corner booth at Mug Shots, Jefferson's only gourmet coffee shop, and watched as a curvy blond woman settled onto the bench seat across from him. The overhead lamps caught the silver highlights in her curls but cast shadows under her clear blue eyes. Once she'd settled, he reached across the table and laid his hand over hers. "Thanks for meeting me on short notice."

Emily Sabian nodded and gave his hand a friendly squeeze. "You said it was urgent, that Alex had a vision."

He nodded and sipped his black coffee. "We were on-scene. She picked up some evidence and the vision hit her. Hard."

"Is she all right?"

"She will be, but . . ." Now that he sat face-to-face with Emily, he wasn't certain if he was doing the right thing. Did Alex's mother really need to know about the vision?

Of course she did, he argued with himself. Emily had to know. If the truth came out now with Alex facing the Tribunal, the repercussions could devastate the Sabian family as well as cast the Bureau into chaos.

"Varik?" Emily touched his arm. "What happened to Alex? What did she see?"

"Bernard. He was with Siobhan."

His words didn't seem to register at first and then realization made the color drain from her face. She bowed her head and closed her eyes, taking a series of deep breaths. Her words were muffled when she spoke. "Did Alex recognize her?"

"No, she said she couldn't see the woman's face."

Emily raised her head. "That's good."

"How is that good? She's going to figure out that Bernard cheated on you, that it wasn't just some random vision."

"As long as she doesn't know it was Siobhan, everything will be fine."

"I don't think you understand what I'm saying. Alex and I are bond-mates. If she has another vision like that, she's going to know I'm lying to her."

"No, she can't find out about Siobhan. Bernard was adamant that Alex never know of the affair."

"And I'm telling you that she's *going* to find out sooner or later."

Emily sighed and began twisting the gold band encircling her left ring finger. They sat in silence for several minutes before she finally spoke, her voice pitched low. "Bernard and I hit a rough patch in our marriage about a year before Alex was born. What caused the split isn't important anymore. The affair only lasted a few months and then Bernard came to his senses and came home. He and I made up and were very happy until the day he was killed."

When she leveled her gaze on him, her blue eyes were a pale shade of gold, like sunlight filtered through autumn leaves. "You were Bernard's partner for a long time, and he thought of you like a second son."

Varik looked out the coffee house's large window and watched the traffic passing by on Jefferson Boulevard.

"I'm asking you—*begging* you—to bury your knowledge of Bernard and Siobhan deep in yourself."

He focused on her again. "I don't know if I can."

"Varik, please . . ."

"I understand your desire to follow Bernard's wishes, Emily. Hell, I certainly don't want to hurt Alex. She idolized her father—still does—but there is *no way*

Bernard could've foreseen any of this, regardless of his Talent."

"But he *did* foresee that Alex would face the Tribunal. He said if she faced the Tribunal ignorant of his past as a Hunter-Talent, as well as of Siobhan, then she would be exonerated."

"Visions change. They're nothing more than educated guesses based on current circumstances. Replace one element and the entire pattern alters."

"He *saw* it, Varik, and he said—"

"He also saw himself at the Tribunal with Alex. That's not likely to happen now, is it?"

Emily drew back as if he'd slapped her.

"I'm sorry." He reached for her hand, and she pulled away. "That came out wrong."

"I should go." She began gathering her things.

"Wait, please."

She slipped out of the booth and shouldered her purse.

Varik stood and grabbed her arm. "Don't leave. Not like this."

"Please remove your hand, Enforcer Baudelaire."

He released her. "Emily, I'm sorry. Please—"

"Thank you for telling me about Alex's vision. Please let me know if she has any more." She hurried away and this time he didn't try to stop her.

The blood-bond suddenly opened and Alex's voice whispered in his mind. *Turn your fucking cell phone on, jackass.*

What's wrong?

Tasha thinks she may have found Mindy Johnson's body.

"Fuck." His troubles with Emily would have to wait. He grabbed his jacket, tossed the rest of his coffee into the trash, and sprinted for his Corvette.

*   *   *

The campus of Nassau County Community College was abuzz with news about the discovery of Mindy Johnson's car. Kirk lounged on top of a concrete bench outside the Union Center, the hub of campus life, and listened to the gossip floating up from adjacent tables.

"I heard the vamps found her severed hands in the glove box," one pampered-princess coed told a small group and then nodded sagely when they gasped in melodramatic horror.

"A guy in my econ class said it was her head," another contradicted.

"Don't be stupid," the first said. "You couldn't *fit* her big head in a glove box. Besides, I learned about this sort of thing in my psych class. It's called . . ." Her mouth worked but no sounds came forth and she finally heaved a disgusted sigh. "It doesn't matter what it's called but just think about it. Hands in a *glove* box—it's so sick."

Kirk chuckled and turned a page of the book he was pretending to read. The princess table moved their conversation to the upcoming formal dance, and he in turn shifted his focus to another table.

". . . heard she was involved with drugs or something," a mousy-haired girl said, pushing her glasses higher on her upturned nose.

"Yeah, she was gonna snitch on somebody on campus," said a boy dressed in the baggy clothing favored by skaters. "But it wasn't drugs she was into. It was blood."

Kirk glanced at the group over his sunglasses and shifted his position so as to better hear their conversation.

"Blood?" a girl with purple-streaked hair asked. "You're full of shit. She wasn't no vamp!"

"No, but she was selling it," the skater boy replied. "I heard there's someone on campus running some kind of black market blood ring. Vamps are having a hard time finding legal blood since Crimson Swan got torched. I heard you can make a helluva lot of cash."

"Like how much?" the mousy girl asked.

The skater boy shrugged. "A lot if you're willing to let the vamp actually bite you, more if you let 'em do it during sex. I heard Mindy had a couple thousand bucks in her car."

The girls exclaimed their disbelief, and Kirk closed the book, grabbed his backpack beside the bench, and stalked away. Since Crimson Swan, the only legal blood bar in Jefferson, was destroyed he'd seen a marked increase in his business but that wouldn't account for the sudden glut of information available among the student population. Someone was talking too much, and he had a suspicion that someone was Piper.

The little whore never could keep her mouth shut.

It probably wasn't wise to recruit on campus, but college kids had the two requirements he most valued: a need for cash and a desire to do whatever it took to obtain it.

He wouldn't take on just anyone though. His clientele were selective and so was he. Unlike some of his more equal-opportunity-minded competition, Kirk specialized in "blood bunnies"—young women who were willing to share both their blood and their bodies. Nothing got the blood pumping like a good fuck, and blood always tasted better when combined with the sweet endorphin rush that was sex.

Clients called him to arrange for a bunny suiting their tastes. Payment was handled electronically and then he sent the girls on their way. Once the meeting was complete and the client was satisfied, he gave the girls five to ten percent of the payment, depending on how well she performed. Any cash tips they received from the client were theirs to keep.

The best part was that he didn't have to answer to the Central Donor Registry bureaucrats. No licenses meant no overhead, such as rent or insurance, and no overhead meant more profit.

But his profit margin would vanish if he didn't plug the information leak, and soon.

Kirk entered one of the classroom buildings and dashed up the stairs, taking the steps two at a time, to the second floor. Piper's class would be ending in a few minutes. He wanted to be certain she understood the risks they both faced if word of his operation should reach the Enforcers.

As he strode down the hall, a door at the end opened and bleary-eyed students shambled from the room. He placed himself along the wall opposite the door and waited.

Piper was one of the last students out of the room, and she stopped in her tracks when she saw him. A male student talking with the instructor ran into her from behind. Amid a flurry of halfhearted apologies to the instructor and other student, she timidly crossed the hall to join Kirk.

He waited for the hall to clear and then seized her arm.

"What did I do?" she whined as he shoved her into the now-empty classroom.

Kirk closed the door and turned off the lights so the only illumination came from the miniblind-encased windows at the rear of the room. "People know."

"About what?"

"My business. Now, how do you suppose they know about it?"

Piper shrugged.

The back of his hand smacked her cheek. "I asked you a question."

Struggling to hold back tears, she shrugged again. "I don't know."

"Someone is talking," he said quietly, closing the distance between them. "Someone who *shouldn't* be talking." He gripped her jaw, digging his fingers into her flesh, and forced her to look at him. "I wonder who."

Realization dawned in her tear-filled eyes. "It wasn't me," she whispered. She clutched at his shirt. "I swear! I've been careful."

"If the Enforcers find out what we're doing, they'll send me away—"

"No! They can't!"

"—and then they'll turn you over to the human authorities. You'll sit in prison for the rest of your life, lumped in with the whores."

She sobbed and buried her face against his chest.

He rolled his eyes. Piper's capacity for easy manipulation never ceased to amaze him.

"I'll find out who's spreading the rumors." Her voice was muffled until she raised her head to stare at him. "I swear. Just promise me you won't let me go to jail if something should happen. I can't live without you."

Kirk gave her a wan smile and brushed away her tears. He gently kissed her lips and enfolded her in his arms. "I promise you'll never see the inside of a jail cell."

She clung to him in the semidarkness while he held her and thought of all the places he could stash her body once she was of no further use.

seven

EMILY ENTERED THE FOYER OF THE HOME STEPHEN shared with Janet, closed the door, and leaned against it. Anger she thought she'd rid herself of decades prior had returned, and the desire to scream was almost more than she could bear.

Before moving farther into the house, she took a moment to compose herself and listen for signs of life. No voices greeted her. No breath sounded in other rooms. No hearts beat save her own.

Satisfied she was alone, Emily moved to the combination living and dining room adjacent to the kitchen and sank onto the beige sofa. Her conversation with Varik ran through her mind in a continuous loop, refining it until only one point remained fixed in her memory.

Alex saw Bernard with Siobhan.

Siobhan Kelly. Vampire. Mistress. Hunter-Talent. Fugitive. And a name Emily hadn't spoken or even thought of in over forty years. Now she couldn't banish Siobhan from her mind.

Maternal instinct arose. Danger stalked her family. Alex's vision was only the beginning. She had to find a way to protect them.

But how? How could she protect them from a past she was sworn to keep secret?

Emily buried her face in her hands. Her mind became a rapid-fire series of questions and scenarios. Each potential solution was rejected as quickly as it formed, until her subconscious dredged forth yet another name she'd forgotten long ago.

Raising her head, she glanced at her cell phone lying on the table before her. If she called, would he answer?

"I have to try." Her whisper echoed like a shout in the stillness of the empty house.

She dialed the number from memory, hoping it still worked. The receiving phone rang once. Twice. It was picked up on the fourth ring and a male voice filtered over the line.

"Hello?"

Her breath caught in her throat.

He repeated the greeting.

Emily couldn't force the words from her lips.

His tone became more forceful. "Who is this?"

"Hello, Gregor," she said in a much calmer voice than she felt. "It's Emily."

Silence descended and stretched for so long she began to fear the call had been lost.

"It's been a long time," Gregor finally said.

"Yes, it has."

"How are you?"

"I'm well." She closed her eyes, gathering her courage. "I know it's a shock that I'm calling out of the blue like this, and you would have every right to refuse, but . . . I have a favor to ask of you."

Another lengthy pause was followed by a few simple words. "What can I do?"

Emily took a deep breath and said in a rush, "I need you to save my daughter."

As Varik eased his Corvette over the cruddy road leading to Coone's Pull-n-Go Salvage Yard, Alex hunkered down in the passenger seat and wondered why she'd ever become an Enforcer.

It wasn't the first time she'd thought of her motivations for joining the Bureau. Naturally the strongest impetus stemmed from her father's murder and a desire for the justice denied her family as her father's murder remained unsolved. She could've become a lawyer and accomplished much the same goal, however. Why had she pursued the role of Enforcer with such single-mindedness that she'd blocked all other options from her consideration?

The afternoon sunlight hit her face as Varik turned off the bumpy county road and onto the equally pock-marked driveway to the salvage yard. Squinting against the light, she reached for a pair of dark sunglasses she'd hung from the neckline of her shirt and slipped them over her eyes. While sunlight didn't cause real vampires to burst into flames, much to the chagrin of block-buster Hollywood productions, intense light did hurt their sensitive eyes. Wearing shades during the day was a small price to pay for the superior night vision they gained in return.

They arrived at the outer perimeter of the salvage yard to find police cars with their strobing blue and white lights scattered about the crude parking area. Uniformed officers in a group near the cars gestured in the direction of the gate and shook their heads. An old man looked on with unbridled curiosity from a mobile home's porch.

"You haven't spoken a word since we left town," Varik said as he parked behind an empty sheriff's department car. He switched off the Corvette's engine and fixed her with a stern look over his dark aviator sunglasses. "You want to tell me what's bugging you?"

"Before I told you about Tasha's call, I got caught by Damian and the Tribunal's Special Investigator."

"Shit, that was quick. I didn't think the SI would be here until later today."

"Apparently SI Morgan Dreyer has a bug up her ass. She's coming to observe me in the field, by the way, so you have to behave as much as I do. Damian's orders."

Varik's spine turned rigid at the mention of Morgan's name.

The blood-bond reacted to his emotional change and anxiety washed over Alex. "Is there something about Morgan I should know?"

Varik opened his door and climbed out, forcing her to scramble to follow.

"When I mentioned your name she acted as though she knew you," Alex said as she joined him as they walked toward the fence separating the parking area from the rest of the salvage yard.

"She and I worked on cases during my pre-Bureau days."

"How many cases?"

He paused, rubbing his chin and lost in thought. "You said she's coming here?"

"She and Damian should be here any minute."

"I think you and I should keep the bond open while she's on-scene."

Alex frowned. "Why?"

"Morgan's an SI. It's her job to provoke you, and you *do* have a temper."

"So you want to use the bond as a way to mellow me out? It's a blood-bond not psychic Prozac, Varik!"

Several humans turned to stare at them.

Alex moved even closer to him, and the scent of sandalwood and cinnamon called to her, enticing her to touch him. She jammed her hands into her jacket pockets and pitched her voice low. "Besides, we can't ignore the fact that opening the bond in close proximity to each other for more than a few minutes has certain effects on us."

He grinned. "Afraid you'll jump my bones, Enforcer Sabian?"

"Don't be gross."

He winked at her over the top of his sunglasses. "You don't hear me complaining, do you?"

"And what would you do if the bond took over? Push me up against a car and go at it with half of Jefferson's police force watching?"

He tilted his head, and she could feel his eyes swiping over her body.

She waved her hand in front of his face. "Varik?"

"I'm thinking."

She slapped his arm. "You're sick."

His laughter was shortened by the sound of an approaching vehicle.

A black Ford Expedition bounced up the rutted drive and parked behind two JPD units. Alex could feel the judging gaze of Morgan Dreyer sweeping over her even from a distance.

"They're heeee-rrrrre," he said in a singsong imitation of a classic horror film.

Morgan stepped down from the Expedition's running board, and Alex instinctively stepped in front of Varik.

He laid a reassuring hand on her shoulder. The blood-bond pulsed between them as he attempted to open it. "Let me in," he whispered.

"What about the side effect?" she said quietly over her shoulder.

He chuckled. "I promise if you throw yourself at me in a lustful manner, I'll resist the temptation to ravish you."

"Asshole," she muttered.

"Do we have a deal?"

"Fine. Deal."

Alex relaxed the shields keeping Varik's psyche from intruding upon her own. The blood-bond surged to life, carrying his thoughts and emotions to her and sending hers to him. She gasped as the circuit completed and a series of recent memories seen from his viewpoint crowded into her mind: a dark-haired doll on a car seat; Alex lying on the rain-slick pavement and screaming at demons only she could see; her mother's face bearing a sadness that tore at Alex's heart.

The memories faded and were replaced with Damian and Morgan striding toward them. Damian still presented his carefully constructed neutrality, while Morgan beamed, her attention clearly focused on Varik.

He maneuvered around Alex to stand a step or two in front of her.

As the primary investigator for the case, it fell to him to greet the new arrivals. Alex could sense the conflicting emotions—anger, anxiety, dread, sadness—roiling within Varik. Pieces of memory filtered through the bond to her, but they were disjointed and she couldn't make sense of them.

"Bonjour, mon amour," Morgan said as Varik stepped up to greet her, hand extended. She ignored his hand and cupped his face in her hands, lightly brushing his lips with her own.

Anger curled Alex's hands into fists.

Don't you dare *move.* His command filled her thoughts and kept her from rushing forward. He gripped Morgan's shoulders and firmly pushed her away. His words dripped acid when he spoke. "Hello, Morgan. Don't ever do that again."

Morgan thrust out her bottom lip in a perfect pout. "What's the matter, lover? Aren't you happy to see me?"

"I'd rather have my fangs pulled."

Alex tried to disguise her stifled snicker as an aborted sneeze and failed miserably.

Morgan pushed her designer sunglasses to the top of

her head. Her hazel eyes had shifted to a bright copper and blazed with contempt.

An approaching vehicle silenced any remark Morgan would've made. Alex watched as what appeared to be a four-wheel-drive golf cart sped through the chain-link fence surrounding the salvage yard and stopped in front of their group. The driver surveyed them with uncertainty before focusing on Varik.

"Are you Enforcer Baudelaire?" the man asked.

"Yes." He moved away from Morgan and Alex fell into step with him. "You must be Buddy Coone."

The man nodded. "Lieutenant Lockwood sent me to pick you up." His eyes darted to Alex then to Damian and Morgan. He took in Morgan's crisp white shirt, navy pencil skirt, and inappropriate high heels. "The terrain's kind of rough in the yard, ma'am. It might be safer if you changed your shoes. Wouldn't want you to twist an ankle."

A quick image of Morgan stepping in a hole, falling to the ground, and breaking her neck flashed through Alex's mind.

Varik hid a laugh in a cough. *Behave yourself.*

Alex glared at him. *I will if you explain where the hell Morgan gets off calling you her lover.*

"I'll be fine," Morgan responded, positioning herself beside Varik.

Buddy looked doubtful. "There are ruts, holes, rusted metal, all kinds of things to trip over. Ma'am, are you sure you can—"

"I assure you, Mr. Coone, I'm perfectly capable of navigating the terrain without injury."

Buddy shrugged. "Suit yourself, but I'll have to make two trips. I've only got room for two of you at a time."

Varik climbed into the cart's flatbed. When Morgan appeared as though she was going to commandeer the remaining spot, Alex pushed forward. She shoved Morgan aside with a well-placed hip, grabbed the cart's roll bar, and pulled herself on the bench seat beside Buddy Coone.

His startled yelp nearly drowned out Varik's stifled laughter and Morgan's curse.

Looking over her shoulder at Morgan, she feigned innocence. "Oh, I'm sorry, SI Dreyer. I thought you wanted to change your shoes."

"Enforcer Sabian, I—"

The whine of the cart's engine covered the rest of Morgan's statement. Alex pointed at her ear and shook her head, shrugging.

Buddy directed the cart onto the path leading into the salvage yard.

Once they were out of sight, Varik's explosion of laughter and pat on the shoulder combined with a surge of warmth over the bond. *I love it when you're jealous.*

Alex sat up straighter and adjusted her sunglasses. *I'm not jealous.*

Oh, yes, you are.

Envy filled the bond and she sighed. *All right. Maybe a little. But can you blame me after Morgan pulled that lover crap back there?*

No, I suppose not.

Are you going to explain it?

We're on our way to a body dump. Now isn't exactly the best time.

The cart jounced down the side of a ditch and fought its way up the other side. Buddy swerved around a row of derelict minivans with clumps of brown weeds growing between them.

Alex noticed gray-black shadows darting among the wrecks and heard the unintelligible whisperings of the spirit world. She wasn't surprised to find restless souls lingering in the salvage yard. After all, it was a cemetery of sorts and spirits often lingered near objects of significance. Could anything be more significant than the vehicle of one's demise?

The blood-bond shivered and a short pornographic film featuring her flashed through her mind.

She twisted in her seat to punch Varik's arm, startling Buddy and causing him to nearly collide with the remains of a compact car. "Knock it off!"

Laughing, Varik flooded the bond with his thoughts. *You put the idea in my head.*

I did not!

Were you or were you not the one who suggested I push you up against a car and—

That was not a suggestion, *and you know it.*

The bond shivered with the heat of his thoughts. *Perhaps not but it's not a bad idea.*

We're on our way to a body dump, as you pointed out. How can you possibly be thinking of sex?

I think the bond is affecting my judgment.

Alex snorted. *I thought it was because you're male and breathing.*

Varik chuckled behind her but didn't respond.

As they neared an isolated corner of the salvage yard, Buddy slowed the cart and stopped behind a white van with the JPD's logo and the words CRIME SCENE RESPONSE UNIT emblazoned on the side. "This is as far as I go," he said. "The lieutenant is over there, other side of the van. Look for a dark blue Ford."

Alex stepped from the cart and she heard Varik scrambling to exit the flatbed.

"I'll go fetch the other two," Buddy said. "Y'all be careful. There's a lot of broken glass around here."

The cart motored away and wind swept across the pasture. Alex breathed deep, instantly regretting it as the overwhelming smell of decay assaulted her. Gagging, she clamped her hand over her nose and mouth, trying in vain to block the odor.

She'd heard humans describe the smell of decomposition as akin to a Dumpster filled with rotting fruit—sickly sweet mixed with a slightly musty odor. To the heightened senses of vampires, the smell was that of both a fruit-filled Dumpster and an open sewage line.

Varik assumed a similar stance to hers. "No need to look for a fucking Ford. Just follow the damn smell."

Tasha appeared from opposite the van. Her clothing was covered by a white Tyvek jumpsuit, plastic booties enveloped her shoes, and a paper cap protected her hair. The overall effect gave the lieutenant the appearance of a displeased Pillsbury Doughboy. "You're going to want to suit up for this one."

Alex and Varik moved to the rear of the van, where Tasha was pulling out matching jumpsuits for them.

"Tony's with the body," Tasha said while they stepped into the Tyvek suits. "What's left of it, anyway."

"Have you found any ID?" Varik asked, slipping plastic coverings over his boots.

"Not yet. Yard owner says the car isn't part of his inventory. One of my guys is running the VIN number on the car now. Hopefully we can at least figure out the owner."

Alex adjusted the paper cap to cover her hair. Cross-contamination of evidence was a huge risk at outdoor scenes. The protective gear they donned couldn't prevent it with one hundred percent certainty but it did greatly reduce the odds. "How sure are you that it's Mindy Johnson?"

"I'm not even sure it's a person."

Neither Alex nor Varik responded, allowing the severity of what they were about to see penetrate their minds. When they'd finished dressing in their protective gear, complete with latex gloves, Tasha led them toward a Ford Focus.

"Were you able to get anything from Mindy's car?" she asked. "Anything that would lead us to suspect she's still alive?"

"No, but I do have a working theory." Varik offered a quick review of the morning's events as the three slowly walked through the waist-high weeds.

"So you think this Dollmaker guy is here, in Jefferson?" Tasha asked. Suspicion and doubt weighted her words.

"It's possible," Varik said. "The similarities between what I saw in 1924 and today are too great for me to ignore and pass off as a coincidence or a copycat."

"But you're not ruling it out," Tasha added.

"No, not yet."

"If you're correct, why would the Dollmaker come here? Everything you told me makes it sound like he prefers larger cities."

"I don't know why he's here or if he even *is* here, Lieutenant. As I said, it's a theory."

Alex blocked out most of their argument in favor of stretching her senses to learn as much as possible about the scene around her. She focused on the battered Ford Focus. Large dents covered its exterior and the windshield was smashed. Mud caked the passenger's side as though it'd been sprayed from the front wheel.

The trunk was open to its widest point, and Tony Maslan, JPD's chief crime scene investigator, dressed in an identical Tyvek jumpsuit, snapped pictures of the trunk's interior with a digital camera. He glanced up as they approached. The green tinge to his skin let Alex know whatever the trunk held was far worse than she was imagining.

She tried to set aside the nauseating smell of decomposition and search for other clues. The wind carried the metallic bite of rust mixed with the earthy scents of various animals. A faint but pungent strand of garlic made her nose wrinkle.

"What have you got, Tony?" Varik asked, bringing Alex out of her musings as they stopped.

"A goddamn mess," the forensics tech responded. "Best I can tell is that we have a Caucasian female with red hair. Anything beyond that will have to be left for the medical examiner to sort out."

Beside her, Varik hissed in disgust.

Alex forced herself to look into the trunk and struggled to make sense of what she saw. She fixated on a cluster of swollen black protrusions. A few of the misshapen lumps sported strange jagged lavender tips, but all rose from a sea of fine coppery threads that were matted and stained with a dark substance. It wasn't until her mind recognized the black masses as fingers and the threads as hair that the gruesome scene fell into place like a macabre jigsaw puzzle.

"Who or what could have done this to a human being?" Tasha asked softly.

Varik moved in for a closer look. "It's hard to say with this level of decomp but it looks almost like some kind of animal."

"An animal?" Tony echoed. "How could an animal do that much damage to a person?"

"We have no way of knowing if it's an animal or something else," Alex answered, moving away from the gruesome sight. She worked her way alongside the car, searching for anything that seemed out of place. "Until Doc Hancock gets her on the table, we won't even know who she is. We shouldn't jump to conclusions until we have more facts."

"She's right," Varik said. "Let's just stick to what we see here and save the speculation for later."

Tony and Tasha mumbled their agreement, and Varik began directing where Tony should concentrate his photos. Tasha stood back and watched, hands on hips and her expression unreadable, but her eyes followed Alex.

Alex ignored Tasha's unusual amount of scrutiny and continued to circle the car. She traced the dents in her mind but avoided touching them until the exterior could be properly examined for prints. A pattern began to form and a sickening realization crept into her thoughts. She focused on the windshield and its spider-webbing cracks.

"Find something?" Varik asked as he joined her.

"Look at this." She pointed to the double impacts from which the cracks radiated. "See the dark spots in the center?"

He leaned forward and after a moment nodded.

"I'll bet a week's pay when Freddy tests those stains it will come back as vampire blood."

"What makes you think it's vampire?" Tasha asked from the opposite side of the car. "Could be from a deer."

Alex shook her head. "A deer is possible but unlikely. I've seen this kind of damage before. Look at the dent pattern." She swept her arms over the crumpled hood. "It's as though something attacked the car, rather than hit it by accident."

"But why attack the car itself?"

"It held something the attacker wanted. Add in the condition of the body, and I think we're looking at a vampire hyped on Midnight."

Midnight was possibly the deadliest drug on the black market. A potent mixture of the human street drug Ecstasy, garlic, aspirin, and animal blood, it was highly addictive for vampires. The garlic and aspirin thinned the vampire's blood, allowing the Ecstasy to have a greater hallucinogenic effect.

Animal blood, however, was the real danger. Vampires

fed on the residual psychic energy in blood, rather than the blood itself. Animal blood carried a more primitive psychic signature, which in turn caused any vampire who consumed the drug to revert to a more animalistic state, and deaths—both vampire and human—were all too common.

"Shit," Varik murmured. "There goes my theory."

"An attack by a Midnight vampire makes sense but at the same time it doesn't." Alex placed her hands on her hips and shook her head. "If that body *is* Mindy Johnson, what the hell was she doing to run afoul of a Midnighter?"

"Mindy is a registered donor with a private recipient waiver," Tasha said. "Maybe her recipient can answer that question."

"Did her parents know who she was donating to?" Varik asked.

"No."

"Even if we find her recipient, we still have the issue of finding whoever ditched her car," Alex interjected. "It's unlikely a Midnighter would even remember attacking her much less have the sense to get rid of her car."

"Plus her car wasn't damaged," Varik added. "This one, on the other hand, has been beaten to Hell and back."

They stared at the battered car, lost in thought. The whir of an approaching motor signaled the return of Buddy Coone and the arrival of Damian and Morgan.

Alex's loathing for the Special Investigator and her anxiety over being forced to perform for the Tribunal's benefit spread over the bond to Varik.

He brushed against her, sliding his hand across her lower back, as he moved into position at the front of the car. The intimacy of his touch shivered up her spine and made her gasp as a memory snapshot of their most recent lovemaking session flashed through her mind.

"Are you all right?" Tasha asked.

Alex nodded, chewing her bottom lip. She glanced at Varik from behind her dark shades and saw the knowing smirk on his face. *You did that on purpose, you bastard.*

His smirk turned to a grin.

"Is there something going on here I need to know about?" Tasha asked, annoyance evident in her tone.

"Yes." Morgan's voice drifted to them from nearby. "Please do fill the rest of us in on your obviously private joke, Enforcer Baudelaire."

Varik's smile disappeared. "If I did then it would no longer be private, would it, SI Dreyer?"

"Then bring us up to speed on everything instead," Damian said, intercepting Morgan's response. He moved to look into the trunk. "Who is she?"

As Varik recited what they knew so far and Tasha interjected information she'd learned from her interview with Mindy's parents, Alex studied the salvage yard, noting the repaired fencing and the car's proximity to it.

Whoever had disposed of the body and the car had gone through considerable effort. The land beyond the fence was flat pasture with a few clumps of oak trees. No road or path was visible along that side of the fence. Whoever ditched the car here would've had to drive or tow it across the neighboring field.

She frowned. But why leave either the car or the body where they could be found? Why not burn the vehicle with the body inside, thus reducing the amount of evidence as well as the odds of making a positive identification?

Movement beside a nearby rusted hulk drew her attention. A black shadow hovered close to the derelict vehicle. The shadow's form wavered, elongated, and shifted into something vaguely humanoid.

Fine hairs on the nape of her neck stood on end. The sense of menace radiating from the shadow caused her to back up.

As she retreated, it moved forward.

"Alex?" Varik asked, heading toward her.

"Don't move. Stand perfectly still."

"What's wrong?"

"Trouble."

"What kind—"

The shadow charged.

Alex clambered to get out of its way but it moved too quickly. It caught her squarely in the chest and seemed to meld with her flesh as though her body were absorbing it. An unearthly cold passed through her, stealing her breath.

Voices rose in alarm around her. Varik's hand clamped onto her shoulder. She could see him shouting her name but heard nothing beyond the increasing beat of her heart.

A presence entered her mind along with a sense of malice, directed not at her but outward. The blood-bond reached a fevered pitch as the entity seized upon it.

NO! Alex screamed at the possessing force.

The intruder left her in a rush, following the path of the open blood-bond. Too late, Varik attempted to throw up protective mental barriers. The shadow slammed into his body, lifting him from his feet and throwing him to the ground several feet away.

"Varik!" Alex hastily erected protective shields around her psyche, severing the bond. She rushed forward and slid to her knees at his side.

His eyes were wide, staring at something only he could see, and his mouth was open but no breath filled his lungs. A tremor traveled the length of his body and became a series of convulsions.

"He's having a seizure!" Tasha shouted for Tony to call paramedics.

"No, he's fucking possessed!" Alex straddled him, trying to hold him still. She used her hands to steady his head. "Where are you, you son of a bitch?"

"Enforcer Sabian!" Morgan shouted. "I demand to know—"

A shadow darted within Varik's eyes.

"Gotcha." Alex threw open the bond and sent her consciousness chasing after the invader.

She was vaguely aware of strength leaving her body. The sensation of falling distracted her for only a moment, and then she was plunging through the darkness, searching for a shadow in an endless void.

eight

"FUCK!" KIRK SLAPPED THE BUTTON TO PAUSE HIS VIDEO game as the doorbell sounded. He jumped to his feet and the handheld controller bounced on the carpeted floor. Whoever was interrupting his playtime was going to get their asses kicked.

The bell chimed again before he reached the foyer, intensifying his anger.

"What?" he demanded, wrenching open the door.

Piper and a tall blond girl both jumped back in surprise. Nearly incoherent words tumbled out of Piper's mouth, her tone rising so it sounded like she was asking a question rather than making a statement. "Hey, Amber Lynn is—I mean, she and I wanted to— You asked me to bring Amber Lynn by."

Kirk glanced from Piper to Amber Lynn, one of his newest bunny recruits. He leaned against the doorjamb. "What *are* you rambling on about?"

Piper laughed nervously and cut her eyes over at the other girl. "You told me about that *thing* this morning and asked me to bring Amber Lynn by to talk to you about it."

The *thing* she rambled about finally clicked into place and he smiled. "Oh, right." He shifted his attention to Amber Lynn, a pretty blond with pale brown eyes. "Come in," he said, moving aside as he gestured for her to enter.

Amber Lynn ducked into the foyer, her long hair brushing against his bare chest as she passed.

Piper moved to follow, and Kirk stopped her by placing his hand in the center of her chest. "Make yourself at home," he called to the other girl and stepped outside. "I'll be right in."

"Kirk, what about—"

He whipped Piper around and led her toward her car. "You need to leave now."

"What? Why?"

"Amber Lynn and I need to have a private conversation, and you still need to find me a replacement redhead."

"But how will Amber Lynn get home?"

He opened the driver's door of Piper's white Nissan Sentra and encouraged her to sit. "Don't worry." He gave her a quick kiss on the lips and then smiled. "I'll take care of her."

Piper seemed on the verge of protesting but then sighed and cranked the car.

Kirk closed the door and waved to her as she backed out of the driveway. Once she was headed down the street, he dropped the caring-boyfriend façade and returned to the house. He entered and found soft music issuing from the living room. Suspecting what he'd find, he strolled through the foyer, down the short hallway, and into the spacious living room.

"Is she gone?" Amber Lynn asked. The cardigan sweater she'd been wearing lay draped over the back of the sofa and her shoes were tucked under the coffee table.

He nodded and sauntered over to the sofa, positioning himself behind her.

She pushed off from the sofa, drifted to him, and wrapped her arms around his neck. "Good, because I've been *dying* for an excuse to see you again."

He pulled back from her attempt to kiss him. "Before we get down to business, Amber Lynn, you and I need to have a little chat."

Unfazed by his rejection, she giggled and slipped her hand over the front of his jeans. "You mean the *thing* Piper was talking about?"

"I have a problem."

"Oh, I can help you with it."

"I'm sure you can." He smiled and stroked her cheek. "Someone's been talking about my little business. Someone with a big mouth." His hand cupped her jaw and tightened until she cried out and her eyes widened in fear. "Who've you been talking to, Amber Lynn?"

"I-I don't know what you mean," she whimpered.

Kirk shoved her, watching as she tumbled over the sofa and onto the floor. The back of her head banged against the corner of the coffee table. A crimson ribbon soaked into her pale hair.

"First, you blab around campus about *my* business, and now you're bleeding on my carpet." He grabbed her hair and dragged her across the floor to the tiled eating area separating the living room from the kitchen. "Do you have any idea how long it takes to get blood out of carpet?"

She screamed and slapped at his hand. Her fingernails sliced his flesh.

His temper exploded. He released her, ripping strands of hair loose, and grabbed the front of her shirt. Shoving her against the kitchen island cabinet, Kirk straddled her, his face inches from hers. "Who did you talk to, bitch?"

Amber Lynn wailed as he slammed her head against the hardwood cabinet. "I-I didn't say anything!"

"Liar!"

Blood and mucus trickled from her nose. "Please, Kirk—"

"Piper wouldn't have brought you here for no reason!" He shook her and she howled again. "Tell me who you talked to and I *may* let you live."

The girl sobbed hysterically but she rattled off several names, people he didn't know.

"That's all of them?" he asked.

She nodded.

He tugged on her shirt, lifting her torso from the floor, and kissed her, tasting the blood that filled her mouth. He shivered as random memories flooded his mind.

She gasped for air when he broke away, only to have it leave in a rush as his fangs sank into the tender flesh of her neck.

Blood gushed into his mouth but he didn't swallow it. He shook his head like a dog with a favorite toy, digging his fangs deeper and shredding tissue.

Amber Lynn's heart raced, pumping more of her blood through her system. Little gurgles were the only noise to escape her rapidly paling lips.

Kirk released his hold on her, and she flopped against the cabinet, struggling for breath. He cocked his head, watching for a moment, and then stood. He walked to the refrigerator and grabbed a beer. Twisting off the cap, he gulped down half of the bottle while listening to Amber Lynn's feeble attempts to draw a breath grow weaker and finally cease.

The lingering smell of blood made his stomach rumble. He set the beer down on the counter and picked through the freezer section of the refrigerator. He selected a couple of Philly Steak & Cheese Hot Pockets and tossed them in the microwave. While they heated, he moved back to Amber Lynn.

Her eyes were wide and staring at a fixed point somewhere beyond Kirk's shoulder.

He squatted beside her, picked up an arm, checked for a pulse, and finding none, allowed her arm to drop. Her hand smacked a puddle of blood, spraying his bare feet with dark droplets.

She'd given him half a dozen names, all students. He knew from experience most could be bought or scared into silence. For now, however, the major information leak was plugged.

Kirk stood, licked the traces of blood from his fingers, and grabbed his Hot Pockets. Sliding them onto a plate, he retrieved his beer and stepped over Amber Lynn's prone body. He settled on the couch, picked up his game controller, turned off the soft music that had continued to play, and resumed his game.

Alex and Varik both lay unconscious on the ground beside the car. Tasha motioned for Tony to follow her. "We have to help them."

Damian held out his arm to stop her. "Do *not* touch them."

"You saw what happened. They could be hurt. We can't just stand by and do nothing."

"You can and you will, Lieutenant."

"They *need* help! We have to get them to the hospital!"

Damian shook his head. "Moving their bodies could put both their lives in jeopardy."

"What?"

"Save your breath, Chief Alberez," the female vamp—Tasha had heard Varik call her Morgan—said. "Humans aren't capable of understanding the metaphysical ramifications of what just occurred."

"Excuse me?" Tasha rounded on her. "I understand a hell of a lot more than you think, lady! I may not *fully* understand this blood-bond thing Alex and Varik share, but I have a pretty good idea that whatever just occurred has something to do with that bond."

Perfectly sculpted brows rose over the rims of Morgan's sunglasses and she focused on Damian. "Blood-bond?"

Her voice dropped an octave. "Why wasn't the Tribunal informed of Enforcers Sabian and Baudelaire's bonding, Chief?"

With Damian glaring at her, Tasha suddenly felt like a child who'd revealed a secret to the one person from whom it was meant to be kept.

"It's a recent development," Damian answered.

Morgan moved to stand over the unconscious Enforcers. "I don't see fresh bites. Scars, yes, but nothing I would declare as recent." She shifted her attention back to Damian. "Would you care to revise your statement, Chief?"

"Alex attacked Varik a month ago," Tasha said, earning a disapproving look from Damian and one of curiosity from Morgan. "I was told that by doing so she reinforced a bond that already existed."

Damian groaned and swiped a hand over his face.

"Interesting." Morgan carefully picked her way through the weeds to stand before Tasha. "And when was this bond first established, Lieutenant?"

Tasha glanced at Damian who kept his gaze heavenward.

"I'm asking you," Morgan said, "since Chief Alberez seems to be either ignorant of the situation or unwilling to share."

"Six years ago, in Louisville."

"I see. How did you come by this information?"

"Stephen, Alex's brother, told me. I was asking him questions about Varik."

"What made you seek out Enforcer Sabian's brother regarding Enforcer Baudelaire?"

"I didn't trust him." Tasha dropped her gaze to Varik's still form. "Still don't."

"Hmm." Morgan moved past Damian. "A word, Chief."

"Does this affect the way the Tribunal will judge Alex's case?" Tasha asked.

Morgan paused and glanced at Tasha over her shoulder. Sharp white fangs gleamed in the sunlight when she smiled. "Oh, yes, it changes everything."

Tasha watched the two vamps move some distance away. The thought that she'd once again betrayed her oath as an officer crept into her head. But did it even matter anymore?

She'd already stolen evidence. She'd already determined she would hand it over to whomever her mystery caller ordered. She would report on everything she'd seen and heard here. Her pledge to protect and serve had become twisted, and the inner voice that taunted her laughed merrily at her rising misery.

"Well, I didn't like the sound of that," Tony said as he finally joined her. He nodded toward the obviously heated argument brewing between Damian and Morgan. "And I don't much like the *looks* of that." He swept his hand out to encompass the unconscious Enforcers. "I think Alex and Varik are going to wish they stayed down once they finally wake up."

In the distance, Tasha noticed a hearse bouncing over the rough terrain. "Coroner's here." She spun away from Tony, anxious to silence the laughter in her mind. "Will you take care of the body transfer? I want to check on something."

"Sure thing, Lieutenant."

She nodded her appreciation and headed in the opposite direction of both the hearse and the arguing vamps. The internal laughter continued as she rounded the remains of a white panel van.

With shaking hands, she pulled a small flask from an inner pocket of her jacket beneath the Tyvek suit. Tipping her head, she let some of the liquid within burn its way down her throat.

Drinking on the job, her internal tormentor chided. *Just like your loser parents.*

Memories of her father coming home early because he'd been fired from yet another construction job for showing up intoxicated swept through her mind. Those shifted to memories of how her mother thought nothing of "having one for the road" before climbing behind the wheel of a school bus.

She swore she'd never be like them. Yet here she was—the latest in a long line of pathetic scum that deserved all the shit they found heaped on their heads.

Maybe Caleb was right. If she continued to be a part of Maya's life, her daughter would be just as screwed up as Tasha's parents had made her.

Tasha took another swig of the bourbon. As it slid into her belly, she slid down the side of the panel van to sit on the cold, dead ground that was a perfect reflection of her soul.

Alex awoke surrounded by dense forest. What little sunlight filtered through the canopy above gave the ground a dappled effect. A cool breeze shifted the leaves and sent shadows skittering.

She was searching for two shadows in particular and turned in a slow circle, stretching her senses to detect them. The scent of sandalwood and cinnamon wafted to her on a breeze from the left. Movement in that same direction drew her attention.

A shadow darted among the trees, and she gave chase. Her feet flew across the ground, churning to catch up with the fleet figure she could now see running ahead. She burst through a thicket and came to a stop in a small clearing, the figure no longer in sight.

"Damn," she muttered. She scanned the trees but all was still.

Voices whispered behind her and she spun, finding no one. The voices swirled around her. Snippets of conversations long forgotten rose to a crescendo and then vanished.

"Where are you, you son of a bitch?"

Over here.

She spun, searching for the source of the voice, and once again found only empty forest.

A hand trailed over her shoulder.

She recoiled from the phantom touch. Her foot snagged on a root and she fell, twisting to land on her back.

A silhouette blocked her view of the dense tree canopy and an uncomfortable weight pinned her. The specter cocked its head, studying her.

"Get off me!"

Alex screamed as a brilliant flash of light left her momentarily blinded. The light disappeared, as did the weight pinning her to the forest floor, and her vision returned. She sat up, looking for her phantom attacker.

The forest remained quiet and still.

"This bullshit is really starting to piss me off," she muttered. Pushing to her feet, she brushed the ground debris from her clothing. "Varik!"

Her call echoed in the forest.

"Where are you?" She drew a deep breath, preparing another call.

A shadow peeled from the base of a nearby tree and stepped forward.

Alex watched as a young boy—she would guess his age to be no more than four or five—moved into the clearing with her. Black hair framed an angelic face dominated by large warm brown eyes that stared at her with open curiosity.

"Hello," he said with a hint of an English accent.

"Hi," Alex responded, uncertain.

"Are you lost?"

"Sort of. I'm looking for a friend."

"I know."

She frowned. "How do you know that?"

"I heard you call his name." He smiled. "My name is Edward. What's your name?"

"Alex."

He giggled. "That's a boy's name."

Alex looked at him more closely, noticing the way his clothing clung to his tiny body as if it was soaked through. Other things began to stand out. The ashen color of his skin. Dark circles under his eyes. Water dripping from his hair onto his collar. But it was the hair, the eyes, and the smile that sent her mind reeling. She'd seen them all before, on someone else. "Edward, who—"

The leaves rustled overhead, and the boy stepped back. "I have to go now."

"No, wait!" Alex followed, but he melded with the shadows once more and disappeared. "Damn it!"

Wind picked up, ruffled her hair, and carried the familiar smell of sandalwood and cinnamon. The breeze settled and a scent of leather wrapped around her, prickling her skin.

Phantom arms encircled her.

She pushed against the unseen force enveloping her. The smell of sandalwood and cinnamon strengthened her. Warmth filled her and she drew on the connection to fight the entity that had her in its grips. She thrust it away from her, leaving the stench of old blood in its wake, and she gagged.

The shadow darted into the trees.

She chased after it, calling to Varik as she ran. His scent grew stronger the farther she ran into the forest.

"Alex!" Varik's call rang out from somewhere to her right. "Where are you?"

The wraith she chased shrieked in fury and shot heavenward.

She stopped her pursuit. "Over here!"

Varik appeared before her, dashing through the trees. He rushed forward and swept her into his arms. He lifted her from her feet, kissed her hard, and spun her around. Even after he broke the kiss, he continued to crush her to him. "I heard that scream and thought I'd lost you."

"No, I'm fine. It was the shadow-thing, and you can put me down now. I'd like to breathe again."

He traded his embrace for a firm grip on her hand. "Where the hell are we?" he asked, looking around at the trees.

Alex's gaze swept the area. "The Shadowlands. It's sort of a—"

"Metaphysical no-man's-land."

She stared at him. "Yeah. How do you know that?"

He tapped his temple. "Blood-bond."

She rolled her eyes.

"Plus, you talk in your sleep."

"I do not!"

"You also have very noisy and vivid dreams."

"Excuse me?"

He grinned. "I especially liked the one featuring you, me, and the chocolate fountain. Seemed a little messy but I'm willing to give it a shot."

Her face warmed. "We agreed to stay out of each other's heads, damn it!"

His arms slipped around her waist, pulling her close. "I'm keeping my end of the bargain. It's not my fault your brain leaks."

Alex grunted in disgust and pushed him away. "Whatever. None of this matters right now. We have to get you out of here before that shadow-thing comes back."

"Me? You mean *us*."

She ignored his correction and pointed to a distant patch of sunlight. "There's a break in the trees over there. Hopefully we can reach it before either the shadow-thing or a sweeper finds us."

"What the fuck is a sweeper?"

"Big tornado that moves through the Shadowlands. It finds unauthorized consciousnesses and kicks them out. You and I qualify as unauthorized."

"What do you have to do to be authorized?"

"You have to be dead."

"That sucks."

"Yeah, so let's go before one shows up."

As she strode forward, Varik dug in his heels, his hold on her hand keeping her from leaving. "Hang on. How do *you* know so much about this place?"

"We don't have time to play twenty questions."

"I know this isn't your first time in the Shadowlands. How many times have you been here?"

She chewed on her lip and avoided making eye contact.

He ducked his head into her line of sight, forcing her to look at him. "Alex?"

"I don't know. I lost count."

"This is how you've been spending your suspension? Wandering the Shadowlands?"

"I wasn't wandering. I had a purpose."

"And that purpose would be what, exactly?"

She sighed and then continued in a rush. "I've been looking for my father's killer."

Varik groaned. "Alex, you know—"

"He's a lost soul," she interrupted. "He told me so. I can't let him roam the Shadowlands forever, and what little information I've gotten on—"

"Whoa, back up." Varik raised his hands to slow her down. "You've seen and talked to Bernard? Here?"

She nodded.

He ran a hand through his hair. "Shit. What has he told you?"

"Not much, just answered questions about the Shadowlands and the Hall of Records. It's not like I've been spending *every* waking moment here. Sometimes I see him, but most times I don't."

"Hall of Records?"

"It's not a real place, but—"

"I know what it is." Anger flashed in the depths of his dark eyes. "Why didn't you tell me you could access the Hall of Records?"

Her own anger rose to meet his. "I didn't know I could, and once I *did* know, I didn't think it mattered! Besides, how am *I* supposed to know *you* know about any of this? It's not like you've been forthcoming with shit from your past."

"Do *not* try to shift this argument to me. You should've told me about Bernard and the Hall from the start."

"You don't tell me everything. Why should I tell you anything?"

"Because we're bond-mates! That's why!" His eyes shifted from dark brown to molten gold. "I can't protect you if you don't fucking *trust* me!"

"Don't lecture to me about trust, Varik! For your information, I *do* trust you, but it's a two-way street and you're making this a hell of a lot harder than it needs to be. And what are you going to protect me from? Sweepers? The Tribunal?" She gestured to the surrounding forest. "That shadow-thing?"

"Yes, all of that."

Alex scoffed and shook her head, muttering, "You're as bad as Stephen." She paced a few steps away then faced him squarely. "I'm not a child. I've been an Enforcer for over twenty years. I can take care of myself. You can't protect me from everything, Varik. I don't *want* you to protect me. Don't you understand that?"

"How can I when you barely talk to me unless we're working a case?"

"I talk to you," she whispered, crossing her arms in front of her.

"No, you don't." He closed the gap between them. "You keep yourself walled away so I can barely sense you through the bond, except for snippets of dreams. Whenever I try to talk to you about our past, or our future, you shut down."

She shivered as he slipped his hands up her arms.

His voice softened. "You don't respond when I say I love you."

"What do you want me to say?"

"I want you to tell me how you feel." He leaned forward and his breath warmed her face. "About me, us."

"I don't know how I feel."

"Such a pity," he murmured and his lips brushed hers.

A primal scream issued from overhead.

They both stepped back, searching the canopy above. "Where is it?" Alex asked. "Do you see it?"

"No." Varik continued to hold her hand. "You said if we could reach that patch of sunlight, then we could get out of here?"

"I think so."

"Right." He tugged on her arm, pulling her along with him. "Let's go."

They ran, dodging trees and hurdling fallen logs. Another scream sounded from above, much closer, and it chilled Alex. Questions raced alongside her.

What chased them?

Why did it first attack her in the salvage yard before turning on Varik?

Why was it fixated on him?

As they neared the patch of sunlight, the specter dropped from an overhead branch. Alex lost her footing, stumbled, and smashed headlong into a tree. The impact left her unsteady until she tripped over an exposed root and sat down hard at the base of the tree she'd hit.

Only a few feet away, the wraith had Varik on the ground on his back. Both snarled and growled as they grappled and exchanged awkwardly swung blows.

Although disoriented, Alex pushed herself to her feet, using the tree's trunk for balance. She added her own rage-filled scream to the chorus and charged the phantom. She pounced on it and her momentum carried them into the underbrush.

They rolled and tumbled, each trying to gain the upper hand. Hissing in anger, the shadow released her and disappeared as the inertia she'd built tipped her over the edge of a steep slope. Her arms and legs worked furiously, attempting to find any purchase that would slow her descent.

She careened off a jagged stump and was pitched into the air. Her sudden flight ended when she crashed into something flat, hard, and cold. She lay for a moment, mentally adjusting to the abrupt termination of motion.

Groaning, Alex lifted her head, expecting to see the forest but was alarmed to find herself lying on a darkly stained hardwood floor in an unfamiliar room. Shelves lined all four walls, even above and below the bank of tall windows. Hundreds of eyes stared at her from the blank faces of dolls lining those shelves.

She sat up slowly.

And then the screaming began.

nine

VARIK FOLLOWED THE WIDE SWATH OF BROKEN TWIGS and churned-up earth that marked Alex's and the shadow's passing. The forest had grown eerily quiet around him, as though it waited, but for what remained a mystery.

He crept through the underbrush, senses on full alert. Reaching the edge of a basinlike hollow, he could see where someone had slid down the steep slope but saw no signs of either Alex or the shadow-thing, as she'd called it. He carefully navigated the slope, tracking the faint smell of jasmine and vanilla—Alex's personal scent—that abruptly ended next to a jagged stump.

Fear kicked his pulse into overdrive. Casting caution aside, he called to her. "Alex!"

Silence.

"Damn it," he muttered and used a controlled slide to reach the bottom of the hollow. He inhaled deeply, searching for any trace of her scent, but found none. "Alex!"

"She's gone," a voice answered from behind him.

Varik spun, lowering himself into a crouch and baring his fangs. When he spotted the man near a half-dead tree, his tension eased. He sighed as he drew himself up to his full height. "Where is she?"

Bernard Sabian stepped forward. The dappled light played off his snowy hair and highlighted the bright copper streak through his bangs that was the only remnant of his once-red hair. Dark green eyes, the same color as Alex's, fixed Varik with an appraising stare. When he spoke, it was with an Irish lilt that never gave way to the Kentucky drawl possessed by his children. "Gone, as I said."

"You made that part clear. Care to expound on it?"

"Her consciousness has slipped back into the physical world, but it didn't return to her body."

Varik stared at the shade of the vampire who'd been his partner and friend for nearly a century. When Varik first joined the Hunters, he'd been singled out as one of the most promising recruits and assigned to the Special Operations unit. Eventually he worked his way into the position of tracking corrupt Hunters and eliminating them, but to find them, he relied on the psychic readings of Bernard Sabian in addition to traditional investigatory methods.

He crossed his arms over his chest. Dread nibbled at his spine and knotted his stomach. "Where is she, Bernard? What's happened to her?"

"For lack of a better term, Alexandra has become a ghost."

"Where is she?"

"I'm not entirely certain."

"Can you track her?"

"Yes, but I need to send you back through the Veil first."

"I'm not leaving without Alex."

"Where she's gone, you cannot follow."

"Bernard—"

He held up his hand to stave off Varik's protest. "*I* will retrieve her, but you have to leave—now. The longer you remain in the Shadowlands, the greater the risk becomes of you never leaving."

"I know the risks. I've been here before, remember?"

"Yes, and if I hadn't pulled you back through the

Veil, you would've been a permanent resident. You barely survived the transition as it was."

Varik dropped his gaze to the leaf-strewn ground. When he was young and still inexperienced, he was given the task of tracking down a vampire who'd killed several humans. He found the rogue, but unbeknownst to Varik or his superiors, the vampire was a moderate Talent. Varik ultimately achieved his goal and eliminated the other but not before he dealt Varik a psychic blow that left him on the wrong side of the Veil.

Bernard had found Varik, saved him, and took it upon himself to train the young Hunter in psychic self-defense. Even though Varik was a Nil, a vampire with no discernible Talent, he learned to construct elaborate shields to protect his mind. A skill he'd found particularly useful blood-bonding with Alex.

A hand clamped on his shoulder, and Varik met the steady gaze of his deceased mentor.

"Once I find Alexandra, returning her consciousness to her body won't be easy. The transition will be difficult, and you must be in the physical realm to provide an anchor for her."

"Blood calls to blood."

Bernard nodded.

"I'll go," he answered the unspoken question in Bernard's eyes. "But answer one question first."

"Yes?"

"How did I get here?"

"I don't know, but given the size of the hole you made, I'd say someone pushed you through the Veil."

"The shadow-thing."

Bernard frowned. "What shadow-thing?"

Varik summarized the attack in the salvage yard and the subsequent encounters since being forced through the Veil. "Have you ever known of something like this happening?" Varik asked when he'd finished his tale.

Bernard scuffed a toe of his shoe against a rotting log. "No, I can't say that I have."

"Why do I get the feeling there's something you aren't telling me?"

"Have you ever known me to be less than honest with you?"

"Well, no, but a lot has changed over the years, the most significant being you're dead."

"Death doesn't negate one's propensity for honesty."

"It doesn't mean you can't fucking lie either."

Bernard huffed and glanced toward the canopy. "Time is drawing short, my friend. The longer we stand here and discuss this matter, the closer we both come to losing Alexandra."

Varik raked a hand through his hair and nodded, relinquishing his hold on the argument.

"I'm trusting you to keep my daughter safe once she's on the other side," Bernard said as they began the process of climbing out of the hollow. "Now let's get you home."

For as long as Peter could remember, the Shadowlands had been his playground. It'd been his second home for over two hundred years, and he'd only encountered a handful of others with the ability to part the Veil and enter this special place, even fewer who could access the Hall of Records.

It was that ability that had first drawn his attention to Alexandra. Even though she was only a child, he'd recognized the potential buried deep within her, a power to rival his own—a true soul mate. He'd wanted to guide her, instruct her in the limitless power that was hers to control.

He'd wanted to teach her.

To care for her.

To love her.

To possess her.

But Bernard had barred his way, thwarting his every attempt to reach her, until he suddenly disappeared.

Peter had rejoiced in her father's death. Because Alexandra had grieved, he made attempts to ease her suffering, wanting only to comfort her. He left offerings for her—food, money, toys—mostly small things that would ensure her health and happiness, but still he was forced to keep his distance.

With Bernard's passing, a new protector had risen in his stead. For years, the Dark One—named so because Peter never knew his true name until now—pursued him before assuming a guardianship role for Alexandra, never allowing him close to her. So Peter watched her from afar as she left childhood behind and grew into womanhood, never achieving her full potential.

Then the Dark One—*Varik*—wooed her, corrupted her.

That would change.

Soon she would come to him.

He would purify her, rid her of Varik's influence.

He'd already begun the process. Using the blood-bond between them, he'd attacked Varik, blasting him through the Veil in an effort to separate them and sever the bond. He hadn't anticipated Alexandra pursuing them and attacking him to save Varik.

However, after their struggle in which she tumbled down a hill, he could sense that she was no longer in the Shadowlands. She had returned to the physical world, leaving Varik behind. It would've been easy enough to keep Varik's consciousness on this side until his physical body died.

If Bernard hadn't chosen that moment to intercede.

Once again, Peter was forced to retreat. He'd fled to the Hall of Records and searched for his rival's records.

Though he hadn't much time, he'd learned enough to know Varik was a danger to Alexandra. The sooner he destroyed the bond between them, the better it would be for her.

Breaking the bond wouldn't be easy. The first step was drawing Alexandra to him. Preparing the path for the ritual that would bring her to him was exhausting but vital. If the proper connections weren't made at the precise moment they were required, the ritual would fail, as it had in the past.

He wouldn't fail this time. Not when he was so close.

As he sat in the center of his ritual circle, mentally rehearsing the complicated ceremony, a shudder passed through the space around him, and the aroma of jasmine and vanilla filled the attic.

His pulse leapt. He opened his eyes, scanning the room, but nothing moved.

The scent intensified, and he knew she was *here*.

She'd finally come to him of her own volition.

Expanding his senses to encompass the entire house, he rose and gleefully began his search.

"Lieutenant!" Tony Maslan's call pulled Tasha from the dream she'd been having.

Blinking away the remnants of sleep, she glanced around, disoriented. Shapes slowly came into focus along with her memory. Salvage yard. Body dump.

The sun was dipping behind the tree line and she knew she had to have been asleep for at least an hour. She stood, brushed the dirt from the seat of her Tyvek jumpsuit, and made certain the flask of bourbon stashed in her pocket wasn't visible. As she rounded the side of the panel van, she popped a stick of peppermint gum in her mouth. If anyone detected alcohol on her breath at a crime scene, her ass would be toast.

She saw Tony striding her way and waved. "What's up?"

"Enforcer Baudelaire's awake."

"And Alex?"

He shook his head. "Not yet."

Tasha could see Varik sitting on the ground looking perplexed. Damian knelt beside him and Morgan stood nearby, fists on her hips. The vampires paid her no attention as she joined them while Tony veered off to oversee the transfer of the abandoned car onto the flatbed tow truck that had finally arrived.

"Something attacked Enforcer Sabian and then you," Damian said. "What happened after it hit you?"

Varik swiped the paper hair cap from his head. "Everything went black and I woke up in a forest. At first I didn't see Alex or the thing that jumped us. I looked for Alex and eventually found her. That's when she confirmed my suspicion that we were in the Shadowlands."

"The what?" Tasha asked, drawing their attention.

"Shadowlands," Varik repeated as Damian helped him stand. "It's what vampires call the buffer zone between the physical and spiritual planes."

"Are you saying you had a near-death experience?"

"No, I'm saying that whatever attacked Alex and me has the ability to drag another's consciousness into a different plane of existence and leave it there."

Tasha's head was spinning. She was a cop. She dealt with the real world and real dangers, and all this metaphysical vampire bullshit was out of her league. "Alex said you were possessed. So this was some kind of demonic force?"

"Not every possession is demonic," Damian said as Varik stripped out of his Tyvek coveralls. "There are other forms but only exceptionally strong Talents are able to perform them."

"Who or what are Talents?"

"That isn't any of your concern, Lieutenant," Morgan said, stepping forward. "In fact, Chief Alberez and Enforcer Baudelaire have said too much already so I'm going to have to ask you to leave."

"Excuse me?" Tasha nearly fell on her ass when she turned to face the vamp and her foot slipped on a patch of weeds. "I'm the liaison officer, and if I'm going to effectively do my job I need to know what the fuck is going on here."

"This is an internal FBPI matter, Lieutenant, and therefore beyond your scope as a liaison officer."

"But I'm a member of this investigation. If it affects the case or if either Varik or Alex is at risk, I need to know."

"I disagree."

"Since we can't generate enough psychic energy to sustain ourselves, we have to look to outside sources," Varik said.

"Enforcer Baudelaire." Morgan said his name like a warning.

He glared at Morgan but continued. "As a side effect of our blood-hunger, most vampires are considered Nils, essentially possessing no or very little psychic talent. However, a very small portion of our population has above-average psychic abilities. We call them Talents." He walked past Tasha, shoving his wadded-up Tyvek coveralls into Morgan's hands. "There, she knows. Now quit being such a fucking bitch."

Morgan threw the coveralls to the ground. "Enforcer Baudelaire!"

Varik ignored her and moved to Alex's side. He dropped to his knees and brushed a loose strand of hair from her face. "I need you to listen to me, baby. You have to come home now."

Tasha was surprised by how quickly Morgan covered the ground between where they stood and Varik.

Morgan grabbed Varik's arm and pulled him to his feet, shoving him away from Alex. "Your behavior is inappropriate, Enforcer Baudelaire."

"As is yours."

"I should report you for insubordination."

"Why? Because I'm not fawning all over you? And it's *Director* Baudelaire."

"You're out of line."

"You're interfering with my investigation."

Morgan replied in French, as did Varik, and Tasha looked to Damian. "I'm assuming they know each other well."

Damian snorted. "What tipped you off?"

"What do we do about Alex?"

"We wait."

She watched as he stepped forward to break up the argument between Varik and Morgan. The three vamps continued to banter while Alex lay crumpled on the ground at their feet.

Tasha glanced around the scene, noting the tow truck readying to leave with the abandoned car. The hearse that had retrieved the body had long since gone.

Sighing, she crossed her legs, lowered herself to the weed-choked ground, and waited.

Alex cowered on the floor, covering her ears in a futile attempt to block the constant wailing that assaulted her. The screams escalated until she added her own to the mix.

A shudder rippled through the room, silencing the voices.

Her ears continued to ring in the ensuing calm. The sudden shift unnerved her, but she used the moment to pick herself up from the floor. She turned in a slow circle, staring at the dolls lining the walls of what could've been a dining room, if it had been furnished with anything other than floor-to-ceiling shelves. Each doll was unique in hair, eye color, dress, and expression. As she examined one shelf, soft murmuring seemed to emanate from the dolls.

So dark.

Please, no!

Can anyone hear me?

He's coming.

Oh, God! No!

As she moved around the room, similar whispers filtered from other shelves. She reached a broad archway that fed into a dark paneled foyer. More voices called to her from beyond the archway. She stepped into the wide hallway and fresh horror hit her.

Clusters of dolls lined the walls, sitting on shelves, tucked into large shadowboxes, staring out from behind the dusty glass of display cases. At the opposite end of the hall, a sprawling staircase swept upward and curved back on itself to access the second floor. More dolls sat between each carved banister spindle.

All doubt of where she was left her. She was in the center of the Dollmaker's lair. The question that remained was how.

Another rippling shudder passed through the house. The wave hit Alex and made her shiver, leaving in its wake the sensation of cobwebs covering her body. They pulled at her hair and tugged at her clothing as though they would draw her deeper into the house. She passed another archway, pausing to peek inside what had probably served as a parlor once upon a time. Shelving identical to the other room lined the walls.

Somewhere overhead a door opened, closed, and a

man's voice drifted down to her. "I know you're here, little one."

The unseen webs tugged more forcefully when the man spoke, excited by his voice. Alex brushed at them while she crept into the shadows beneath the winding stairs.

"Let's play a game." Footsteps echoed on hardwood in the distance. "Hide-and-seek."

Alex froze.

"Remember how that used to be one of your favorite games?"

She began to tremble. Childhood memories flittered before her, narrated by a stranger.

"Darting among the headstones of that cemetery near your house. Hiding under your parents' bed." Another door opened and closed. "The way you shrieked when you were found. So precious."

How could he know about that? Panic threatened to overwhelm her.

Footsteps neared the stairs and paused at their apex. "Come out, come out, wherever you are."

Another ripple cascaded down the stairs and throughout the first floor but avoided her hiding place. The cobwebs that had pulled at her seemed to loosen and fall away.

Movement on the stairs above stilled her breath.

"Tricky, tricky," her still-unseen pursuer muttered, then raised his voice. "Oh, you're good, but I'll find you, chickie." Feet rapidly descended the stairs. "Chickie chickie, boom *boom.*" He laughed as he stomped on the last two stairs.

The scent of leather and old blood wafted to her, and Alex retreated farther into the shadows. She could see him now—the Dollmaker—standing with his back to her at the foot of the stairs.

She estimated his height at over six feet. He swiveled

his head from side to side, scanning the wide hallway. Short blond hair clung to his skull as though it was damp. When he finally moved, his long legs covered the distance between the stairs and the front of the house with purposeful strides. He paused next to the archway into the dining room, and she caught a glimpse of his profile before he disappeared from view.

She had to move, had to find a way out. Keeping her focus on the archway where he'd disappeared, Alex slipped from the shadows, hugging the wall as best she could while avoiding display cases and doll-filled shelves. She came to a closed door and reached for the porcelain knob.

Her hand passed through it as though made of air. Laughter filled the hall, and she glanced toward the archway.

The Dollmaker leaned against the doorjamb. His blue eyes sparkled and white fangs flashed as he grinned. "Tag, chickie," he whispered. "You're it."

Alex sprinted for the stairs. She could hear him giving chase. Grabbing for the stair's railing, she stumbled as her hand once again failed to make contact.

Behind her, the Dollmaker whooped in delight.

A shadow darted down the stairs, forcing Alex to duck as it sped by overhead. It slammed into the Dollmaker's chest and sent him sliding backward along the hardwood floors.

He crashed into a display case, toppling it and spilling the contents. A chorus of screams erupted as porcelain doll faces shattered. Wisps of silvery-white mist drifted up from the remains.

"No!" The Dollmaker reached for the tiny puffs of mists, but they easily slipped through his fingers and evaporated. Rising to his knees, he threw his head back and howled like a wounded animal.

Alex covered her ears as hundreds of voices matched his wail.

The shadow that had slammed into the Dollmaker dropped to the stairs in front of her, taking on the form of a man in a dark suit. He extended his hand to her. "Time to go, Princess."

She gaped at her father but clapped her hand in his without question.

As they raced up the stairs, the Dollmaker shouted from below. "No! She's mine!"

Alex and her father reached the second floor and plunged down a hall nearly identical to the foyer. The dolls were fewer in number here, interspersed with artwork, photos, and mirrors. A large multipane window glowed with fading sunlight at the opposite end.

"You have to get to the light and cross the Veil," her father said as they ran. "Find Varik. He's waiting for you."

She dug in her heels in the center of the hall, staring at one of the dolls encased in glass like a priceless piece of art.

"Alexandra, we don't have time for sightseeing."

"Hang on." She pulled away from her father and stepped closer to the glass enclosure.

Dressed in overalls and a red-and-blue striped shirt, the doll held a miniature bouquet of daisies in its hands. Red hair styled in pigtails framed a familiar smiling face. Dark green eyes rimmed in gold stared back at her.

"That's me," she whispered. She looked at the other dolls encased in similar glass boxes. Each wore a different outfit and hairstyle but the face remained the same. "They're all *me*."

"Alexandra," her father said, spinning her around to face him. He glanced toward the sound of the Dollmaker charging up the stairs. "We have to go. *Now!*"

The Dollmaker reached the top of the stairs and stopped, glaring at them, his face twisted in rage. "Back away, old man."

Her father moved in front of her, shielding her. He backed up slowly, forcing her to match his steps, and shook his head. "I don't think so."

"She came to me." The Dollmaker advanced. "She's mine."

"Keep dreaming, buddy," Alex muttered.

Her father shot her a withering glance over his shoulder.

The Dollmaker stretched his arms wide and continued to advance. He voice softened as he focused on her. "I made them all for you—gifts for my soul mate. Don't you like them?"

"They're fucking creepy as hell. You're a sick bastard, and I'm *not* your fucking soul mate."

"Such ugly language from such a pretty mouth." He grinned, showing the full extent of his fangs. "I like it."

Alex and her father had nearly reached the window when the Dollmaker lunged forward.

"Daddy!" she screamed as her father rushed ahead, meeting the attack head-on.

A burst of energy struck the Dollmaker, knocking him back. He growled but didn't charge again. "Impressive, old man. I didn't think you had it in you."

"There is much you don't know about me." Her father took up a low fighting stance in the center of the hall.

"Perhaps, but I'm not the only one." He focused on Alex and smiled. "Am I?"

"You'll not lay a hand on my daughter," her father growled. Not shifting his attention, he asked over his shoulder, "Princess, do you remember when we used to play rocket ship?"

"Daddy's little princess," the Dollmaker sneered, pacing like a predator trapped in a cage. "Not for long, old man."

"Yes," she answered her father's question, ignoring the other's taunts.

"Get ready."

She dropped into a crouch.

"Blast off!"

Alex and her father both sprang into action. He turned and ran for her. She leapt into the air, arms outstretched. The Dollmaker's roar of fury echoed the childhood sound effect in her mind. Her father caught her in midair as he jumped forward, and they both sailed through the window, into the twilight.

ten

EMILY FOUND HERSELF IN AN ALL-TOO-FAMILIAR POSI-
tion: pacing the floor while she waited for the phone to
ring. How many times had she performed the same ritual when Stephen and Alex were teens? Being a vampire didn't free her from the worry all mothers carried
for their children. If anything, the worry was com-
pounded, especially with the Sabians' family history.

She waited for a call from Gregor Wahl. He'd been a
Hunter during the time before the formation of the
FBPI and had known Bernard well. While Gregor had
retired from active duty, he remained with the Bureau
as an instructor at the Academy located on a portion
of the Fort Knox base outside of Louisville. His years of
service had provided him with an extensive network of
contacts within the Bureau, and Emily hoped it could
be used to influence the Tribunal into either sparing
Alex's life or dropping the charges altogether.

Restless, she paced to the bay window overlooking
the oak tree–lined street in front of Stephen and Janet's
shared home, and her thoughts turned to the past, to
the day she discovered her beloved husband wasn't the
man she thought him to be.

It was early May 1962, and she and Bernard had
been married for two hundred and thirteen years. She
dropped off Stephen at a friend's house for a sleepover
birthday party and was looking forward to a quiet
evening at home with her husband.

When she entered their small home east of downtown Louisville, she found Bernard sitting in his favorite chair, staring out the front window.

"I wasn't expecting you home, dear," she said, and gave him a peck on the cheek. The stiffness of his reception took her aback. "Is something wrong?"

"Siobhan's pregnant," he replied softly.

Emily tried to place the name. "Siobhan Kelly? She's one of the other Talents, right?"

He nodded.

She beamed. "Well, that's wonderful, isn't it?" When he didn't answer, she frowned. "Siobhan's married, isn't she?"

"No."

Then Bernard looked at her and his expression carried such remorse—Emily knew even before asking. "Who's the father?"

Almost inaudibly, he answered. "I am."

An electronic version of "Greensleeves" began playing and shattered her reverie, bringing her back to the present.

She picked up her cell phone from the coffee table and answered. "I'm here, Gregor. What were you able to find?"

"Not much and what I did find isn't good news," he answered.

"What do you mean?"

"The Tribunal isn't going to drop the charges. Alex will have to face them next month."

"Why won't they—"

"Hang on," Gregor interrupted. "That's not the worst of it. I was able to find out that Woody Phelps has taken a personal interest in Alex's case."

Emily felt her heart sink as she dropped onto the sofa's edge. Woody Phelps, Chief Magistrate of the Tribunal, was known for his hard-line stance against corruption among Enforcers. The Bureau's retention of the death penalty for Enforcers convicted of the offense was largely due to Phelps's influence. "Why is he so interested in Alex?"

"I don't know, but I can tell you Phelps and the other magistrates have been holding regular meetings over the past few weeks. They've called in Enforcers from all across the country and questioned them behind closed doors. The scuttlebutt is that it's some sort of massive internal investigation."

"Does it have any bearing on Alex's case?"

"I'm trying to find that out."

"It's an awfully big coincidence, wouldn't you say?"

"It does seem odd."

Emily stood up and began pacing again. "If they won't drop the charges, what are the chances of at least influencing the Tribunal toward leniency? Alex has had a spotless record until now."

"Given Phelps's interest, not good."

"There has to be a way to save her."

Silence filled the line for a moment. "You won't like it."

"I won't sit idly by while they take her from me. I'll be the judge of what I like or don't like."

"Siobhan."

"What about her?"

"She's still wanted by the Bureau."

Emily stopped pacing. "Gregor—"

"If you know where to find Siobhan, you may be able to barter her location for leniency."

"You're asking me to trade my daughter's life for another woman's."

"Siobhan killed three Hunters."

"You have no proof of that. Even if I knew where to begin looking for Siobhan, I can't do what you're suggesting. There has to be another option."

He sighed. "I'll see what I can do."

"Thank you, Gregor."

He grunted his acknowledgment and the line fell silent.

Emily pushed the button to end the call, Gregor's suggestion still echoing in her mind, and she wondered, once again, had she made the right decision—both in calling Gregor and when she made a promise on a cold January night more than forty years ago.

The window before him was unbroken even though he'd seen Alexandra and Bernard crash it. They were nowhere to be found once he'd reached the window, but he hadn't expected to find them.

Ghosts left no visible tracks.

Turning from the rapidly darkening window, Peter breathed deeply, inhaling her lingering scent, and smiled. She had come to him, just as he'd predicted. He hadn't counted on her father's appearance, but it also didn't surprise him. Bernard had always been her greatest protector, even surpassing Varik.

But it no longer mattered.

She had come. She had proven she wanted to be with him.

He paused by the replica doll she'd been admiring. Varik and Bernard would try to prevent her return, try to keep them apart.

They would fail and he knew precisely how to guarantee their failure.

He strode down the hall to the oversized print of Duchamp's painting. His fingers swept along the side of the frame and found the dual triggers that released the lock. It clicked and he swung open the hidden door leading to the attic. The door closed soundlessly behind him as he jogged up the stairs.

His latest acquisition stared at him from across the

spacious room. He picked up one of the scalpels he used for delicate sculpting work from his table as he passed.

She remained immobilized with his special restraint system but whimpered when he stroked her hair.

"Shh," he cooed. "Everything's fine."

The scalpel flashed in the light and her breathing increased, as did her futile pitiful sniveling. Blood welled from the tiny cut he made along her shoulder. Her skin was soft beneath his tongue as he licked away the crimson beads. Images of her life darted before his eyes and he drank them in, coveting each as though it were a rare jewel.

Peter pressed close to her naked body. The need to find solace from the inner fire that burned his flesh and tortured his mind consumed him. He wanted to bury himself within her, plunge his fangs into the tenderness of her neck, and quench the fire with her blood.

It took all his strength to step away from her. He couldn't seek the release he desperately wanted, that he'd denied himself for so long. He must save it for Alexandra. Once she was his and his alone, then he could satisfy his desires.

He returned to his worktable and picked up the newly completed doll's head. Its porcelain face was a perfect copy of Alexandra's as he'd seen her in the Hall of Records. Holding it delicately, he turned it so the neck revealed the cavity within the head—the perfect vessel to ensure his soul mate remained with him forever.

Turning back to the girl, he could see her fear. He stroked her new penny-colored hair. Tears rimmed her jade green eyes. As his eyes and hands admired the lines of her body, the smoothness of her unblemished skin, she trembled and sobbed.

"Shh," he said and wiped her tears. "It will all be over soon. I'm going to release you."

"You're letting me go?" she croaked, the first words she'd spoken in days. A spark of hope flared deep in her eyes.

He smiled. The scalpel he'd tucked in his belt now pressed into the soft flesh of her neck. "I said I would release you. I said nothing of you leaving."

With a practiced flick of his wrist, the scalpel flashed red in the light.

A dizzying kaleidoscope spun around Alex. Wind whistled past her ears and ripped away her scream as she fell. Vivid colors flashed, searing her eyes, until everything turned black seconds before she slammed into the ground.

Her eyes snapped open, and she bolted to her feet, only to immediately collapse, struggling for breath. Darkness enveloped her. She swatted at the hands that tried to pin her as voices shouted all around her. "Daddy!"

"Alex!" The scent of sandalwood and cinnamon cut through the chaos, easing the panic that consumed her. "It's me, baby. Calm down. You're safe now."

"Varik?"

"Yes, baby. It's me."

She closed her eyes and melted in the warm safety of his arms. "It was him. He was chasing me. I was so scared. Where is he? Did he follow me?"

"What is she talking about?" a woman—Morgan, Alex remembered—asked.

"Baby, Bernard's dead. If you saw him it was in the Shadowlands," Varik said calmly.

Images flashed through her mind in a confused jumble. "No, not Daddy—the Dollmaker. Did he follow me?"

Varik's hold tightened. "You saw the Dollmaker?"

She nodded, feeling the soft scrape of his shirt against her cheek. "I saw him *and* his house."

"The Dollmaker's been on our Most Wanted list for decades," Morgan said. "If you saw him, who is he? What's his name?"

"I don't know," Alex grumbled, pushing away from Varik. "I was running for my life so I didn't stop to swap recipes and Twitter handles." She felt as though fine grit coated her eyes and she blinked rapidly, trying to clear them. When that didn't work, she tried rubbing them.

"Is there something wrong?" someone else—Tasha, Alex placed the voice—asked.

"I'm not sure." Alex frowned. "Varik, do I have something in my eyes?"

He tilted her head back. His breath was warm on her face and his hands gentle. "No, I don't think so. Why?"

"Because I can't see shit." A chill flashed up her spine. Her hands tightened on his arms. "I'm fucking blind!"

Kirk nursed his amaretto cappuccino while he gauged the appearance and reactions of the girl seated in front of him.

Jennifer Lee was petite, barely five feet tall, and maybe a hundred pounds when weighed soaking wet. Bright red hair surrounded her head like a giant puffball. She would glance at him with her bright blue eyes and quickly look away.

Piper sat beside him in the corner of the booth they all shared in the back of Mug Shots. She yammered on about an assignment she and Jennifer had recently been given in a psychology class.

He hadn't expected Piper to actually find a willing redhead to replace her cousin so quickly. He liked having a variety on hand and natural redheads were the hardest to find. Hopefully Jennifer would prove more loyal than Amber Lynn, whose body had been safely deposited in three separate Dumpsters around town. Steam cleaning the stains out of the carpet had taken longer than depositing the bitch's body.

"So, Jennifer," he cut into the girls' conversation, earning a startled look from the new bunny. "Piper tells me you're looking for work."

Jennifer glanced at Piper, who nodded encouragingly just as he'd taught her. "Yeah, I got laid off from my job and my rent's already late. If I don't pay my landlord soon, he's going to kick me out."

He nodded sympathetically. "This economy is tough on everyone. What kind of work do you do?"

She shrugged and sipped her chai tea latte. "Whatever I can find. What about you?"

"I'm in the entertainment business." Kirk leaned back in the booth and slipped an arm around Piper's shoulders. "I supply goods and services to a select clientele."

"Sounds fascinating."

"Oh, it is."

"Do you ever meet anyone famous?"

"It's been known to happen."

"Like when the vampire band Primal Dark was playing in Jackson," Piper said in a rush. "Kirk set them up with—"

He squeezed her shoulder, a silent warning to shut her mouth.

Jennifer sat forward. "Primal Dark? I love them!" She closed her eyes and began swaying in her seat, singing off-key. "She was my lover, my bloody lover, my dancer. . . ." She giggled and when she looked at Kirk, her eyes sparkled with visions and dreams of fame. "Do you *really* know them?"

He nodded and sipped his cappuccino.

"Wow. I'd give *anything* to meet them. I'm, like, their biggest fan."

Kirk smiled, showing his fangs, and knew he had her.

"*Vita in nex,*" Peter intoned and poured a few drops of blood on the first sigil. "Life in death."

Stripped of his clothing, he knelt within the circle he'd carved into the attic's wooden floor. His latest acquisition lay to the left of the center, on the side of death. The newly completed Alexandra replica was to the right, on the side of life. The ritual was a delicate process and if performed incorrectly could result in his own soul becoming splintered and trapped within the doll.

He moved clockwise around the circle to the second sigil and dribbled more of the girl's blood. "*Pectus pectoris nutritor nex*—the heart feeds death."

The girl moaned softly. He'd drained as much of her blood as he dared, bringing her near death. She needed to be hovering on the edge of the abyss in order for the ritual to work. Shattering a soul required precision timing and over the years he'd become adept at making it quick. However, there was no way to make it painless.

He followed the outline of the circle to the third sigil. Three liquid rubies fell in its center and were greedily absorbed by the dry flooring. "*Nex nutritor obscurum*—death feeds the darkness."

Power hummed within the circle. It crackled in the air and made the tiny hairs on his neck and arms stand erect.

"*Totus animus servo obscurum,*" he droned and added the last of the blood to the final sigil. "All souls serve the darkness."

The circle snapped closed, sending a charge through

his body. His breath hissed over his teeth as he sucked in the electrified air.

The initial rush of power was always the sweetest and the hardest to control. Peter forced himself to relax and open his mind to the energies now swirling within the confines of his circle. Gradually, with each measured breath, a balance was achieved both within him and within the circle.

Now the ritual could truly begin.

He paced to the center of the circle and knelt between the girl and the doll. Picking up the ceremonial dagger, he held it over the girl, blade directed toward her heart.

"*Ut quod est recipio, quod novus visum est instituo in obscurum,*" he recited as he had done countless times prior. "That which is, recedes, and new vision is found in darkness."

He positioned the dagger over the doll. "*Memento vivere,*" he said. "A reminder of life."

The girl moaned as he laid his free hand on her bare chest, over her heart. "*Viva enim mortuorum in memoria vivorum est posita.*" He placed the dagger against her throat. "The life of the dead is retained in the memory of the living."

The dagger sliced through her flesh. Bright red arterial blood sprayed upward, coating his arms and chest.

Power surged around the circle's perimeter, flowed through him, and into the girl. She convulsed beneath his hold as her life drained away, pushed into the abyss by the energies now coursing through her—the same energies that caused his back to bow and his penis to stand erect, energies he had to control and direct into the doll.

Peter gasped and groaned as another surge of power hit him. "*Vita mutatur . . .* life is changed. . . ."

The girl stilled and the power receded, but he knew it was only a momentary pause—the eye of the storm.

The girl's mouth fell slack and a pulsing blue-white stream of mist rose before him.

He speared the mist with the dagger. Coldness spread over the blade, up the hilt, and into his arm. ". . . *non tollitur* . . . not taken away," he completed the incantation as the energies ripped the girl's soul from her body.

A piercing shriek filled the circle and he answered it with his own howl of pain. The mist quivered and writhed on the dagger's blade. Power rushed into him.

The girl's soul shattered like glass, leaving a small piece clinging to the dagger's blade.

Peter positioned the blade over the doll, reciting the words he'd used to seal the circle in reverse order. "*Totus animus servo obscurum. Nex nutritor obscurum. Pectus pectoris nutritor nex. Vita in nex.*"

The soul shard slipped from the blade and melded with the doll.

He covered the doll's chest with his hand, feeling the final surge of power building within him. "*Ego sum obscurum quod vestri nex sustineo mihi.*"

The dagger fell from his hand. The last of the circle's energy coursed through him. His hips bucked violently as he climaxed and then collapsed to the floor between the doll and the girl's corpse.

Panting from his exertion, he gazed at Alexandra's replica, glowing brightly with life. He stroked the doll's fine red hair and a spike of power jolted his fingertips.

He smiled and whispered to the doll. "I am the darkness and your death sustains me."

eleven

ALEX PERCHED ON THE END OF A GURNEY AND CURSED the darkness that her own stupidity had thrust upon her. The rapid transition through the Veil had been too much for her psyche to handle. As a result, her brain had blocked all visual input as a defensive measure. Even though it was a natural reaction, she still berated herself for following the possessing entity into the Shadowlands. She did it to save Varik, but now Morgan, and therefore the Tribunal, would know about her abilities as well as the blood-bond.

Blood-bonds were rare and a bond shared by two Enforcers even more so. The FBPI had no policy against its agents fraternizing, dating, or even marrying so long as their work performance didn't suffer. However, having two Enforcers bound by blood increased the danger to both, especially if they worked in the field together. The attack in the salvage yard proved she and Varik were vulnerable, and with her temporary blindness, the Tribunal was sure to use it as an excuse to widen the scope of their inquiry.

"Well, Ms. Sabian, there doesn't appear to be anything physically wrong with your eyes," an unseen doctor said. "However, I'd really like you to have a CT scan."

"No." Alex rubbed her eyes and sighed when the darkness remained unchanged. She slipped on her sunglasses, not because she needed them, but because she felt weird staring into nothing.

"We need to be certain there isn't an underlying cause that—"

"The underlying cause is psychic trauma." She heard the emergency room treatment door open and the scent of sandalwood and cinnamon announced Varik's return. "Your scans and tests aren't going to find diddly shit."

The doctor huffed loudly and seemed to be preparing his next argument when Varik cut him off. "Save your breath, Doc. You're not going to win with her. Believe me."

Alex flipped him off, earning a laugh from Varik and another huff from the doctor.

"When can we expect her eyesight to return?" Varik asked.

"Could be anywhere from hours to days. In the meanwhile, if you should develop any headaches or eye pain, come back to the ER right away."

"Understood," Alex said.

"How's your pain now?"

"Better after that nurse shot me in the ass." Ever since she'd returned from the Shadowlands, she'd felt as though she'd fallen from a great height and her body was a giant bruise. Whatever drug the nurse had given her dulled the hurt to a tolerable ache. Too bad it wouldn't last more than an hour or two due to Alex's high vampire metabolism.

"It's probably best if you aren't left alone for the next few hours, at least until the medication wears off. Will someone be around to help you?"

Varik answered before Alex could respond. "Don't worry. She'll be well supervised. I'll see to it personally."

Alex frowned in the direction of his voice. Vampires were fiercely independent, even in childhood, and a blind vampire was often viewed as a burden both on their family and on the community. Long ago, any disabled vampires, whether caused by the rare birth defect or through artificial means, were killed in order to preserve the community's hidden status from humans.

Alex was already facing a potential death sentence because she'd turned rogue. Damian's reinstatement didn't change the fact that she still must face the Tribunal, nor did her blindness. In fact, her current self-made predicament would be viewed as further evidence of her recklessness and would undoubtedly weigh heavily against her.

The room's door scraped open, startling her. She heard retreating footsteps and the hiss of hydraulics as the door closed. The soft scuff of shoes on linoleum and the intensified smell of sandalwood and cinnamon told her Varik remained and had moved closer. She reached for him and was surprised when he pressed a warm cylinder into her hand. "What's this?"

"Fresh blood. It'll help the healing process."

"Where did you get it?"

He chuckled. "We're in a hospital and you have to ask that question? What kind of drugs did they give you? I think they're affecting your brain."

"What I meant was—"

"I know what you meant, and no, I didn't steal it or bite anyone. I found a registered donor who volunteered to have some drawn by one of the nurses." He nudged her hands toward her mouth. "Now be a good girl and make the superyummy treat disappear."

"Fuck you."

"I've never done it on a bed with wheels. Could be fun."

Alex let his attempt at humor slide and drank the cooling blood. The thick liquid reminded her of licking a salt-encrusted spoon—brackish with a metallic edge—as it coated her tongue and slid down her throat.

Flashes of memory from the donor's life sparked in her mind: the rush of freedom that came from riding a bicycle for the first time without training wheels, a profound sense of loss as a hearse passed on its way into a small cemetery, the soaring joy of seeing a newly born son lying at his mother's breast.

The memories faded as quickly as they appeared, leaving lingering warmth that spread throughout her body and made her fingertips tingle.

Varik removed the cylinder from her hand. "Feel better now?"

She nodded. "What about you? How are you feeling?"

"Fine. You want to tell me about your little adventure with the Dollmaker?"

"I told you all there was to tell on the way here." She tucked her hair behind her ears. "Somehow I ended up in what I'm assuming was his house. There were dolls everywhere. My dad showed up. They fought."

"Then you and Bernard jumped through a window and you woke up in the salvage yard."

"Blind as a fucking bat."

"You got a good look at the Dollmaker?"

"Tall, blond, and creepy."

"But you could identify him?"

"As soon as I can see again, yeah, I can do that."

"Good, because I really want to nail this son of a bitch."

Silence crept into the room as they both became lost in their own thoughts. The memory of the screams emanating from the dolls rose unbidden from her subconscious, making her shiver.

She reached for Varik, eager to feel his touch, to have him banish the screams, and was rewarded with his fingers interlacing with hers. "I'm sorry," she whispered.

"For what?"

"I fucked up in front of Morgan. I was stupid."

"No, you weren't," Varik said softly, his body pressing against her knees. "We were both attacked. If you hadn't followed the possessing entity into the Shadowlands, I might still be there. I don't have the ability to part the Veil like you."

"I know."

"Why didn't you tell me you could access the Hall of Records?"

She shrugged. "I didn't think it was that big of a deal. I'm sure there are plenty of others who can do it."

"No, there aren't. It's a rare ability, even rarer than parting the Veil."

"Dad could do it."

"I know, that's why he was—" Varik abruptly stopped speaking and pulled away from her.

"Why he was what?" Alex reached for him and found only dead air. "For that matter, how did you know my father? He was just a history professor." She felt pressure on her legs as he returned and laid his hands on her thighs.

"You know how close-knit the vampire community is in Louisville," he said and she could hear the smile in his voice. He traced lazy patterns on top of her jeans, sending small electric pulses through her body. "The same was true back then. Bernard had a reputation for being a great professor. It was my job to know certain things about prominent members of the community."

She stopped the motion of his hands, and his fingers entwined with hers. "That's it?"

"That's it," he echoed and then chuckled. "Would I lie to you?"

"In a fucking heartbeat."

"Only if it was in your best interests."

"Or yours."

"Remember our conversation in the Shadowlands about trust?"

"I remember it, but I know you, Varik. You keep secrets like some people keep houseplants. Your brain is a greenhouse for lies and half-truths."

"At least I'm honest about it."

Alex sighed and leaned forward, striking her nose against his shoulder. Hissing in pain, she pulled back and fought to restrain the tears that threatened to spill over. "Damn it! How the hell am I supposed to do anything when I can't fucking see?"

Varik removed her sunglasses and his gentle hands cupped her face. The blood-bond pulsated and warmed as Varik's voice slipped into her thoughts. *You let me help you.*

A clear image formed in her mind. She saw herself— hair tangled, face streaked with dust, and clothes rumpled—sitting on a gurney. Seen through Varik's point of view, it was disorienting at first when he looked around the room. Bandages, gauze, and tape littered a rolling tray near the door. Gray cabinets hung on pale blue cinder-block walls. Then he focused on her once more.

Alex smirked and saw the action mirrored by the image in her head. "This is like watching yourself on live television. It's freaking me out."

"I can help with that, too." The image faded as Varik closed the bond's connection. "You just need to relax."

Excitement pulsed through her body as his lips found hers. Her hands slipped around his neck and her fingers curled in his shortened hair while his arms encircled her waist. She parted her legs to allow him to step forward, pressing close.

His hands slid down her back to cup her bottom and pulled her even closer. Their natural scents of jasmine and vanilla, sandalwood and cinnamon swirled around them and enticed them to explore their desire.

A new vision, one born of fantasy, pushed its way into her mind. Muscles in her lower abdomen contracted in anticipation and she gasped.

Varik chuckled and kissed the scar on her neck. *See what you've been missing by ignoring me all day?*

I haven't been ignoring you. We were working.

You've avoided me, avoided this. He nibbled her earlobe, teasing it with his fangs.

Coherent thought faltered and fled before his pleasurable onslaught. She wrapped her legs around him and shivered as his fangs grazed her neck.

I want you. His hand edged under her shirt, tracing her jean's waistband and prickling her flesh.

Alex giggled. *You* do *realize we're still technically on duty.*

He leaned forward, gently pushing her onto the bed. One hand remained at the small of her back while the other left a trail of tingling fire over her ribs and cupped her breast. His lips reclaimed hers. *Fuck duty.*

Raised voices in the hallway made them pause, and a knock on the door forced them apart. One voice outside rose above the others and Varik groaned. "Your brother's here."

Alex sat up, smoothing her clothing. She sensed Varik moving to her side as the door opened and an intoxicating mix of new scents mingled with hers and Varik's. Her nostrils flared as she replaced her sunglasses, and she recognized the fragrance of musk and cloves Stephen possessed, her mother's natural perfume of lilac and lavender, and the spicy ginger and sage combination that was Damian.

The air vibrated with the intensity of their emotions. Fear, sadness, and concern washed over her followed by anger. Alex shrank from them, seeking to find a refuge from the emotional storm that assaulted her.

Varik's weight on the bed beside her and the protective arm that snaked around her waist reassured her. She leaned into him, letting the aura of calm he projected encompass her.

"Oh, honey." Emily's voice was heavy with the bulk of the fear and sadness Alex sensed. Her hands smoothed Alex's hair away from her face. "Damian told me what happened."

Alex grabbed her mother's hands, guiding them away from her head. "I'm okay, Mom. It's not as bad as it sounds. I was really fucking stupid, that's all."

"Nonsense," her mother said and Alex could hear the half-smile in her voice. "You were doing your job. These things happen. I'm just glad you're all right."

"These things seem to be happening a lot more often now that *he's* in town," Stephen grumbled from across the room.

Alex felt Varik stiffen and the carefully constructed bubble of calmness around her popped. "Varik had nothing to do with this. We were attacked."

"Which wouldn't have happened if he hadn't dragged you into the case."

"He asked for my help."

"He's a fucking Enforcer, or at least claims to be. Let him deal with it himself."

"Oh, grow up, Stephen."

"That's enough, both of you," Emily scolded. "Stephen, now is not the time for you to launch into an anti-Varik campaign. If you can't calm yourself, then you can wait outside in the car."

"Why is everyone determined to defend this guy?" Anger and frustration carried Stephen's voice into a higher octave. "For that matter, why aren't *you* defending yourself? Why are you hiding behind my sister and mother?"

"I'm not hiding," Varik said softly. "I'm showing respect."

"Respect?" Stephen laughed. "How is letting them fight your battles respectful?"

"Firstly, I haven't killed you. Yet."

"You son of a—"

"Knock it off," Alex growled. "Either beat the shit out of each other—right here, right now—or get the fuck over it because I'm tired of listening to your pissing contest every time you're in the same fucking room."

"Language, Alexandra," her mother hissed.

"Sabian's right," Damian said, silencing everyone. "We've got a body to identify and a missing girl to find. This isn't the time for you two to be comparing dick sizes."

Varik's hand brushed against Alex's back and his voice filtered into her thoughts. *Mine's bigger.*

Stop it.

I'm just saying, but then again you've—

Alex elbowed his ribs and was satisfied to hear a sharp grunt.

"None of this even matters, anyway," Stephen said. The direction of his voice changed as he spoke. "There's no way you can keep working."

Alex turned her head, following the sound movements. "Like hell I'm going to stop now."

"You can*not* be serious," Stephen sneered.

"As a damn heart attack."

"How can you possibly work? You can't fucking see!"

"Not with my *eyes,* but I see just fine in other ways."

Stephen snarled in frustration. "Mom, talk some sense into her."

"What would you have me do?" Emily asked softly. "She's a grown woman. She can make her own decisions."

"Damian?" Stephen asked. "You're her commanding officer. Surely you don't expect her to return to duty."

The silence that followed was menacing in the way it cloaked the room. Finally, Damian spoke.

"Normally I would agree with you and tell her to go home," he said. His tone switched to a more formal cadence as he continued. "However, given the present circumstances of the Mindy Johnson case and with the upcoming Tribunal inquiry, I expect Enforcer Alexandra Sabian to fulfill her duties as best she can and in whatever capacity she is able."

She released her held breath in a slow exhale. By using her title and full name, he had made his statement an official decree. Although her duties in the field would obviously be curtailed due to her physical limitations, he wasn't going to send her home.

"This is bullshit," Stephen spat. He grabbed Alex's shoulders. "Listen to me—"

"Let go," Alex said through clenched teeth.

His grip tightened. "No, you're going to listen to me for once, damn it!"

"Stephen, I'm warning you."

"Don't do this. Just walk away from it, all of it."

"I can't do that."

"*Yes,* you can."

"What about Mindy Johnson? Can she walk away? Can her family?"

"That's not fair, and you know it."

"I understand your concern, Stephen, but like Damian said, there's a missing girl whose life is in danger. If I can do something, *anything,* to help find her, then that's what I have to do." She laid her hands over his and gently pulled them away.

"I don't want to stand over my baby sister's grave."

"We're not kids anymore. You can't protect me from all the bullies."

"I can try," he growled.

Varik's arm tightened possessively around her waist.

"And what will you do?" she asked. "Beat up anyone who says something negative about me?"

"Of course not, but—"

"What about the Tribunal? Are you going to take them on as well?"

"You're blowing this out of proportion."

"Am I? You're throwing barbs at Varik every chance you get because of what happened in Louisville. Did you even once stop to consider that maybe he and I have worked past that, and maybe I *want* him to be a part of my life?"

The bond pulsed with Varik's surprise and excitement even though he remained still beside her.

"He's going to hurt you again," Stephen said.

"You don't know that, and I can't keep denying the fact that he and I are bond-mates." Another ripple of emotion jolted the bond. "Regardless of what kind of relationship we had in the past or may have in the future, the bond remains the same. The past can't be changed. I have to accept that, and so do you."

A moment of tense silence was followed by the sound of boots on linoleum and the door scraping open.

"I don't have to accept a damn thing," Stephen said from the doorway. "Not when it concerns that ass-hole."

The door's hydraulics hissed as it shut. Alex hung her head and sighed, lost in a quagmire of confusing thoughts and emotions. The scent of lavender and lilacs and a gentle hand on her arm lifted her head.

"Don't pay any attention to him, honey," her mother said softly. "He'll come around in time."

Alex nodded, unable to speak past the lump that had formed in her throat.

"I should go. I know the three of you probably have official business to discuss." Her mother gave her a quick hug. "I'll call and check on you later."

Alex nodded and a moment later she heard the door open and close. Tilting her head slightly, she was able to zero in on the area of the room where Damian stood by listening for the steady rhythm of his breathing. "So, how much trouble am I in with Morgan and the Tribunal?"

"Considerable," Damian rumbled. The rustle of clothing indicated he moved out of the corner to stand in front of her. "Morgan knows about the blood-bond, which hadn't been previously recorded with the Bureau. She also knows you can part the Veil. She's on the phone with the Tribunal now."

"Getting orders to haul my ass into jail, no doubt."

"Possibly but unlikely," Varik said. "I don't think the Tribunal will rush into any sort of judgment based on one incident. My guess is they'll tell Morgan to keep an eye on you, but I don't think they'll throw you in jail."

"Not yet," Damian agreed. "Regardless of what they do, the Tribunal will have to proceed with caution. Until the Black investigation, you had a spotless record, plus you're Bernard Sabian's daughter. Public opinion will play a role in the inquiry whether the Tribunal wants it to or not."

Alex knew they both spoke the truth, but she wasn't certain she fully believed it. Her father's murder had been the catalyst for the vampire community's decision to reveal itself to humanity, a decision most thought had been for the betterment of the community. However, there were those who thought they should've remained hidden, living in the shadows. No one knew how many of these holdouts there were among the community or where they may rise. Her inquiry could become a political hotbed with two sides of the community fighting for dominance, leaving her defenseless in the middle.

The steady beep of a cell phone interrupted the downward spiral of her thoughts.

"Alberez," Damian answered, silencing the beeping, and then paused. "You're certain?" Pause. "Keep me updated."

Alex heard the snap of his phone closing. "What's going on?"

"Just bureaucratic bullshit at headquarters."

The slight waver she detected in his voice told her there was more to his excuse but she wasn't in a position to push.

"Damian," Varik said as he stood up. "It's late. Freddy and Reyes aren't going to have full results on any evidence until tomorrow. I think it's probably best if I took Alex home for the night."

"Good idea," Damian agreed. "Both of you get some sleep."

The brief flash of thought that flooded the bond let Alex know sleep was the last thing on Varik's mind, and for once, she couldn't have agreed with him more.

twelve

TASHA OPENED THE DOOR OF THE DUCK 'N' COVER AND was greeted with a chorus of raised voices and drinks from the scattered regulars. She nodded and waved to them in turn as she picked her way through the tables to the bar.

The Duck 'n' Cover was a popular bar located outside Jefferson's city limits and therefore had no need to worry about noise ordinances when bands played. Housed in a converted cotton gin building, it featured a rusted tin exterior and a worn and uneven plank floor. The tables and chairs were all garage sale or flea market finds of differing shapes and sizes. Neon signs advertising the various brands of beer on tap clung to the exposed wall beams that supported the intricate open-framework rafters. The most distinctive feature, however, was the countless names and messages that had been written on every available and reachable space—walls, tables, bar, signs, and even the mismatched curtains covering the wavy-paned windows.

Tasha reached the bar and hoisted herself onto one of the secondhand bar stools. While she waited for the bartender, she checked the cryptic text message she'd received on her cell phone.

MEET TONIGHT, 7:00 AT DUCK 'N' COVER. BRING JOURNAL.

The message itself didn't concern her as much as it probably should. It was the number displayed as the message's origin—12-29-1995, her daughter Maya's birthday—that worried her most. She knew a trace would prove fruitless. Countless websites allowed text messages to be sent from false numbers. Staring at the number displayed on her screen, she wondered how much of her personal life, of Maya's life, could her mysterious callers access?

"Hey, shug," Dinky Kincaid, the Duck 'n' Cover's owner and bartender, greeted Tasha with her trademark smile. Drawn-on black eyebrows that arched too far up her forehead made her look as though her face had frozen in a scandalized expression. Short, round, and proudly displaying her ample cleavage, Dinky was a force to be reckoned with and few in the bar ever dared to cross her. She set a bowl of popcorn in front of Tasha and tilted her head. "You're looking a little long in the face tonight, honey. Rough day?"

Tasha crunched a few kernels of the stale unbuttered popcorn and nodded. "Got a letter from my ex. He wants sole custody of my kid."

Dinky pursed her bright red lips and shook her head as she began mixing liquids from different bottles. "My ex tried that once. He didn't get very far though."

"How did you deal with it?"

"Start with the one on the right." Two shot glasses thumped on the bar in front of Tasha. "I shot him in the ass," Dinky said with a wink.

Tasha's eyes widened.

The other woman cackled and fluttered a pudgy hand against her chest. "Oh, Lordy! I'm joking. I hired a lawyer and took him to the cleaners. We wrung enough money out of his sorry ass for me to buy this place."

Tasha picked up the first of the shot glasses. "Maybe I should talk to your lawyer." She slammed the drink back and swallowed. The chilled liquid left an acid trail to her stomach, where heat bloomed and seared its way to the back of her throat. Coughing and sputtering, she grabbed the second glass and downed it. The heat dissipated. When she could speak again, she asked, "What the hell is that?"

Dinky smiled. "I call it a Bayou Bomb. Couple of drops of Tabasco in the first one give it a real kick." She swept the glasses from the bar. "As for my lawyer, I don't think he lives around here anymore, but you could probably track him down. Name was Caleb Lockwood."

Tasha choked on her popcorn. Coughing, she beat her chest in an attempt to clear the obstruction. Tears gathered in the corners of her eyes and spilled down her cheeks. She struggled for a clean breath.

"Lean forward," a masculine voice instructed as a strong hand smacked her back a few times.

She complied and was rewarded with a dislodged kernel and fresh air.

"There you go," her savior said. "Dinky, grab her some water."

Tasha gratefully accepted the glass Dinky handed to her with a worried expression. She gulped the clear liquid. Her body rebelled and she returned to coughing.

A few more sharp pats on her back helped to ease the air back into her lungs. "Sip it."

She sipped the water as directed and when she didn't cough, she used one glorious deep breath to sigh in relief. "Thanks," she whispered hoarsely and turned to her rescuer only to have her breath stolen away again by coffee brown skin and black eyes.

"My pleasure," he said, flashing a lopsided grin. "Rueben."

Her gaze slipped over his broad shoulders, down the

muscular and tattooed arm. She weakly clasped his hand. "Tasha."

"Well, take care of yourself, Tasha." Rueben pushed away from the bar, still smiling. "And lay off that corn."

Tasha nodded mutely, watching him as he backed away a few steps before turning and striding confidently toward the stage on the opposite side of the building. She saw him slap high fives to a few of the patrons along the way before hopping on the stage, where a band had begun to set up their equipment.

"Dinky," she called and waved for the older woman to join her. "Who was that guy?"

Dinky looked toward the stage and sighed. "Rueben—I don't know his last name. He plays drums for one of the bands that comes through here once in a while."

"Does he live in Jefferson?"

"I'm not sure. I don't see him in here except when his band is playing." Dinky removed the popcorn bowl and wiped down the bar. "Can I get you another one of them Bayou Bombs, honey?"

Tasha nodded, her eyes trained on the stage. Whomever she was to make contact with here was running late. At least she would have something to occupy her until they showed.

"Rueben," she whispered, liking the warm feeling saying his name gave her, and settled in to wait.

Alex's leg caught an unseen corner as she exited the bathroom and pain sliced across her shin. "Ow! Fucking hell!"

"Steady," Varik muttered. His hands settled at her waist, keeping her upright.

After leaving the hospital, he tried to convince her to spend the night at his apartment, but she insisted on returning to the hotel and checking on Dweezil. She also thought she'd be safer in her hotel room, having lived there for weeks and being familiar with its floor plan. The throbbing pain in her shin told her otherwise. "I hate being blind."

"You'll adjust in time."

"I don't want to adjust. I want to see, damn it!"

He slipped his arms around her, pulled her against him, and nestled his chin on her shoulder. "You will, baby, but until you can, you need to relax a little and let your other senses take over."

"Easy for you to say. You're not the one stumbling in the dark."

"I said I would help you."

"Aside from keeping the bond constantly open so I can see through your eyes, what can you do, Varik?"

"Make you more aware of your surroundings by heightening your other senses."

"How?"

Warm breath prickled her flesh as he sighed. A wash of sandalwood and cinnamon enveloped her and made her pulse jump. Soft lips traced the scar along her neck. Alex inhaled sharply and shifted her stance, exposing more of her throat to him.

Fingertips replaced his lips, featherlight as they explored the length of her scar from collarbone to ear. He pulled her earlobe into his mouth, grazing her flesh with the tip of one fang.

She shivered as his hands cupped her face. "Varik—"

His mouth slanted over hers and his tongue raked across her lips, demanding entry.

She opened to him and his tongue curled around hers. Fangs grazed her lower lip, teasing her with their points until her knees threatened to give way.

Alex drew in a breath when he broke the kiss. "Varik, I can't—"

"Shh," he hissed, pressing a finger to her lips.

She opened the blood-bond. *We shouldn't*—

He closed the bond, sealing himself away, and kissed her forehead. "Do you trust me?"

She nodded.

"Then shut up," he murmured, recapturing her lips.

Alex twisted his hair around her fingers as they kissed, while his arms encircled her waist, holding her tightly against him as he lifted her and spun.

He pinned her against a wall, pressing close. Jasmine and vanilla mingled with sandalwood and cinnamon and set her mind spiraling into a series of memories and half-formed fantasies. His hands trailed up her arms and gently pulled her hands away.

Her pulse jumped again as he held her arms above her head, moving his kiss from her lips to her neck. Fangs grazed her scar and she moaned from a combination of anticipation and anxiety. Lips sealed over the slick mark, and his tongue danced along its edges. She inhaled and muscles tensed along her shoulders, her body's way of preparing for the bite to come.

Cool air rushed over her, jolting her to reality and the awareness Varik no longer held her. She stood in darkness with her back to a wall, her arms still over her head, and her pulse racing.

"Find me," Varik whispered from somewhere to her left.

"What kind of sick game are you playing?"

"No game. Now find me."

"I can't fucking see," she snarled.

"That doesn't matter." His words drifted up from her right. "You have other senses. Use them."

She opened the bond and winced as he slammed the connection closed.

"That's cheating," he taunted, his voice and breath inches from her face.

Alex jerked away, startled. "Goddamn it, Varik! You said you'd help me."

He pinned her against the wall once more. "I am."

"How is this helping me?"

His fingers trailed along her arm and left prickled flesh in their wake. "Consider it motivation."

"Seems like foreplay to me."

A grin lay behind his words as he spoke, moving away again. "You know what they say—all work and no play makes for really boring sex."

She pushed off from the wall, following the soft sounds of his footsteps on carpet. "What makes you think I'm going to sleep with you?"

"Sleeping isn't what I had in mind."

Alex spun as his voice issued from behind. She was certain he'd been in front of her. How was he moving around her so quickly and without her hearing him move?

Arms wrapped around her waist and his body molded to her back so she felt *all* of him. "You're thinking too much, *ma poule*. Stop thinking and trust your instincts."

"Right now my instincts are to turn around and beat the shit out of you."

"It's a start." He laughed and released her with a playful swat on her butt cheeks.

She yelped, whirled, and reached for him but found only emptiness. "Oh, you're going to pay for that."

More laughter followed another smack to her backside. "I eagerly await your reprimand, *if* you can catch me."

Alex inhaled the familiar scent of sandalwood and cinnamon that permeated the room. Another quick breath and she noticed a fresh waft to her right. She moved in that direction and was rewarded with the faint sound of retreating footsteps.

"You may be better at this than I initially estimated."

She smiled, following the stronger trails of his scent. "Don't tell me the big bad Hunter is afraid of a blind woman?"

No taunt answered her as she crept along, using the wall as a guide. Her hand brushed against a doorjamb and the sense of a yawning void opened to her left. The trail of Varik's scent was strongest here. Envisioning that he'd moved into what could only be the bathroom, Alex crouched beside the jamb, listening.

Only her own heartbeat and the soft *whir-ka-thunk* of the fifth floor's ice machine in the distance filled the silence.

She rushed into the void and ripped through a soft barrier before crashing into a hard vertical surface. The force of the impact rocked her and made her stumble back.

"You're still thinking too much," Varik chastised to her right. "You're also assuming I'm playing fairly."

She rubbed the sore spot on her forehead where it had hit the wall of what she now knew to be the closet. The soft barrier she'd encountered became his discarded shirt, still warm from his body's heat. Alex snarled and threw the shirt to the floor. "You're being an ass. That much I know for certain."

Thinking of the room's layout as she faced the closet, she knew the exit would be to her left and the bathroom behind her. She extended her arm along the wall opposite the closet, following the surface until she reached the bathroom door and discovered it closed. She pressed her ear to the door and heard only the soft crunching sounds of Dweezil enjoying his nightly meal.

She followed the wall until she reached a corner. The sensation of open space stretching before her told her she'd come to the bedroom portion of the room.

Waving both arms in front of her and taking tentative steps, she located the rolling chair in front of the desk, the dresser and flat-screen television, and finally the curtains covering the windows.

Varik's scent grew stronger, more concentrated on this side of the room.

Alex paused and listened to the sounds around her. Elevator machinery whirred and beeped as the carriages passed different floors. Cars whizzed by on the street outside. Her heart beat out a stereo rhythm in the relative silence.

Excitement zinged through her as she narrowed her focus on the heartbeat. Her heart wasn't beating twice but *two* hearts were beating in synch. A smile pulled the corners of her mouth and she whirled, her hands rising to press against the warm and familiar solidity of Varik's bare torso. "Gotcha."

"Are you sure of that?"

A thin chain circled her neck and a weight thumped against her chest. Frowning, Alex reached for it. Her fingers recognized the well-known edges of a faceted teardrop, flanked by two smaller drops, and the smoothness of a metal band still warm from where it had been nestled against his skin. It was the engagement ring she'd returned six years prior. "Why are you giving me this?"

"To illustrate a point," Varik answered from her left. The sound of springs compressing under weight, the rustle of clothing, and the change in direction of his voice signaled he'd sat down. "Even when you believe you've cornered your opponent, you can't let down your guard. He can still distract you and get away."

She moved toward his voice, clutching the ring in one hand and searching for him with the other. Her fingers laced with his as he pulled her close. "I understand what you're saying, and I know why you chose to use this as your demonstration but I can't keep it."

He stopped her when she raised her hand to remove the chained ring. "Listen to me." He drew a breath. "I've lived my life surrounded by death. I've seen and done what many would consider to be terrible things, and there are few I regret."

Alex waited as he gathered his thoughts before continuing. Varik rarely opened up to her about his past. Huge chunks of his life were a mystery to her while her past was openly debated in the public domain.

"Today, when we were separated in the Shadowlands, I thought I might truly lose you and it frightened me."

The tremor in his voice felt like a knife twisting in her heart.

"My biggest regret is letting you walk away from me—from *us*. I know you've resisted talking to me about what happened because you're afraid the Tribunal is going to find you guilty and we won't have a future."

"Varik—"

"I don't care how long we have, Alex. Whether it's weeks or centuries, it doesn't matter to me. I want to know you feel the same way. I want to know you're mine. I want to know you forgive me."

Alex hesitated and then released her hold on the ring, letting it fall against her chest. Her free hand brushed his cheek and she was surprised to find it slick from tears. "I do forgive you, Varik."

His arms encircled her waist. He buried his face against her stomach.

"And I *am* yours."

A bone-weary sigh racked his body.

Her hands settled on his shoulders. "But I can't wear—"

"No," he whispered, tightening his hold and moving

his head so she knew he was looking up at her. "Wear it. Just for tonight."

"Varik—"

"Please. For me."

Alex couldn't speak as her throat closed with emotion and she nodded.

Varik slipped his hands up her spine and leaned back, pulling her down on top of him. *Thank you,* he whispered in her mind.

She shivered as the desire and longing he felt poured over the blood-bond. Any response she may have voiced was lost when his mouth closed over the scar on her neck, teasing her with the scrape of his fangs and the quick feathery strokes of his tongue.

Images flashed across the bond. Memories of their life together in Louisville. Dreams of a future that never came to be. With these came a fragile hope that the future they'd once envisioned could still be possible. The bond laid bare all the emotions and desires Varik couldn't express in words.

Tears gathered in the corners of her eyes as her own desires for reconciliation echoed his. Years of bottled shame and anger exploded and burned within her, leaving only sorrow and regret. She closed her eyes in a vain attempt to keep her tears from showing.

"Don't cry, baby." Varik wiped each one away. *"J'allais mourir un millier de morts à garder vos larmes."* He kissed first one cheek then the other. "I would die a thousand deaths to keep your tears away."

A new emotion rose within her, flooding the bond, feeding their shared hope, and chasing away the momentary sorrow she'd felt. Her hands slipped between his head and the bed, and her fingers knotted in his hair as she kissed him with a passion she hadn't felt in years.

He returned her kiss with equal fervor, rolling them both on the bed until he lay stretched beside her. They separated only long enough for Varik to slip her shirt over her head.

When she attempted to unfasten his belt, he swatted her hands and she hissed in protest. "Not yet, *chérie*," he murmured. His hand slipped over her stomach, followed by his lips. Her flesh prickled when his breath blew over it in puffs as he spoke. His voice changed, dropping in pitch and carrying a seductive promise. "I intend to take my time with you."

"What happened to you eagerly awaiting my reprimand?" she demanded, not wanting to wait. "I *did* catch you."

"Yes, and I also got away so your argument is moot, *ma puce.*"

"You cheated, and what did you just call me?"

He surged forward, silencing her with a deep kiss that stole her breath. One hand cupped her face while the other deftly removed her bra.

She sucked in air while his lips and hands left a blazing trail down her neck to her exposed breasts. Though darkness ruled her vision, the sensations she felt as he varied his touch from featherlight strokes to more demanding as he silently guided her into position overwhelmed her.

Her fingers raked through his hair and she whispered his name while his mouth clamped over one swollen nipple, his tongue alternately flickering over its surface and lazily circling the hardened flesh.

He slid down the bed. His hands and mouth exploring her flesh and making her entire body tingle.

She chewed her bottom lip when he reached the top of her jeans. She drew in a sharp breath as his hands worked the button loose. A barely audible moan escaped her lips, lost in the sound of the zipper being pulled down. She shivered with anticipation as he first slowly slid the heavy denim off her hips and legs and then her soft cotton panties.

Varik shifted his position so his partially clothed body tented her naked form. His fingers traced the curve of her lips. "If you want to stop, tell me now."

Alex captured his hand in hers and guided him to the throbbing sensation centered deep between her thighs. "Don't stop."

An animalistic growl issued from him as he kissed her and his fingers slipped inside her. He rubbed her clitoris with practiced strokes while he drank in her small cries of pleasure.

She protested when he moved away, leaving her exposed to the room's cool air. Her objections turned to gasps and moans as he settled between her thighs, darting tongue replacing deft fingers. As he explored her innermost areas, electric currents zinged over her skin and along her spine. A pressure built in her loins and her breathing turned ragged as he merrily led her to the brink of wondrous oblivion.

He moved away at the last moment, and she snarled her frustration. Varik laughed, deep and throaty, as he kissed his way up her stomach to her breasts. "I'm not letting you off so easily, *chérie*. After all, I have six years to make up."

"In one night?" she puffed.

Varik hesitated before giving her left nipple a teasing scrape with his fangs and a flick of his tongue. "I may need to rest in between our sessions, but I'm willing to give it a try."

Alex laughed and wrapped her arms around his neck, pulling him to her. She kissed him and savored the smell of their combined scents. She reveled in the electric tingle she felt as the smooth plane of his chest glided over her breasts.

He used his long legs to open her thighs wider.

Somehow he'd managed to remove his jeans without her notice. One hand slipped under her hips, lifting her to meet his slow thrust as he entered her.

She gasped from the multitude of sensations that exploded within her and unexpected words tumbled from her lips. "I love you."

Varik froze and a tremor rippled through his body. A hand brushed her cheek and breath warmed her face. "Do you mean that?"

Alex bit her lower lip. She hadn't said those words to him for a long time, despite his having said them to her repeatedly since arriving in Jefferson. Conflicting emotions swirled around her but one shone above all others, and she nodded.

"Then say it again," he whispered.

"I love you."

He flexed his hips. "Again."

"I love you," she rasped as he thrust into her.

He asked her to repeat it again and again, creating a steady rhythm until there was no more need for words. His low grunts and her soft moans became their soundtrack. As the pressure once again built in her loins, Alex clung to him, wrapping her legs around his waist. Her nails dug into his back and he responded by increasing his pace.

Thousands of tiny electrical pulses raced up her spine. She sank her fangs into his chest. Hot blood pumped into her mouth as she drew on the wound.

He groaned and thrust into her with a renewed speed and force.

Alex threw her head back and cried out with the intensity of the orgasm that rocked her. Fire seared every nerve ending in her body. Everywhere their skin touched burned and she never wanted it to end.

Varik's fangs pierced her shoulder, and he buried himself within her for the final time as wave after wave of tremors swept through him. His mouth clamped around the wound, drawing her blood into him as he in turn gave a vital part of himself to her.

When the last of his tremors faded and the fire beneath her skin had been quenched, Varik rolled onto his side, wrapping her in his arms and holding her close. They said nothing. Everything that needed to be said had been voiced in their lovemaking.

Alex lay in the darkness that continued to plague her and listened to the rhythm of Varik's breathing slow and level out with sleep. She silently fingered the ring hanging on the chain around her neck.

Her profession of love, although unexpected, was accurate. Her feelings for him hadn't changed in the years they'd been separated. She truly did love him. She knew that now, but she wondered, with facing a possible death sentence from the Tribunal, was it too little too late?

Peter awoke screaming. Visions of Alexandra giving herself to the Dark One continued to play through his mind.

He slapped the sides of his head trying to rid himself of the sight of Varik caressing her, kissing her.

Fucking her.

"No!" He bolted from his bed and ripped open his door. He stormed down the second-floor hallway toward the master bedroom.

Each specially crafted Alexandra replica doll—one for each year of her life—stared at him from behind their glass enclosures. Whispers and moans filled the air, tormenting and taunting him.

He opened the hidden door to his attic sanctuary and rushed up the stairs. The smell of blood lingered in the windowless space. Sinking to his knees in the center of the circle, he pounded the wooden planks with his fists until his skin split and left bloody smears on the cracked boards.

"Why?" he whispered to no one.

No answer came.

Peter retraced the ritual steps in his mind. The offerings. The incantations. The sacrifice. Everything had been performed correctly and yet it had failed.

Again.

"Why does she still go to him?"

He'd entered a trance as he had done so often, desiring to see Alexandra, wanting to know if the ritual had yet taken hold. Using a doll that had been a favored toy of hers in childhood as a focusing object, he sent a ribbon of his consciousness to her. He'd performed the same action countless times to observe her, learn of her likes and dislikes, and share in her joys and sorrows.

But *this* time, he discovered her in mid-coitus with Varik. Peter was horrified that she would still give herself to him, a clear signal that the ritual had failed, and yet entranced by the beauty of her naked form as she writhed in pleasure. He'd been unable to look away.

Rage consumed him as he sensed all his carefully laid plans slipping away. *She* was slipping away.

"No," he snarled. "She's *mine*."

He would take her.

He would make her love him.

She *would* be his.

Forever.

thirteen

VARIK SLAMMED HIS CORVETTE'S DOOR AND ROUNDED the car to help Alex out of the passenger seat. "Watch your footing. There's a slight slope here."

She eased out of the car, holding on to his hand for balance and guidance. "I'd really hoped my eyesight would be better this morning."

"The doctor said it would take time. We'll get through this." He closed her door and set the alarm.

"I don't know how much use I'll be until my sight comes back, *if* it comes back."

"Don't talk like that. Of course it'll come back, and you're a valuable member of my investigative team."

"Why? Because I'm psychic or because you're afraid I'll get into trouble if you don't keep your eye on me?"

Varik smirked. "Both."

She linked her arm with his as they walked in silence through the Nassau County Municipal Center's parking lot toward the FBPI's mobile lab.

The sun was already above the trees and approaching midday. They'd spent the morning making love and finding some much-needed solace in each other's company. Their euphoria had been interrupted by an urgent call from Reyes Cott, who reported they'd found something disturbing regarding the doll from Mindy Johnson's car.

While examining the doll, Reyes had determined the soft material used to make the doll's body was some type of leather. He thought he might be able to trace it to a specific manufacturer and then follow the bread crumbs to a possible suspect. His logic was sound enough but sustained a fatal blow when he discovered the leather was in fact human skin.

This latest development had pulled Alex and Varik from their bed and set them on a course for Nassau County Municipal Center. As they walked toward the lab, Varik sensed the hesitancy in Alex's steps and the distraction in her mind. He'd noticed it earlier but hadn't pressed. She would tell him what was bothering her when she was ready.

"Here we are," he said when they reached the front of the converted RV.

Alex nodded and then sighed and stopped, tugging on his arm. "There's something I didn't tell you yesterday. Something happened after we were attacked and you were pulled into the Shadowlands."

"Does it involve the Dollmaker?"

She shook her head. "No, it was before then, before I found you. I ran into the spirit of a little boy."

"As I understand things, it's not uncommon to meet spirits when you part the Veil."

"It's not, but this boy couldn't have been more than four or five years old. His clothes were wet like he'd been swimming in them. He said his name was Edward."

Dread knotted his stomach. Memories long supressed pushed against the barrier between his subconscious and conscious minds. He drove them back, only to have them resurge, demanding his attention. "What did he look like?"

Sunlight reflected in the dark glasses she still wore to cover her sightless eyes. "He looked like you, actually."

Varik felt as though he'd been punched in the gut.

The barrier keeping the memories at bay broke and unleashed them.

It was a frigid night in early January 1928. He was in London on an assignment—tracking a vampire accused of slaughtering three families north of the city. He'd finally managed to get a solid lead on the vampire's location. All he needed to pursue the rogue was to gather a few supplies from the basement flat he was leasing.

As he rounded a corner, a wave of water rushed past him, nearly knocking him from his feet. Then came the cries and pleas for help. Panicked, he slogged through the rising water, desperate to reach his flat.

His own cries mingled with those of others until the water became too deep. It swept him from his feet and carried him through the narrow winding streets, another piece of flotsam eventually left abandoned in a dank alleyway.

A warm hand on his arm chased away the cold memories. "Varik?" Alex asked. Her other hand cupped his cheek and her voice was soft. "What is it? Talk to me. Who is Edward?"

"Someone I haven't talked about to anyone in a very long time."

"I don't understand."

Varik sighed, gently removed her hand from his face, and kissed her knuckles. "The spirit you met was Edward Lucien Baudelaire," he whispered hoarsely. "My son."

"Your son?" She tried to pull away but he tightened his grip on her hand. "How can you— Why didn't you ever tell me?"

"It was a long time ago. He was only four when he died, drowned when the Thames River flooded parts of London. I never thought the two of you would meet."

"I'm so sorry," she whispered and hugged him.

He closed his eyes, returned her embrace, and drew

strength from her warmth. A day didn't pass when he didn't think of Edward at least once. Edward was one reason he hadn't killed in over fifty years. Seeing the anguished parents of a teenaged vampire he killed because of faulty information reminded him of the loss he'd suffered. He swore he'd never cause that kind of pain again.

"Well, isn't this cozy," Morgan's voice drifted up from behind them.

Alex stepped away as Varik whirled to face Morgan. "How long have you been standing there?" he demanded.

Morgan leaned against the side of an SUV, arms crossed in front of her with a file folder tucked between one arm and her side. "Long enough to know you've intentionally kept Enforcer Sabian in the dark about a great many things."

"Don't," he warned, his voice hard.

"Don't what, *Director* Baudelaire?" she taunted. "She already knows of Edward. Why not tell her the full story?"

"What is she talking about?" Alex asked.

"Nothing important," he said.

Morgan laughed. "Isn't it obvious? He doesn't want you to know the identity of the mother of his only child."

"Morgan, now isn't the time for this discussion."

"And when would be a good time?" Morgan asked. "Perhaps you'd like to avoid the issue for another eight decades?"

He turned to leave.

"Varik." Alex touched his arm, making him pause. "Talk to me. Who is Edward's mother?"

"I am," Morgan responded.

He glared at her as Alex's hand first tightened on his arm and then jerked away. He grabbed it. "Alex, wait. Let me explain."

She shoved him.

"Alex, will you please—"

"Anything else I should know? I mean, are any of your other ex-girlfriends going to show up here wanting to kill me? If so, I'd like to know now so I can be ready to defend myself."

"Stop!" He grabbed her upper arms. "Just stop it!"

She pulled away. "No, you stop it!" She opened her mouth as if she was about to say something, and then thought better of it. "Just leave me alone, Varik."

He watched her turn away, reaching out with her hands to find the front of the RV and following it around the side to the door. Once she had disappeared around the corner, he shifted his attention to Morgan, who still leaned against an SUV but who now sported a broad grin.

"Well, that was entertaining," she said.

Varik closed the distance between them in two steps. He wrapped his hand around her throat, slamming her against the SUV's side. "Why did you do that?"

"Remove your hand," she growled. "Or I'll remove it for you."

"Answer my question."

"It's my job."

Centuries of hiding among humans had ingrained subterfuge into the vampire cultural psyche. Special Investigators like Morgan were trained to manipulate and provoke responses from their targets and observe their reactions. The reasoning was simple: those innocent of corruption allegations maintained their innocence, and the guilty turned defensive. It was effective if not always accurate.

Varik released her and paced a short distance away before rounding on her again. "But why Edward? Why would you choose *our* son to provoke Alex?"

"I didn't use Edward," she said, rubbing her neck

and glaring at him with copper eyes. "I used our prior relationship, which you apparently haven't shared with your latest conquest."

"Alex isn't a conquest," he muttered.

"Be that as it may, you've kept secrets from her." She flashed the file she'd been holding. "And she's done the same to you."

"What the hell are you talking about?"

"Were you aware Enforcer Sabian possesses a psychic Talent strong enough to access a metaphysical storehouse known as the Hall of Records?"

Varik weighed his answer before speaking. "Yes, I knew she possessed a Talent, but I was only recently made aware of its full extent."

"Did she also tell you that she's accessed the Hall of Records on numerous occasions since her suspension?"

"I don't see where it's any of your or the Bureau's business what she's done during that time."

"It's very much our business considering there are hundreds of records missing from the Hall."

"What do you mean missing?"

"Disappeared, gone, as if that person never existed."

"You can't possibly think Alex had anything to do with it," Varik retorted. "She wouldn't even begin to know how to delete a record."

"But you don't deny she knows how to access the Hall?"

"No, but— Where are you getting your information?"

"We have our sources."

He folded his arms in front of him. "How many records are missing in total?"

"At least three hundred and sixteen, possibly more."

"Human or vampire?"

"Both, but mostly human and nearly all female."

"Damn it," he spat. "The Dollmaker."

"What about him?"

He stared at the front of the lab for a moment, arguing with himself on how much information to reveal to Morgan. If he told her everything, she could use it against Alex during the Tribunal's proceedings. If he withheld information, could he potentially be putting Alex at risk with the Dollmaker?

Finally he looked back to Morgan. "Alex heard screams coming from the dolls when she was in the Dollmaker's house. While she was there, some of the dolls were broken. She saw what she described as spirits rising from them."

Blood drained from Morgan's face. "Are you suggesting that he is somehow trapping the souls of his victims in those dolls?"

Varik nodded. "That would explain your missing records." He glanced over his shoulder at the lab. "And now he's after Alex."

The morning's shadows had lengthened and crept into the corners of Kirk's bedroom. He lay on his bed with his head nestled between Jennifer Lee's widespread legs. She gasped and then moaned softly as he licked the blood from the twin punctures in her upper thigh.

Piper's attitude toward the new girl had progressively deteriorated the longer Kirk had interviewed Jennifer at Mug Shots the previous night. When he'd suggested returning to his place to finalize their new working arrangement, Piper had insisted on coming with them.

He'd denied her and sent her home. She hadn't been happy but a few well-placed kisses and whispered promises and she'd relented. Once she was gone, he drove Jennifer back to his place and the two of them partied until late in the night. As a blood bunny, she was working out just fine.

He sank his fangs into Jennifer's thigh once more. He drew on the wound and blood rushed into his mouth along with discordant memories. She squealed and begged him to do more than bite her.

It was all the encouragement he needed. He grabbed her wrist and spun her around on the bed. Shoving her onto her hands and knees, he knelt behind her and clutched her thin hips, maneuvering her into the desired position. He grabbed both her wrists, yanked her arms behind her back while pulling her toward him, and thrust into her roughly.

She cried out and tried to pull away.

Kirk's firm hold kept her immobile. He quickly found his rhythm, rapidly sliding in and out of her. Soon they were both panting and lost in the pursuit of their own release, performing a frantic dance to the beat of slapping flesh.

Kirk was closing in on his pleasure when he heard footsteps in the hallway outside the bedroom seconds before the door opened.

Piper entered, carrying two plastic bags and trailing the scent of fried chicken, rice, and soy sauce. "Hey, sweetheart, I thought you might—" She stopped, mouth and eyes wide. The bags hit the floor, spilling their contents.

He never slowed his pace, despite Jennifer's sudden lack of enthusiasm and pleas for him to stop. "Hi, Piper," he sneered between sharp intakes of breath. "Be with you in a moment. Almost done here."

His last word became a loud groan as he climaxed. Breathing heavily, he separated from Jennifer, who ran sobbing to the adjoining bathroom. Kirk collapsed on the bed, smiling. He reached for the beer he'd left on the bedside table, then turned to the still-motionless girl standing in the doorway. Gesturing to the spilled food, he said, "Be a dear, would you, and clean that up before it stains the carpet." He took a swig of beer. "I'm wiped out."

Piper seemed to snap out of whatever trance she'd entered, glanced at the mess on the floor, and then back at him. Anger and defiance shone in her previously lackluster eyes. "Clean it up your own damn self," she shouted and spun on her heel, stomping down the hall to the stairs.

"Get back here!" He threw the beer after her and jumped from the bed to follow.

The bottle shattered on the wall above her head as she scooted down the stairs, screaming.

Kirk vaulted over the banister to land heavily on the sofa, tipping it and breaking the supports underneath. His ankle twisted painfully beneath him.

Piper ran past him, trying to reach the front door.

"Come here, bitch," he snarled and pounced onto her back, driving them both into a wall. He pinned her between the wall and his naked body. "Do *not* talk back to me! You understand? Don't *ever* talk back to me!"

"You said you don't fuck the new girls!"

He laughed. "You honestly believed that bullshit? I've fucked every single one of my bunnies, including your cousin before I sent her off to be sucked and fucked by someone else, just like the good little whores you all are."

"Fuck you," she spat, awkwardly kicking first one leg and then another behind her in an attempt to gain her freedom.

He reached around her and stuck his hand between her legs. "Been there, had that, wasn't impressed."

Piper shrieked and lashed out with her fists.

He laughed, dodging her ill-aimed blows until a kick

made him move to the right and her fist found its mark in the tender flesh above his groin. All strength left his body and his knees buckled. His stomach churned, and he felt as though he would be sick.

She didn't offer taunts or more punches. Piper bolted for the door, flung it open, and fled into the midday light, leaving Kirk groaning in pain among the shattered remains of his living room.

"Is there something wrong, Mom?" Stephen asked quietly. His voice was pitched so as to be both intimate and audible over the low, indistinct conversations of other diners around them.

Emily looked up, noted the worry in her son's clear blue eyes, and offered a halfhearted smile. "No, honey, I'm fine."

"You haven't touched your lasagna."

She set her fork onto the side of her undisturbed plate. Stephen had offered to take her out for a nice lunch since Janet was in class until late afternoon. She'd looked forward to spending time with her son, but now all she could do was think of how to keep her daughter alive. "I guess I'm not very hungry."

Stephen pushed his empty plate aside and a passing waiter grabbed it on his way to the kitchen. He steepled his fingers and tapped them against his pursed lips, studying her. "You're worried about Alex, aren't you?"

She settled farther in the corner of their booth. "Of course I'm worried about her. I'm always worried about her."

"No, this is different." Stephen leaned forward and dropped his voice even lower. "What's going on, Mom? I haven't seen you this distracted in a long time."

"I said it's nothing."

"Is it the Tribunal? Varik?"

"Oh, Stephen, not all of this family's problems stem from Varik Baudelaire. In fact, he's probably the last person who'd want to harm any of us."

"Could've fooled me with the way he tried to choke me a month ago."

"You provoked him, and you know it," Emily scolded. "And, for Alex's sake, until this Tribunal business is over, the less you antagonize Varik, the better."

"Why are you always so quick to defend him? I don't understand why I'm the only one who sees this guy is trouble."

"Because you're protective of Alex and you want what *you* think is best for her." She reached across the table and squeezed his hand. "But, honey, Alex is a grown woman. She can make her own decisions, and if she chooses to try and work things out with Varik, you need to step back and let her."

Stephen slumped in his seat, arms folded across his chest, brooding and silent.

Emily scooted out of the booth and handed her purse to him. "I'm going to the little girls' room. Watch this for me?"

He took the bag with a terse nod.

She ruffled his curls and earned a half-smile. As she navigated the maze of tables, Emily thought of the days following Bernard's murder.

Suddenly finding herself as a single mother in 1968 with two young children had been the least of her worries. She and Bernard shared a blood-bond and when that connection was severed, she'd fallen into a deep depression.

The week immediately after Bernard died had been the worst. She'd lain in bed, unable to move, speak, or eat. Pearlie Marker, her human neighbor, and a few others had taken it upon themselves to care for Emily, as well as Stephen and Alex, and Alex had needed just

as much care as Emily. The poor child had been the one
to find her beloved father's staked and beheaded body.

It was ten-year-old Stephen, however, who had taken
on the bulk of Alex's care. He made sure she received
the proper amount of blood daily, even making certain
the humans knew nothing of it. He read bedtime stories
to her and comforted her during the night when she
woke screaming for Bernard. Even though he was griev-
ing himself, he'd taken on the mantle of "man of the
house" and cared for his sister when Emily couldn't.

Bernard's funeral, however, was the turning point for
Emily. The service had been closed casket, per Bernard's
will, and she and the children had been allowed into the
chapel to say good-bye in private. Even now Emily
could close her eyes and still smell the roses and lilies
that draped the casket in red and white.

Stephen was stoic as he approached the sleek silver
casket. Five-year-old Alex was quiet. She'd hardly spoken at all since finding Bernard. Emily had been . . .
numb, as if she drifted through a haze. It wasn't until
Alex began crying, screaming that her father wasn't
dead, that she could hear him calling to her, and tried
to rip open the coffin that Emily had finally snapped
out of her stupor.

After the funeral, her days had been rote: wake the
kids, feed them, greet the endless stream of sympathiz-
ers, avoid the media seeking to know more about "the
first family of the vampire community" as they dubbed
the Sabians once vampires revealed themselves, bathe
the kids, send the kids to bed, and then collapse into a
sobbing heap of misery. She would then rise the next
morning to start the cycle again.

Throughout it all had been Varik Baudelaire. He
hadn't made any grand displays of watching over the
mourning family, but Emily had been aware of him on
the periphery. She would find envelopes stuffed with

cash slipped under the front door. Vials of fresh blood would mysteriously appear in the refrigerator overnight. Stephen and Alex were provided with armed bodyguards when the vampire rights movement reached its peak. There were other small events as well, but perhaps the most comforting were the occasional gifts sent to Alex.

Emily had never understood why Varik left gifts for Alex and not Stephen, but perhaps he'd felt Alex needed more attention, more support to overcome the trauma of her father's death. Whatever his reasons, Emily still felt indebted to him four decades later, and as she made her way back to the table where Stephen waited, she decided it was time she let Varik know just how much she appreciated everything he'd done for her family.

Smiling, she slid into the booth, opposite Stephen. Her smile soon disappeared as she noticed his once-clear blue eyes had shifted to vivid amber. "What is it? Did something happen to Alex?"

He slid her cell phone across the table in silence.

"Stephen, what's—" Her question faltered and died as she noticed the displayed number of the last call received. The time stamp was only minutes ago, while she'd been in the restroom.

"Gregor Wahl called." His tone was dark and full of anger.

"I see that. Did he leave a message?"

"He said to tell you he had a possible lead on Siobhan's whereabouts, and he was going to check it out."

Emily felt her heart sink into her stomach.

"Why is Gregor calling you, Mom? Who is this Siobhan?"

Emily closed her eyes and took a deep breath in an effort to calm her own rapidly shifting emotions. She'd hoped to keep her inquiries into the Tribunal a secret from Stephen and Alex.

"Mom?"

"I called him," she said quietly. She squared her shoulders and met Stephen's angry gaze. "I asked him to find out any information he could on the Tribunal's proceedings, anything that could help save Alex."

"He's the one who suggested using us as the public face for the vampire rights movement after Dad died. He made our lives hell for seven years. *Why* would you call him?"

"I know you like Gregor about as much as you like Varik, but we—*Alex* needs all the allies she can find right now. I trust Gregor, just as I trust Varik."

"Mom, you—"

"There is more going on with the Tribunal than we've been told, Stephen."

He frowned. "What do you mean?"

"Woody Phelps has taken a personal interest in Alex's inquiry, and the Magistrates are calling in Enforcers from all over the country in some sort of massive internal investigation."

"Why would—"

"I don't know. Gregor was going to find out what he could and call me." Emily punched the button to redial Gregor's number. The line rang several times without anyone picking up. "That's odd. Now he's not answering."

"So who is Siobhan?" Stephen repeated his earlier question.

She listened to a few more rings before ending the call. "A woman who worked with your father."

"At the university?"

"Yes."

"Is she the one Dad got pregnant?"

Emily wordlessly stared at him for several moments before finding her barely audible voice. "How do you know about that?"

"I heard you and Dad talking—arguing, at night. I may've been a kid but I wasn't stupid. I knew Dad had an affair with a woman at work, but I didn't know her name."

"Oh, honey. This isn't something I ever wanted to burden you and Alex with. You were both so young when he was killed." She paused and drew a deep breath to keep her voice from shaking. "I didn't want this to be a part of either of your memories."

"Alex doesn't know about the affair. I never told her." Stephen shook his head. "She has such an ideal-ized view of Dad. I couldn't hurt her like that."

Before Emily could respond, Stephen's cell phone rang, giving her time to truly assimilate what she'd learned. Stephen knew about Bernard's affair and that there was a pregnancy. But how much of the rest of the story did he know? Did he know about the accusations against Siobhan?

She fingered the small shamrock charm hidden be-neath her blouse. What about the child? Did he know—

"That was Janet," Stephen announced, breaking into her thoughts. "She's getting out of class early."

"Well, I guess you'll want to go home and meet her, then." Emily scooted out of the booth.

Stephen rose and handed over her purse. They wove their way through the tables, out of the restaurant, and into the cool November afternoon. As they walked through the parking lot, Emily's thoughts returned again to her husband, his mistress, and their child.

A child born during a night of fear and blood.

A child whose true identity must remain hidden.

If certain individuals within the vampire community learned the child survived, Bernard's murder—his *sacrifice*—would've been an exercise in futility, and Emily refused to allow his death, and her family's pain, to ever be meaningless.

fourteen

"NOW, THAT'S JUST FUCKING CREEPY," FREDDY HAVER said. "How can you trap a soul in a doll?"

"I don't know." Alex ground her fingertips into her closed eyes until sparks invaded the darkness in which she was confined. "But that's what I saw. Once the dolls were broken, the souls within were released, and the Dollmaker was seriously pissed off."

Varik had finally made his way into the mobile lab, and they were discussing Freddy's and Reyes's findings on the doll left with Mindy Johnson's car, as well as other evidence. Morgan had thankfully gone back inside the Municipal Center.

Alex sighed and rapidly blinked her eyes. The starbursts cleared from her vision, leaving an unending darkness in their wake. She squinted and slowly looked from side to side. The inky blackness remained unchanged.

Sandalwood and cinnamon washed over her along with the rustle of clothing as Varik shifted beside her. *Are you all right? Is the pain getting worse?*

His thoughts slipped easily into her mind. She frowned and once again covered her eyes with her sunglasses. Ever since she'd pursued the shadow entity into the Shadowlands, the blood-bond had been harder to seal. She was now developing a headache from attempting to keep her mental shields clamped tight enough to prevent Varik's thoughts from trickling over into her own, and it wasn't working.

Plus, she was still pissed at him for not telling her about his past relationship with Morgan. Not telling her about Edward she understood, but failing to mention the woman whose investigation could be the deciding factor in whether Alex lived or died—that was inexcusable. *I'm fine,* she replied. *Just a headache.*

"If he is trapping souls, why do it?" Freddy asked, drawing their attention. "What would be the point?"

"Blood substitute," Reyes answered from across the lab. "Think about it. As vampires we don't physically need to feed on blood to survive. It's the residual psychic energy in the blood that we really need. If you could trap a soul, or even a portion of one, and then find a way to feed off that energy, you could theoretically sustain yourself on it and forgo the need for blood."

"But we crave the taste of blood," Alex countered. "It's why Vlad's Tears were invented, to curb our blood-hunger between feedings."

"True," Reyes said. "However, you're forgetting that blood-hunger for us is similar to a human craving nicotine. It's a form of addiction and most addictions can be broken with time, training, and practice."

"So *if* the Dollmaker is trapping souls, and *if* he's found a way to feed off those souls, why do it at all?" Varik asked. "Like Reyes said, blood-hunger is an addiction. Why break the addiction in favor of something as elaborate as soul trapping?"

"Maybe something happened and he can't feed normally," Freddy offered. "Alex, during your encounter with him, did you notice if he still had fangs or had them filed down?"

The image of the Dollmaker screaming in rage as he charged toward her and her father drifted before Alex in the black sea of her vision. "He still had fangs." She shuddered. "I think whatever made him start trapping souls wasn't a physical problem. I think it may be psychological."

"What do you mean?" Varik asked.

Alex sighed and drummed her fingers on top of the workstation at which she sat. "He's a collector. Yes, he makes these dolls, but the dolls themselves aren't that important to him. If they were, he wouldn't have given up even one of them. The dolls are vessels. It's the souls that matter. He's collecting *them* so there has to be a reason for it, something beyond just feeding off the residual energy." She stopped drumming her fingers. "Reyes, the doll left with Mindy's car, was it damaged in some way?"

"Yeah, a hairline fracture in the back of the porcelain head," he answered. "It was partially obscured by the wig but I noticed one tail end of it along the neck where the head joins the body."

"So the doll was damaged and no longer capable of containing a soul," Freddy said.

"That would be my guess." Alex stifled a yawn. The lack of sleep from the previous night was starting to catch up to her. She propped her chin on the palm of her hand and rested her elbow on the workstation. "Porcelain heads and bodies made of human skin aren't easy to make. He's not doing it in a weekend. He's taking his time with them."

"Maybe he takes his time with the victims as well," Varik said. "If preserving a soul is that important to him, he'd probably want to spend time with the victim."

"It's possible." Alex's eyes drooped and closed behind her sunglasses. Sleep tugged at her consciousness and made her body feel heavy. "We should call Doc Hancock and ask if he's finished the autopsy on our Jane Doe from the salvage yard. If we can establish an identity and time of death, I think—"

"I think it's probably best if we take a break and grab some food," Varik interrupted. "We're all hungry. I've heard Freddy's stomach grumbling for the past ten minutes. We can pick this up in an hour or two."

For once, Alex didn't argue. She was tired but as soon as he mentioned food, her stomach rumbled to remind her she hadn't eaten since that morning. She reluctantly allowed Varik to help her to her feet and guide her down the steps of the mobile lab. The November air was much colder now than when they arrived and she leaned into him for added warmth as they traversed the parking lot in silence.

They slowed and she assumed they were close to Varik's Corvette.

Varik sighed. "Alex, I'm sorry about earlier, with Morgan. I should've told you about our past relationship when you told me she was coming here."

"Why didn't you?"

"I couldn't. We were on-scene and with everything that happened afterward—I don't know what you want me to say, Alex. You expect me to be either some squeaky-clean schoolboy without a past or to bare my soul to you and fill you in on all the dirty, gory details. Well, I'm not and I can't."

"I know you have a past, Varik, and it's trying to kill me."

"That's not fair, and you know it."

"Fair?" she scoffed. "You want to talk about what's *fair*? You keep saying I should tell you everything because we're bond-mates, but you're not willing to do the same. And you wonder *why* I have a hard time trusting you?"

"I'm trying to protect you."

"Protect me from *what*?" she shouted. "I hear that a lot, too, but ever since you showed up I've been shot, beaten up, possessed, and blinded, and yet you haven't offered one *single* scrap of evidence that suggests I need protection from anything other than *you*!"

Her voice echoed across the parking lot, and Alex realized what she'd said. She reached for him, clutching at his shirt. "Varik, I'm sorry. I didn't mean that."

She expected him to shy away but he took both her hands in his and pulled her into an embrace. "Yes, you did."

She shook her head. "No, I—"

He silenced her with a kiss.

Alex returned the kiss, pressing herself to him as if she could take back her words and soothe the pain she'd inflicted in a single act.

Varik broke the kiss and touched his forehead to hers. "I'm sorry," he murmured.

When she tried to protest, he touched a finger to her lips.

"I haven't been completely honest with you about my past, about Morgan, about Edward—a lot of things— but baby, you have to understand. There are people in my past who wouldn't hesitate to use you to get to me. I *have* to keep some secrets because I *have* to keep you safe." He wrapped her in his arms once more. "I nearly went insane when Edward died. The thought of losing you . . ."

"I understand," she murmured. "And I'm sorry I said all those things."

"They needed to be said."

Alex tightened her hold. "That's no excuse though."

He peeled away from her. "Perhaps not but let's put it behind us for now and go have lunch. I'm starving."

She couldn't keep the smile from her face.

They reached his Corvette, and he assisted her with settling into the passenger seat before closing the door.

"Excuse me, sir," a man's muffled voice materialized

outside. "My battery seems to be dead. You wouldn't happen to have any jumper cables, would you?"

Alex frowned. Alarm bells sounded in her head. Something about the voice sounded familiar.

"Uh, yeah," Varik responded warily. "I have a set in the trunk."

She heard the two move away from her door, their voices growing fainter. A weak odor filtered into the car, wrinkling her nose. She inhaled, trying to place the scent.

Leather and old blood.

"Varik!" she called. She managed to open the door as the sounds of a struggle arose from the rear of the car. "It's him! It's the Dollmaker!"

Something heavy slammed into the car beside her, knocking Alex from her feet. The back of her head banged painfully against the window as she fell. She heard the sound of flesh striking flesh, a series of loud grunts, and then silence except for one person's heavy breathing and her own heartbeat.

"Varik?" she said softly, inwardly cursing the blindness that still afflicted her. "What's happening?"

She heard someone kneel in front of her. The smell of leather and old blood covered her.

"Hello, chickie," the Dollmaker whispered. A rough hand grabbed her arm, and she felt a sharp pinprick in her wrist.

She fought to free herself as the drug he'd injected rushed through her body. Whatever he'd given her worked rapidly, as her movements slowed and her words slurred. "What have you done to Varik?"

"Put him out of his misery." He hauled her to her feet. "And now you're going to be mine. Forever."

Tasha groaned and rubbed the sleep from her eyes as she sat up. She yawned and blinked against the sunlight filtering through the west-facing windows of her bedroom. Squinting against the light, she tried to reason why the sun was rising in the west.

"Shit," she hissed and then moaned as her head thumped with pain and her stomach lurched. She rolled from the bed, grabbing for any nearby clothing. "I'm such a fucking idiot."

"Something wrong, Mama?"

Tasha screamed, dropping the clothes she gathered, and patted her hip, reaching for a sidearm that wasn't present. She backed up against the closet door, staring at the obviously amused—and naked—man in her bed. "Who are you? What are you doing here?"

He chuckled and stretched, thick corded muscles rippling under dark skin. "If you don't remember *that,* then I did *not* do my job right last night."

"Last night?" Tasha scratched her head.

She remembered going to the Duck 'n' Cover last night to meet someone who never showed. Dinky had supplied her with Bayou Bombs—the thought of which made Tasha's stomach somersault—and there was a band. "Rueben."

He grinned. "Ah, so you *do* remember. I don't think my ego could take it if you didn't."

A draft blew across her bare legs. She looked down and cursed, grabbing a short satin robe from the closet doorknob and slipping it on to cover her nakedness. Another glance at the windows made her groan. "I am so fucking fired."

"No, you're not."

Tasha frowned at Rueben as she tied her robe. "What do you mean by that and can you please cover yourself?"

Rueben pushed himself up, leaned against the headboard, and draped a corner of her comforter over his lap. "Someone called here looking for you this morning. I told them you were sick and couldn't make it in today."

"And they believed you?"

He laughed. "Yes. Would you have preferred I told them you were passed out in an alcohol-induced sexual stupor?"

"Absolutely not!" Tasha hugged herself and sat on the edge of the bed. "Did they want to know who you were?"

"I told them I was a friend and you'd asked me to come over to take care of you."

Tasha hid her face in her hands, silently cursing her stupidity. How could she let herself get so drunk she brought home a strange man, had sex with him, and then failed to report to work the next day? Tears pressed against her closed eyes and she could no longer hold them back.

"Whoa, hold on," Rueben said behind her. "What did I say?"

Deep sobs racked her body and she was unable to speak.

"Hey, if it was what I said about the sex, I was joking. I didn't touch you. I swear."

"What?" Tasha asked, looking over her shoulder.

He shrugged and offered her a lopsided smile. "It was a joke. We had such a good time last night joking around I didn't think you'd think I was serious."

She used the hem of one sleeve to wipe her eyes and shifted her position so she could see him without craning her neck.

He skimmed a hand over his bald head. "The truth is that I drove you home because you didn't need to drive yourself. You got sick as soon as we got inside the house and passed out. I didn't want to leave you alone."

Her gaze dropped to his bare chest and his own followed.

"Did I mention you got sick *on* me?"

Tasha whimpered and hid her face again.

Rueben chuckled and pulled her hands away. "I got you in bed, washed my clothes, and took a shower. I lay down here with you so I could keep an eye on you and must have fallen asleep. I *swear* I never laid a hand on you for any other reason."

Staring into his coal black eyes, Tasha believed him. Snippets of their conversation at the bar were coming back to her. He'd kept her company in between sets with the band while she waited for—

She jumped to her feet and began searching through the pile of clothing on the floor. "Where is it?" she muttered, turning pockets inside out. "No, no, no . . . come on . . . be here . . ."

"What's wrong?" Rueben asked from the bed.

"I had a journal, a little pink leather-bound book, last night. I have to find it."

"I didn't see a book."

Tasha stopped her search and stared at him.

"I'm sorry, but I think I would've seen a book."

Fear and guilt slithered up her spine like twin snakes and she collapsed on the bed. As soon as it was discovered that she was the one who'd stolen the journal from the lab, her career would be over.

Without the journal, her mystery callers were bound to withdraw their offer of assistance. Without their assistance, she couldn't fight Caleb.

And she'd lose Maya.

Kirk was fucked and he knew it. He'd let Piper get away. Now he had to find the bitch before she went to the cops and told them everything about his operation.

He parked his silver Porsche down the street from her apartment, making sure he had a good view of the exit. When she left, he'd follow her, and when the time was right, he'd swoop in and grab her. The scenario that would follow played out in his head like a movie scene. He'd take her somewhere secluded, fuck her until she begged him to kill her, and then he'd fuck her some more. Only when he was satisfied he'd had her every way he could imagine, then he'd drain her dry and leave her battered corpse for the birds.

A car approached the entrance of the apartment complex and he tensed for a moment, but it wasn't Piper. He sighed and picked up the small Thermos beside him. The mixture of blood and vodka burned his throat as he swallowed. Images of the fight he'd had with Piper, seen from above and intensified by the alcohol, flitted through his mind and he shuddered.

It'd been a shame to kill the new bunny—Jennifer, wasn't that her name?—and leave her body behind an abandoned hardware store, but she'd seen and heard too much after Piper's outburst. At least her blood was useful. He capped the Thermos as he settled in his seat to wait with the lingering taste of blood coating his tongue.

His thoughts once more turned to his plans for Piper. Anticipation made his dick hard and had him squirming in his seat. He'd need to be careful and not kill her too quickly. He'd made that mistake in the past and the satisfaction hadn't been nearly as intense as he'd hoped.

No one turned on Kirk Beljean and lived. *No one.*

Another car approached the complex's entrance and he perked up. A white Nissan Sentra paused at the entrance as a garbage truck passed and then turned right, heading up the street and away from Kirk.

"Gotcha, bitch," he muttered and started the Porsche's engine. He waited until the Nissan had reached the stop

sign at the other end of the street, left turn signal wink-
ing like a spasmodic eye, before he steered his car onto
the street and into pursuit.

He paused at the stop sign long enough to see Piper's
car turning right down another street. The Porsche
lurched forward and tires squealed as he took the next
turn a little too fast.

Keeping the Nissan in sight, he followed at a safe distance so as not to spook the driver, but after several
more turns onto side streets, Kirk frowned. The route
the Nissan carved through the town was taking them
farther into downtown Jefferson.

"Where the fuck are you going?" he asked. Realization hit him when he caught a glimpse of the Nassau
County Municipal Center's roofline, now only blocks
away. "Fucking goddamn bitch! You are so fucking
dead!"

He couldn't allow her to reach the Center and the police. A train's horn sounded in the distance and he
grinned. The railroad tracks were between their current
position and the Municipal Center. If the timing was
right, he could use the delay caused by the train to his
advantage. His foot pressed the gas pedal to the floor
and the Porsche shot forward.

Kirk whooped as warning bells combined with a
blast of a train's horn. Red-and-white-striped barriers
lowered across the road, trapping Piper's car between
an eighteen-wheeler semi and his Porsche. He skidded
to a stop behind the Nissan, angling his vehicle to cut
off her escape route.

Jumping from the car, he could see the panic on
Piper's face that increased to horror when he reached
the driver's-side door and lifted the handle.

It didn't budge. She'd locked the damn thing.

"Open this goddamn door, bitch!" He could hear her
sobs even over the noise of the passing train as she fum-

bled with her cell phone. Rage and impatience overrode his senses. His fist connected with the window, shattering it and releasing Piper's high-pitched screams. "Com'ere, you fucking whore!"

"Hey!" a man shouted from nearby. "Get your hands off the lady, mister!"

Snarling in fury, Kirk whirled toward the voice, to find the truck driver slowly approaching from the rear of his rig with a .22-caliber revolver already drawn and aimed at Kirk. "Fuck off."

"Step away from the car," the truck driver ordered.

"If you insist." Kirk leapt over the Nissan's hood. Gunfire echoed off the surrounding buildings. He roared in pain as a bullet grazed his ribs. He reached the driver, knocked the revolver aside, and wrapped his hand around the man's throat.

The force of the impact knocked the smaller driver into the back of his rig. Kirk held him suspended by the throat with his feet frantically searching for the ground inches below. Soft tissue collapsed beneath the increasing pressure he applied to the driver's throat until he heard a *pop* and the man ceased to struggle.

Kirk dropped the driver and he collapsed in a heap. Turning back to Piper's car, he growled when he saw the open door and the empty driver's seat. More angry shouts rang out from farther up the street and sirens sounded in the distance.

He picked up the driver's revolver and darted for his car. The pain intensified with his movements. Wincing and clutching his side, he slid behind the Porsche's steering wheel and jammed the car into reverse. Seconds later he was rocketing through the downtown streets, heading for the one person who might offer him sanctuary.

He just had to convince her it was in her best interests to do so if she wanted to live.

* * *

The fading vestiges of daylight pierced the remainder of the alcohol-induced fog that veiled Tasha's mind. She rubbed her temple, trying to ease the ache in her head, and focused on Varik Baudelaire as he stood—battered and bruised—on the steps in front of Jefferson PD and described a vampire known only as The Dollmaker.

"He's approximately six feet, four inches tall," Varik announced in a hoarse voice. The line of bruises around his neck was plainly visible even in the dim light. A cut on his right cheek had been stitched closed and dark bruises ringed both eyes. "Short blond hair, blue eyes that turn a very pale yellow." He paused and swallowed, wincing, before addressing the vampires standing to one side of the gathered crowd of officers. "Enforcers, be advised, the Dollmaker has a scent similar to leather and old blood."

A murmur passed among the human officers and Tasha shuddered. She'd known all vampires had a particular scent that was unique to each individual but it wasn't common knowledge. Despite four decades of living openly, vampires were still a secretive lot and information regarding them was often hard to obtain. The fact that the FBPI was sharing this much information with humans underscored the gravity of what had transpired in the past few hours.

"Enforcer Sabian—" Varik's broken voice fractured even more, forcing him to pause yet again. "Enforcer Sabian was abducted—" He stopped, and when he attempted to speak again, no words came forth.

Damian Alberez stepped forward, laid a hand on Varik's shoulder, and Varik turned away, unable to continue with the briefing. Damian's dark eyes swept the crowd as he picked up where Varik faltered. "Enforcer Sabian was abducted at approximately fifteen hundred hours, or three p.m., local time. That was almost five hours ago. I know most of you have worked through the day on other assignments and I know you're tired. Despite what you may have heard about events of weeks prior, Enforcer Sabian *is* a federal agent. She's one of us. Let's bring her home."

The crowd dispersed, with the Enforcers gathering around Damian, who appeared to be issuing additional instructions. The human officers moved away in pairs or small groups. Those who'd been working through the day gave the new arrivals a brief rundown of the events. All officers had been called in for the search, even Tasha, despite her status on the sick roster.

Still trying to massage away the pain in her temples, Tasha entered the deserted Municipal Center lobby and strode toward the wing housing the Jefferson Police Department. A rush of air and noise signaled that someone had entered behind her. She glanced over her shoulder to see Varik limping toward her.

"We need to talk," he croaked.

Tasha didn't respond and entered the JPD offices, breathing in the smells of stale coffee, gun oil, and sweat as she passed through the rows of empty desks on her way to the employee break room.

"Where the hell were you earlier today?" Varik's ragged voice carried an edge of anger that quickened her pace.

"Sick."

"I left messages for you to meet Alex and me at the mobile lab."

Tasha reached the break room and rounded on him. She braced one hand against the doorjamb to keep from falling over as the world suddenly spun at a much faster rate than normal. "And I told you I was sick. It happens to humans from time to time. We're not as robust as your kind."

"You should've been there."

"I'm not some rookie you can jerk around from one place to the other, or threaten, for that matter."

Varik shoved her inside and closed the door behind him.

"Get your grubby hands off me!" Tasha pulled free of him. "Goddamn vamps think you can just barge in whenever the hell you feel like it and manhandle people—"

Varik clutched her shoulder, yanked her from her feet, and slammed her into the door. Fury twisted his face into a dark mask. "I haven't begun to manhandle you, Lieutenant," he growled, fangs flashing as he spoke. "Alex is gone, abducted by the Dollmaker, and if you'd been where you were supposed to be, it might not have happened."

"You are *not* going to pin this shit on me." She tried to push him away but she might as well have been trying to move a brick wall. Human strength was no match against a pissed-off vampire. "What happened to Alex isn't my fault."

"I ask you again: where were you?" His dark chocolate eyes became two kaleidoscopic maelstroms as they shifted from brown to gold.

Tasha's stomach churned violently. She gagged and he released her. She ran to the sink, expecting to heave the contents of her stomach into it, but nothing came forth. Once the nausea had passed, she splashed cool water on her face, praying that Varik would be gone when she turned around.

He still stood in front of the closed door, arms folded over his chest and glaring at her.

She returned his hostile stare, trying not to wince at the extent of his injuries. The limp he now sported was the result of a savage kick to his leg that had dislocated his right knee.

When the Dollmaker took Alex, he attacked Varik first, using the ruse of a stranded motorist to move in close. Once Varik's guard was down, he'd severely beaten the Enforcer and then wrapped Varik's own jumper cables around his neck, choking him into unconsciousness. The cables had been left tied around Varik's neck, slowly stealing his breath. If Freddy and Reyes hadn't found him, drawn out of the lab by Alex's screams, he would've died. He'd been very lucky.

Although, looking at him now, Tasha was certain he didn't consider himself so.

"You could've helped save her," he whispered. "Why weren't you there?"

Tasha held his gaze for a moment and then looked away. The memory of finding Rueben naked in her bed zipped through her mind like a movie. "It was a personal matter."

"That is the best answer you can give me?"

"It's the only one you're going to get."

"When you compromised evidence by giving it to Sheriff Manser—"

Tasha shuffled her feet and frowned, avoiding eye contact.

"—Alex covered your ass. *I* covered your ass." He stalked toward her, hands clenching into fists. "Now Alex is in trouble, and you're going to stand there and play these stupid games?"

"I answered your question." She backed away from him until her shoulders bumped into a corner. "You can threaten me all you want, but you should know by now, I don't respond well to threats."

He leaned in close so his face was only inches from hers. "And I don't respond well to losing people I care about."

The door opened and Damian Alberez's hulking form entered the break room. His dark eyes swept the scene as he placed his hands on his hips. "Is there a problem in here?"

Varik fell back a few steps but never looked away from Tasha. "No, no problem, just a misunderstanding. Right, Lieutenant?"

Tasha remained silent.

Damian grunted. "If you're finished correcting it, the medical examiner has the report on the Jane Doe from the salvage yard."

"On my way."

"Lieutenant."

Tasha glanced at Damian.

"Someone needs to follow up with the owner of the property next to the salvage yard. You're it."

"Whatever."

Damian shot Varik a final parting glare and left.

Varik turned to follow but paused in the doorway. "This isn't over between us, Lieutenant. Far from it."

Tasha listened to his retreating footsteps as he limped down the hall toward the central office area. Her ears rang in the ensuing silence, and she struggled to control the hatred growing in her heart. Shaking like a rookie hyped on adrenaline, she vowed she would no longer allow herself to be pushed around by vampires.

Varik scared her, especially now that Alex had been abducted, but what frightened her even more was the prospect of people discovering where Tasha had been: drunk and in bed with a man whose last name she didn't know.

Just like your fucking mother, the nagging voice in her head taunted. *How long did she wait after your father split to shack up with someone? One week? Two? You're just as pathetic as she was.*

Tasha bolted from the room, trying to outdistance the voice that sought to break her spirit and drove the self-destructive thirst building within her.

"Lieutenant," a woman's voice called from the hallway behind her.

Tasha stopped and glared at Morgan as the vampire approached. "What is it, SI Dreyer? I'm in a hurry."

"Running from the ghosts of your conversation with Director Baudelaire?"

Tasha tensed. "Excuse me?"

"I couldn't help but overhear what Director Baudelaire said to you, specifically the threats." Morgan slipped her hands into the pockets of her tailored designer slacks. "Such behavior is unbecoming for someone of his rank. If you'd like to file a formal complaint, I can see that it receives the appropriate attention at FBPI headquarters."

"Wouldn't that start an inquiry against him?"

"It's possible, depending on the severity of his threats and if he's made any against you in the past." She shrugged. "Just something to think about," she said as she sauntered past.

Tasha replayed in her mind her encounter with Varik, absently rubbing her shoulder where he'd grabbed her. "Ah, hell," she muttered to herself then raised her voice. "SI Dreyer?"

Morgan stopped at the end of the hall and half turned toward her.

"I think I'd like to file that complaint."

As Morgan strode back down the hall, her smile wide enough to show her fangs, Tasha couldn't help but think she'd just made a deal with the devil.

fifteen

A GENTLE BREEZE RUFFLING HER HAIR AND THE SCENT of wildflowers forced Alex's eyes open. The wind brushed her again and something slithering over her outstretched arm sent her heart into a frantic rhythm. She pushed herself away from whatever had touched her.

Soft things encircled her, and her mind began to piece together her environment from touch and smell. She lay on what she surmised was a huge bed, surrounded by mounds of pillows and a fluffy comforter. Sheer drapes billowing in the breeze from an open window beside the bed had brushed against her arm, startling her.

Wildflowers permeated the air with their sweet fragrances. Frowning, she searched for the bouquet. Her hand encountered a crystal vase on a table nestled between the bed and the open window. The flowers felt real enough, but how was it possible to have fresh-cut wildflowers in November?

A foreboding she couldn't shake settled over her like a mantle.

She swung her legs over the side of the bed and was surprised when her feet didn't touch the floor. Blood pounded in her head and the world threatened to spin out of control as she slipped off the bed and landed unsteadily with a loud *thump*. She closed her eyes and groaned, waiting for the dizziness to pass.

Once the sensation had eased, she opened her eyes

and, sweeping her hands in front of her, slowly made her way to the window. Darkness still ruled her sight.

Alex heard the footsteps approaching seconds before a door opposite the bed opened. She spun to face the door and groaned loudly as the floor tilted beneath her feet. Her head pounded in response and her stomach threatened to release its contents. She slumped against the wall and sank to the floor, drawing her knees to her chest in misery.

"Darling, what are you doing?" A familiar man's voice filled the room. "You shouldn't be out of bed. You need your rest."

Fear clutched her heart as the shadow of recognition nibbled at the edges of her brain. "Who are you?" she croaked. "What is this place?"

The man sighed. "You see? This is precisely why you shouldn't be out of bed. You're not fully recovered."

She batted away his hands when he grabbed her arms. "Don't fucking touch me."

An image of Varik, along with the muffled sounds of a struggle and then a horrible silence filled her mind. She opened the blood-bond, searching for Varik's comforting presence, and was met with only a mind-numbing cold. An overwhelming sense of loss gripped her, constricting her lungs and turning her breath into short, rapid gasps.

"Easy, now," the unknown man murmured. He clasped her hands in his, retaining a firm but gentle grip when she struggled to free herself. "Deep breaths. That's it. Just take deep breaths."

"What have you done to me?" she asked between gasps.

He brushed a strand of hair away from her face. "Why, nothing, darling."

"Where am I? I want to go home."

"You *are* home."

She shook her head. "No."

"You'll come to love it here."

"No."

"But first, we need to get you off this cold floor."

Before she could protest, he'd shifted to one side and scooped her into his arms. He laid her on the bed and then she could hear him rummaging in a table drawer.

She heard the tinny *pop* of a needle through thin rubber and the soft slide and gurgle of a syringe being filled. Alarm raced through Alex. She scooted away from him. "What is that?"

"Just something to help you relax so you can rest."

"I don't want it."

"Now, this won't hurt—"

Alex sprang toward what she hoped was the foot of the bed and the door.

A hand grabbed her ankle, knocking her to the bed, and she felt the sharp sting of a needle in the back of her thigh. Warmth spread through her and her muscles seemed to collapse under their own weight. She tried to push herself up, to no avail.

She heard him return the syringe and vial to the drawer.

He rolled her onto her back, slid her around until her head rested on an overstuffed pillow, and pulled a fluffy comforter over her once more. "There we go. That wasn't so bad. Now, you get some rest."

She tried to resist when he leaned forward and his mouth found hers. His tongue brushed across her lips, seeking entry. She made a noise of protest and turned her head.

His voice held a smile. "I have some work to finish, but if you need anything, just call."

"Your name." She struggled to get the words out as she sank deeper and deeper into the haze that had suddenly filled the room. "Tell me your name."

"Peter," he whispered and his voice shook as he continued. "Now get some rest. I'll check on you in a little while."

As the last vestiges of consciousness slipped away, her whisper was consumed by the darkness. "Varik . . ."

The Nassau County medical examiner's office was housed in a little-used wing of Jefferson Memorial Hospital and shared a morgue with the facility. However, the county officials had thought to secure a separate entrance for the ME's office, a feature Varik was grateful for as he slowly made his way up a loading ramp to a gray metal fire door.

He pushed a button on the security pad next to the door and heard a faint buzzing from inside. He waited a moment and then waved his FBPI credentials in front of the small camera attached to the security pad. A red light on the pad turned green and a series of clicks sounded as the door unlocked. Entering the hallway, he paused to allow his eyes to adjust to the fluorescent lights before limping toward the distant offices and autopsy room.

A young human carrying a clipboard appeared from around a corner and stopped as he caught a glimpse of Varik. "Holy shit!" Jeffery Stringer exclaimed. "You look like reheated hell."

"Where's Doctor Hancock?" Varik asked, stopping in front of the deputy medical examiner.

"Autopsy room, finishing up his notes on Trunk Girl."

Varik pushed past him.

"Do I want to know what the other guy looks like?" Jeffery called after him.

"Not nearly as bad as he will once I get my hands on him again," Varik shot over his shoulder.

Jeffery emitted a low whistle and quickly picked up his route to wherever he'd been going.

Varik winced as he turned a corner. The pain in his leg was decreasing, but the muscles still protested being used so quickly after his fight with the Dollmaker. He'd been stupid, had let his guard down, and now he was paying the price.

Alex was paying the price.

He replayed his confrontation with the Dollmaker, looking for anything that would give him a hint of who he was and where he might be holding Alex. However, nothing presented itself. The only trace left in the wake of Alex's abduction was the diamond ring he'd given to her last night—its chain broken.

The physical pain he could manage. He'd certainly been hurt much worse during his time as a Hunter. It was the pain of knowing the Dollmaker had Alex that made his heart ache until he felt it would explode.

Thoughts of what could possibly be happening to her crowded around him. He refused to acknowledge them, to give them weight. If he did, he would break down and become immobile. He had to keep going, had to find her, had to save her.

Ever since the attack, he'd kept the blood-bond open, hoping for some sign of life from her. The bond remained cold and empty. No welcoming warmth greeted him when he extended his thoughts in search of Alex. Not feeling the constant weight of her mind pressing against his filled him with grief and rage. Desperation gnawed at him, filled his thoughts with chaos once more.

What if she was dead?

No, she's couldn't be dead. He would know.

But the Dollmaker had her and could be—

Varik forced himself to focus on the door ahead of

him and not allow his imagination free rein. He refused to accept she could be taken away so easily.

Doctor Philip Hancock looked up from his notes as Varik entered the autopsy room. A gleaming bald head and thick bottle glasses that enlarged his brown eyes gave the rotund man the appearance of a startled owl. "Enforcer Baudelaire, I wasn't expecting to see you so soon after your unfortunate encounter."

Since taking over from Alex as the official Enforcer for Jefferson, Varik had gotten to know Doc Hancock much better after their initial frosty meeting. Doc was human but accepting of vampires, quick-witted, and a closet Lady Gaga fan, a fact Varik had discovered by accident and had since been sworn to secrecy.

Varik reached the stainless steel autopsy table and leaned against it heavily as a muscle spasm momentarily weakened his right leg. "I'm full of surprises, Doc."

"Are you sure you should even be working?"

Varik nodded. "I have to find Alex."

"Still no word from the son of a bitch who grabbed her?"

"No, and there won't be. We figure he's a collector and Alex is his prize possession."

"Hmm, well, that may work in your favor. As long as he continues to think of her that way, he's less likely to actually hurt her."

"Doesn't stop me from thinking of the ways he could though."

"No, I suppose not."

Varik sighed and pushed away from the table, eager to find out what Doc Hancock knew. "You got an identification on our salvage yard Jane Doe?"

"Dental records do *not* match Mindy Johnson. That's the good news. Bad news is the forensic odontologist in Jackson *was* able to match it to a girl who's been missing for two weeks: Vicki Pettersson."

Varik flipped open the file the doctor handed over. Scanning the reports, he frowned. "How did a girl from Vegas end up in the trunk of a car in Jefferson, Mississippi?"

Doc Hancock slipped a new report on top of the file. "Jumped a bus and went as far as her money would take her, which was apparently here."

"That still doesn't explain how she got in the trunk."

"Well, now, that's your job, but I can tell you she had help." Doc Hancock grunted as he slipped off the stool on which he'd been perched. His knees popped and crackled as he made his way across the room to an X-ray display panel.

Varik followed and squinted against the sudden bright illumination before focusing on the large black-and-gray photo negatives. "Are those *all* broken?"

"Poor girl's rib cage was crushed like an egg, and look here." Doc Hancock pointed to an X ray of a skull. "Multiple fractures of the jaw as well as at the back of the skull. Not to mention one leg and both arms were also broken."

"So she was tortured?"

"Yes and no." Doc Hancock switched off the display panel. "All the breaks and fractures occurred post-mortem, after she was already dead."

"Where does the torture fit in?"

He handed Varik a stack of color photos. "I found evidence of starvation and dehydration. She also had multiple lacerations around her neck, but they're so shallow I can't even begin to speculate the reason."

"Only her neck?"

Doc Hancock nodded. "And I didn't see any signs of sexual assault."

Varik frowned as he studied the photos. Several showed long regular patches of exposed tissue. "What about these areas?"

"Those are the weird bits. They're concentrated on her back, stomach, and legs. I saw no evidence of healing so it had to have been done after she was killed. Very precise cuts and tissue removal. Someone skinned this poor girl. My question is, Why?"

"That's what the Dollmaker does. He uses skin from his victims to make dolls in their likenesses."

"I've heard of a lot of strange things in my time, but that's just fucked-up, as my granddaughter would say."

Varik sighed and handed the photos back to him. "What was the official cause of death?"

"Exsanguination. Her throat was slit from ear to ear."

An upbeat techno rhythm filled the room and Varik pulled his cell phone from its holster at his hip. He checked the caller display before answering. "Any word, Damian?"

"Not yet. Teams are still sweeping the area and fanning out into other sections of town."

"We have to find her, Damian. Bring in more Enforcers from Jackson or Hattiesburg if you have to."

"We're doing everything we possibly can."

"Doc Hancock and I are finishing up." He glanced at the medical examiner and received a confirming nod. "I'm going to join the sweeper teams when I leave here. The bond isn't working but maybe if I get close to her location then I can—"

"Negative," Damian interrupted. "I need you back here as soon as you wrap up with the ME."

Anger flared within him, hot and blinding. "What the fucking hell for? I'm not going to sit on my ass while that psycho has Alex!"

"Did I say anything about you sitting on your ass? There's someone here you need to interview."

"Get someone else to do it."

"Her name is Piper Garver. She's Mindy Johnson's

cousin, and someone tried to kidnap her a few blocks from JPD, killed a truck driver in the process. She's got one hell of a story, but the important part is the guy who tried to abduct her knows a vampire who likes redheads."

Adrenaline surged through his system and melted away the pain in his legs as he sprinted from the room.

Tasha closed the door of her sedan and paused to take in the grandeur that had once been Cottonwood Plantation.

A sweeping oak-lined drive nearly half a mile long led to the multistory home that had seen better days. What had once been a simple farmhouse had been expanded over the years. Each generation of the Corman family had added their own touch to the house until it became a mishmash of various architectural styles.

The house sat on a couple of hundred acres of mixed pasture and groves. Once the plantation had grown cotton but it had switched to pecans sometime in the 1950s. Cottonwood had been well-known in southwestern Mississippi for producing some of the finest pecans in the region until Benjamin Corman died. After his passing a few years prior, the house sat vacant and fell into disrepair while the estate searched for an heir.

One had finally stepped forward and it was that heir Tasha had come to see.

She eyed the crumbling front steps and lack of hand railing but climbed the steps nonetheless. Boards creaked and bowed beneath her as she crossed the porch to the front entrance, its protective outer screen door hanging to the side by a single hinge. She knocked on the weather-beaten wooden door and waited.

A large group of crows took flight from a field adjacent to the house, startling her. The black birds cawed and squawked to one another, flying farther out to field, and Tasha remembered reading the technical name for a flock of crows was a "murder." She'd never understood why and seeing so many so close to a house made the hairs on the nape of her neck prickle.

She knocked on the door again. "Hello," she called. "Anyone home?"

Only the distant call of the crows answered her.

Tasha stepped around a missing board to reach one of the windows near the door. She cupped her hands to the side of her eyes and pressed her face to the torn screen, trying to see inside.

Heavy curtains blocked her view. She tried the windows on the opposite side of the entrance and discovered their broken panes had been boarded over from the inside. Sighing, she returned to the door and knocked a final time. "Hello! I'm Lieutenant Tasha Lockwood with the Jefferson police. If you can hear me, please open the door."

Again, no answer came from within the house.

"Shit," she muttered. She pulled a business card from her pocket, wrote a brief note asking the homeowner to call her, and stuck it in the crack between the door and the jamb.

She retraced her steps to her car and hesitated as she opened the door. For a moment she thought she saw movement in an upstairs window. She caught sight of it again and realized it was simply drapes blowing in the breeze from an open window. She slipped behind the steering wheel and headed back to Jefferson, cursing Damian for sending her on a wild-goose chase.

Today was the second day the police had come to his door. Peter knew it would only be a matter of time before they returned. He'd hoped to have more time to prep Alexandra before leaving this town to start their new life together but it wasn't meant to be.

He thought of how much work he had before him. He would have to accelerate his plans to separate her from Varik. It carried a risk of damaging her beyond repair, but it was a possibility he must accept nonetheless.

Peter slowly opened the bedroom door, careful not to wake Alexandra. She was finally his to possess. He slipped into the room and crept to the side of the bed.

Her breathing remained steady and unchanged. The last rays of sunlight from the window turned her auburn hair into a blaze of deep reds, mahogany browns, and copper. Beneath closed lids, he imagined her gold-rimmed emerald eyes sought him in their rapid-dreaming movements.

Watching her sleep, he ached to touch her, to climb into the bed and make her his for always.

But he couldn't. Not yet. She had not yet given herself to him willingly and he wouldn't accept her any other way. Much work needed to be done before their bodies could finally join the way their souls had already combined so long ago.

First he had to purge her of Varik's influence.

He kissed her forehead, closed his eyes, and inhaled her exotic scent of jasmine and vanilla.

She moaned and shifted in her sleep.

"Soon, my darling," he whispered, smoothing her hair. "I promise."

He straightened, made his way to the door, opened it quietly, and slipped into the hallway beyond.

As he closed the door, she shifted in her slumber once more, mumbling incoherently but one word struck like a dagger to his very core.

"Varik . . ."

Rage surged through him, hot and blinding.

He stormed up the hall to his own bedroom and

flung himself onto the low, narrow bed. Beating and strangling his rival wasn't enough to sever their bond. He'd known it wouldn't be, but he'd foolishly allowed himself a small hope that it would at least weaken it. As soon as he accessed the Hall of Records and used the information he'd gleaned from its vast store, she would forget all about him.

"And then you *will* love me," he whispered and closed his eyes, surrendering himself to the void as he parted the Veil and entered the Shadowlands.

Emily felt as though she were in a nightmare dreamscape and unable to wake. Numbness had settled into her brain, dampening all thought and dulling her senses. She could only sit at the kitchen counter, an untouched mug of coffee and her cell phone before her, and stare at the small photo she always carried with her.

It was taken eight years ago during a family vacation to Cumberland Falls in the southeastern part of Kentucky. The photo had been taken at night as she stood between Stephen and Alex on the observation deck overlooking the falls. Light from the full moon played through the spray and created a beautiful moonbow that hung in the air behind three smiling faces. It had been a magical week for them all.

It'd also been the last vacation the three had spent together.

Fast-forward to their present, and Emily found herself in a mother's Hell. Only a few weeks had passed since Stephen was kidnapped by drug runners looking to get even for Crimson Swan stealing a large portion of their customers. He didn't talk about what happened to him and most of his physical wounds had healed, but Emily knew the psychological healing would take much longer.

Now Alex was missing—abducted by a madman who Varik said was obsessed with her.

Emily traced the outline of Alex with her finger. Tears welled in her eyes. No matter how much she fought, how much she tried to protect them, it seemed the world was determined to rip her family apart, and she couldn't let that happen.

She angrily brushed away her tears and traded the photograph for her cell phone. She dialed Gregor's number and listened to the steady ringing on the other end, counting each tone as they passed unanswered. After ten rings, she sighed and hit the button to end the call. Where was he?

Lost in her own thoughts, she ignored the chime of the doorbell and Janet's hurried footsteps. Stephen had left earlier for a meeting with investors regarding the rebuilding of Crimson Swan. Emily had insisted he keep the appointment despite what had happened with Alex. He needed the distraction. He would've gone insane with worry had he stayed home.

A startled shout and the sound of a man's angry voice drew Emily from the kitchen. "Janet?" she called, hurrying into the living room. "What's wro—"

The barrel of a revolver shoved in her face stole her words. Angry golden eyes bored into her from behind stringy and sweat-soaked brown bangs. The scent of blood, pepper, and sage was strong in the air. The hand holding the revolver wavered slightly as the stranger spoke, showing fangs. "Who the fuck are you?"

Her gaze flicked to the frightened Janet, held tightly against the unknown vampire's side. "Emily," she replied, surprised by her own calm. "I'm a friend of Janet's."

The stranger inhaled sharply. "You smell like a vampire, but I don't see fangs."

"I had them filed down and capped a long time ago."

He grunted. "You're one of Janet's clients?" He didn't wait for Emily to respond before tightening his hold. "I never knew you swung both ways, Janet. That would've made for more interesting suck and fucks. A little girl-on-girl action, huh?"

"You're hurting me," Janet whined.

"Let her go," Emily said.

"You are *not* the boss here, bitch!" He cocked the revolver's hammer and Janet sobbed. "*I am!*"

Despite the wild pounding of her heart, Emily spoke calmly. "Yes, you're in charge, but you're obviously injured. I can smell the blood. If you let Janet go, I can help you. That's what you want, isn't it? You want someone to help you?"

Several moments passed in silence while the stranger stared at her and Janet sobbed at his side. Finally, he shoved Janet into Emily's arms, where the girl sobbed even harder and clung to Emily like a frightened child. "No tricks," the stranger rasped. "Or you're both dead."

Emily nodded her understanding. "Come into the kitchen where there's better light."

She guided Janet into the kitchen with the stranger following slowly. They reached the counter where Emily had been sitting, and she indicated for Janet to sit on one of the stools.

The stranger entered, eyes darting from one side to the other, revolver held at the ready.

Emily swiped her coffee mug and cell phone from the counter while he was distracted. She slipped the phone into her bra and dumped the coffee into the sink. "No one else is here," she said with her back to Janet and the stranger. Turning to face him, she pointed to the stool most distant from Janet and grabbed a clean dish-cloth. "Sit there."

Wincing in pain, he obediently climbed onto the stool.

Emily patted Janet's arm as she passed. "Show me," she ordered the stranger. Standing next to him, she could not only smell the blood but see where it had soaked through the side of both his shirt and jacket. She also caught the faint scent of alcohol on his breath.

He clumsily removed his jacket and lifted his shirt. Blood seeped from an angry gash along his ribs. It was short but deep, and its placement made for a painful wound.

She pressed the small towel against the gash and he hissed in response. "I've seen worse but you're going to need stitches."

"No doctors," he growled.

"I thought you'd say that. I can do it but I'll need to get some supplies from the bathroom."

He leveled the revolver on the counter, aiming at Janet, and fixed his golden gaze on Emily. "If you're not back in two minutes, I start shooting."

She dropped the towel on the counter, and Janet whimpered as Emily stepped around the stranger, leaving the frightened girl in his direct line of fire.

"Wait," he said, grabbing Emily's wrist as she passed. "Empty your pockets."

Emily slowly turned out her pockets, placing a few coins and an old crumpled shopping list on the counter. "Satisfied?"

"No. You." He motioned for Janet to join Emily. "Pat her down." His face contoured into a wicked grin. "I'm sure you remember how it's done."

Janet's hands shook as she quickly ran them over Emily's waist, legs, and torso. "She's clean," the girl muttered.

"Check her bra."

Emily kept very still as Janet tentatively ran her hands over her chest.

Janet stepped back. "Nothing."

The stranger smacked the back of Janet's head, making her cry in pain. "Get your hand in there and feel between her tits, you stupid cow."

Anger rippled through Emily but she forced herself to remain still. If she attacked him, he would undoubtedly kill them both. She could only hope Janet didn't betray her and left behind the phone she hid in her cleavage.

"I'm sorry," Janet whispered.

"It's okay, dear. Just do what you need to do, and we'll get out of this."

Emily kept her focus on Janet as the girl reached inside her blouse. She felt Janet's hesitation at finding the cell phone and saw the question in her eyes before extracting her empty hand.

"She's clean," Janet said, her voice a little more steady.

"Good." He grabbed Janet's arm, pulled her roughly against him, digging the revolver's barrel into her side, and glared at Emily. "Your two minutes start now."

Emily purposefully kept her pace to a brisk walk, determined not to let him see either her anger or her anxiety. Once in the hallway bathroom, she pulled her cell phone from her bra and grabbed bottles of rubbing alcohol and hydrogen peroxide from beneath the sink. She used a hand towel to muffle the sound of her phone's keys as she quickly typed in a text message:

NEED HELP. GUN.

"One minute," the stranger called from the kitchen.

Emily hit the send button, dialed a preprogrammed number, and then switched the phone to silent mode. She stuffed it back into her bra and rummaged through the medicine cabinet, grabbing dental floss, tweezers, bandages, and a roll of tape. She gathered the supplies and hurried back to the kitchen as the stranger began a countdown from twenty.

"Took you long enough," he grumbled when she dropped the supplies on the counter. He pushed Janet onto the stool beside him. "You stay there, where I can see you. I'll need a snack after this, anyway."

She ignored him and focused on Janet. "I need a needle. Do you have a sewing kit?"

Janet nodded. "Top drawer beneath the microwave."

Under the stranger's watchful gaze, Emily opened the drawer and riffled through the various take-out menus, expired coupons for Vlad's Tears, paper clips, used twist-ties, and spare batteries until she located the small travel-sized sewing kit. She added three bowls, a roll of paper towels, and another clean dish towel to her pile of supplies.

Silence reigned between them as she filled one bowl with water and poured equal amounts of alcohol and hydrogen peroxide into the other two. She measured out several lengths of floss and dropped them into the alcohol along with the two small needles from the sewing kit. Finally she scrubbed her hands with hot water and a liberal amount of antibacterial soap. Using the water in the bowl and the towel she'd first used on the wound, she cleaned the site until she could see the edges.

"What's your name?" she asked the stranger while she carefully threaded one of the needles with the sterilized floss.

"Why do you want to know?"

"Because I'd like to know the name of the man whose flesh I'm about to stick a needle into."

He studied her for a moment before answering. "Kirk."

"Well, Kirk, I'm going to need you to hold very still

and bite down on this." She handed him the clean dish towel.

He looked at her in confusion.

"I don't have any way of numbing this wound," she explained. "It's going to hurt. A lot. Unless you want the neighbors to hear you screaming and call the cops, I suggest you bite down on that towel."

Kirk hesitated, apparently gauging her seriousness. "Just make it quick," he said and stuffed the towel in his mouth.

"I'll do my best," Emily replied and drew a steadying breath.

As she guided the needle into Kirk's side, the first of his muffled cries filled the kitchen.

sixteen

VARIK ENTERED THE INTERVIEW ROOM IN WHICH PIPER Garver sat, and waited for the girl to acknowledge his presence.

She looked up from the soda she nursed and flinched. "Who are you?"

"My name is Varik Baudelaire," he said as he crossed the room, trying not to limp. "I'm an Enforcer with the Federal Bureau of Preternatural Investigation."

"You're a vamp?"

He nodded and sat down opposite her.

Her eyes scanned his battered appearance. "I didn't think vamps could bruise like that."

"No, we bruise same as humans. It just takes more force to do it and they fade quicker."

She nodded and sipped her drink. "I'm going to jail, aren't I?"

"Why would you think that? As I understand it, you're one of the victims here."

"I saw him kill that man and I didn't do anything." She choked back a sob. "I *couldn't* do anything but run."

"That was the smartest thing you could've done, Piper," he said gently. He waited, watching her wipe away her silent tears with a shaky hand.

Damian had filled him in on the details of the attack. A vampire had tried to drag Piper from her car, and when a Good Samaritan intervened, the vampire had killed the truck driver coming to Piper's aid. The man had left behind a wife and five kids.

When it seemed as though she'd composed herself enough, he leaned forward. "Tell me what happened."

"I already told that other vamp. Didn't he tell you anything?"

"Yes, but I'd like to hear your story from *you*."

Piper sighed and took a swallow of her soda. "Okay."

As she related her story, Varik listened, stopping her every now and then to ask a question. She finished talking and he nodded. "That's good, Piper. That's very good."

She gave him a weak smile.

"I have a couple of more questions for you though."

"Okay."

"You said you and your cousin, Mindy Johnson, worked for your boyfriend, Kirk Beljean?"

She nodded.

"What kind of work?"

"He called us blood bunnies. He would send us out to clients—vampires—so they could bite us." She toyed with a loose thread on the arm cuff of her sweatshirt. "We were paid more if we also had sex with them."

Varik had encountered similar operations in the past. Taking girls and turning them into blood whores disgusted him. Many of the humans caught in illegal blood rings were desperate for money or were enamored with vampires to the point they weren't able to pass the rigorous psychological testing registered donors faced.

Operations such as Beljean's were dangerous because of the potential for a vampire to lose control and accidentally—or intentionally—kill their human donor. It was the reason the Central Donor Registry existed and legal blood bars were established.

"Do you know where Kirk may have gone after he attacked you?"

"No."

"What about Mindy? Do you know who he sent her to last before she disappeared?"

Fresh tears tracked down her cheeks. "No. All Kirk would tell me is that it was a new client and the guy had a thing for redheads." She buried her face in her hands and sobbed. "She's dead. I know she is. I hooked her up with Kirk. I killed her. Oh, God! Mindy, I'm so sorry."

She fell into a pattern of repeating "I'm sorry," and the interview was over.

Alex knew she was dreaming from the moment she opened her eyes. She sat in a straight-backed chair with her arms and legs chained to the bare cement floor. An odd oily sheen coated the dark walls only a few feet from her. The only light source came from a large video monitor, its screen a fuzzy haze of black-and-white pixels.

Sensing movement behind her, she turned as far as the chains would allow. "Who's there?"

No answer.

"What is this place? What's going on?"

The screen before her snapped to a flat blackness, plunging her into darkness for a moment, before returning with what appeared to be a film. A man and woman snuggled close in the flickering dimness of candlelight.

Alex felt her heart skip a beat. "Varik."

The woman tossed her long dark hair over her shoulder and smiled. Focusing on the woman, she now recognized her as Morgan Dreyer. Varik stroked Morgan's hair, brushing his fingers along her cheek and throat. "You're so beautiful," he whispered.

Betrayal speared Alex.

"You must say that to all your women," Morgan replied.

Varik smiled, showing the full extent of his fangs. "No, just you, *ma puce.*"

Morgan laughed and playfully slapped him.

He easily caught her wrists and pulled her closer. "*Je t'aime, ma puce,*" he murmured and kissed her.

Alex looked away, tears stinging her eyes. She knew Varik had a prior relationship with Morgan, but knowing and seeing were two very different things.

A hand slid across her shoulders, caressing her.

Startled, she searched for the source but saw no one. Soft moans and whispers emanated from the video screen, demanding her attention.

Varik and Morgan had progressed from kissing to foreplay. Morgan ran her fingers through Varik's hair as he trailed kisses down her exposed stomach and settled between her thighs.

Alex closed her eyes and strained against the chains that bound her. She tried to stand and was forced back into the chair by the short length of the chains. "What the fuck do you want from me?"

The unseen hands stroked her shoulders as one lover would comfort another. "He doesn't really care for you."

She looked for the source of the voice but it seemed to originate from everywhere and echoed throughout the small room.

"You're just one of a long line of women."

The image on the screen changed, shifting from Morgan and Varik to Varik and a parade of unknown women making love. Dozens of women's faces flashed on the screen, ending with hers.

"You're nothing to him," the voice whispered.

"You're wrong."

"Do you truly believe he no longer has feelings for this one?"

The screen showed Morgan holding an infant, speaking to it in soft tones. Varik entered the room and Morgan smiled. "Look," she whispered to the infant. "Papa is home."

He gently took the baby from her arms. A mixture of love, joy, and pride shone in his eyes. "Hello, Edward," he cooed and the infant gurgled in response.

Morgan wrapped her arms around Varik's waist, leaning on his shoulder. He kissed the top of her head in the picture of domestic bliss. More images flickered across the screen. Scenes of Varik chasing a growing child with dark hair, of holding Morgan in his arms while she slept with a sleeping Edward in her arms, and family walks in the sunlight flashed before her.

"See?" the voice intoned. "How could you ever compete with the mother of his child?"

"Stop it," Alex murmured, feeling the warm trickle of tears on her cheeks.

The images of Varik, Morgan, and Edward faded and were replaced with a view of Alex, dressed in shorts and a T-shirt, humming as she busily chopped carrots in a galley-style kitchen.

"No," she said. "Not this."

Varik entered the kitchen, his face pale and drawn, a bandage on his arm.

The Alex on the screen looked up, smiling, but her smile quickly turned to a frown. "Holy shit," she said, stopping her prep work. "What happened?"

Varik shrugged. "A Midnighter clipped me." He fingered the bandage covering his biceps. "Took a plug out of my arm."

"Are you okay? Do you need a doctor? A donor?"

"No, I'm fine. It's not that bad."

Screen Alex eyed him uncertainly. "Are you sure?"

"Yes." Varik grabbed a piece of chopped raw carrot and popped it in his mouth. "But I'm starving. How long until this is ready?"

Screen Alex returned to chopping vegetables. "Not that long if you'll help. Would you— Ow!" She dropped her knife and grabbed a towel. "Damn it."

"Stop this," Alex whispered to her unseen tormentor. "Shut it off."

No response met her plea.

Screen Alex was asking Varik to find her a bandage. He didn't respond except to move closer, his dark eyes shifting rapidly to molten gold.

"Stop it!" Alex shouted as Varik attacked her twin on the screen.

The attack was swift. He pushed her to the floor, straddling her and pinning her to the cold linoleum. Screen Alex screamed for him to stop, to get off, but her cries were silenced as his fangs ripped into the soft tissue of her neck. The picture froze as Varik rose onto his knees, fangs bared and her blood dripping from his gaping mouth.

Alex sobbed and covered her face with her hands, trying unsuccessfully to block the memory of the attack. "Why?" she whispered into her hands. "Why are you doing this to me?"

"To help you."

Her anger flared, bright and hot. Chains rattled and groaned as she gained her feet and cast her chair aside, shouting, "How is torturing me helping? How is keeping me chained helping?"

"*He* is the one who has bound you, not I. *He* bound you to him. *He* wants to control you, limit you." The voice drew closer and the unseen hands returned to briefly grip her shoulders before sliding lightly down her arms. "*I* would free you. No restrictions. No boundaries."

The video screen flickered, refocusing her attention on the still image of a savage and bloody Varik crouched over her.

"No pain," the voice whispered in her ear. "Accept me and I will make certain he never harms you again."

"And if I don't?"

"You will. In time."

The video sprang to life once more, playing out a memory Alex had tried very hard to forget. Unable to look away, she sank to her knees and wept.

Tasha sat in front of a closed-circuit video monitor and watched a clearly distraught Piper Garver attempt to pull herself together. She couldn't blame the girl for being upset. It wasn't every day someone watched a person—even if the person in question was a vampire—kill another human with their bare hands.

Sighing, she turned in her chair to face Damian and Varik, who were speaking in hushed tones a few feet away. "So what happens now?"

They looked at her.

"What's going to happen to Piper now? She's clearly a victim here."

"She's also an accomplice," Damian said. "She admitted to recruiting girls for Beljean's operation."

"He forced her. He took every opportunity to abuse and threaten her."

"He *paid* her," Varik snapped. Ever since Alex was taken, his normally dark eyes had remained a bright gold, evidence of his intense emotional state. "The Bureau will take her situation and relationship with Beljean—*all* aspects of it—into consideration, but we can't let her walk. We have to charge her as an accessory."

"That's bullshit and you know it." Her anger flared.

"That girl is an emotional wreck and if you charge her with anything, she's likely to shut down completely and not give you any more information."

"Don't tell me how to run my investigation!"

"I would *never* consider telling the great high-and-mighty Varik Baudelaire how to wipe his ass much less run an investigation! But I *am* telling you that you're making one hell of a big mistake right now!"

"Lieutenant Lockwood makes a valid argument," Morgan said as she entered the small observation room, cutting off Varik's potential response. "It would be more logical to cut a deal with Ms. Garver in exchange for information."

Varik rounded on her. "I don't recall asking for your fucking opinion on the subject."

Morgan's brows rose sharply as Damian laid a warning hand on Varik's shoulder. Her voice sliced the air like a blade made of ice. "I will remind you *once* more to whom you are speaking, *Director* Baudelaire."

"I know perfectly well to whom I'm speaking, and you aren't going to intimidate me, Morgan." He brushed away Damian's hand. "So drop the SI shit."

As Morgan closed the distance between her and Varik, Tasha scooted her rolling chair as far away from the two vampires as the small room would allow.

"You seem to be laboring under the false impression that *I* answer to *you*," Morgan hissed. "Enforcer Sabian's abduction doesn't negate my role here. I will continue following my orders to find evidence of corruption, and if that means calling your actions into question along with Sabian's, which I'm beginning to suspect would be a fair assessment, then so be it."

"You fucking bitch. You have no cause to open an inquiry on me."

"Oh, really?" Morgan's gaze slipped to Tasha.

Tasha's blood turned to ice, despite her racing heart, as three sets of golden eyes shifted their focus to her.

"What did you do?" Varik rasped, taking a step toward her.

Tasha stood and maneuvered her chair to stand between them. She glanced at Morgan, who nodded her encouragement. "After you cornered me in the break room, Morgan approached me, told me I should—"

A continuous loud beeping filled the room. Varik swore loudly as he ripped his cell phone from the holster at his hip. The anger in his face drained away as he checked the display.

"What is it?" Damian asked, moving to stand next to Varik.

"It's a text from Emily but—" A techno beat sounded from his phone. He pushed the button to answer and raised it to his ear but didn't speak. Seconds ticked by in silence.

Tasha dug her fingers into the fabric of the chair back, anxious to know what was happening.

Varik and Damian were suddenly in motion, reacting to something she hadn't heard. Varik darted from the room with Damian only steps behind, his own cell phone now glued to his ear as he shouted orders.

Tasha found herself alone in the observation room with Morgan. "What the hell just happened?"

"I couldn't hear everything, just enough to know that call was from Emily Sabian," Morgan answered. "Apparently she and another woman are being held at gunpoint."

"Shit." Tasha raced to catch up with Varik and Damian with visions of blood-spattered walls and crime scene tape already filling her head.

*   *   *

Pain seared Kirk's side whenever he moved. The stitches were holding and the blood loss had stopped but his entire side felt like it was on fire. Adding to his unhappiness was a growing blood-hunger. He'd have to feed soon if he wanted to heal properly.

Luckily, there was a donor nearby.

He focused on the sight of Janet on her hands and knees, wiping up droplets of his blood. He watched as she helped the woman who'd stitched him up, Emily, clear away the remaining bandages, supplies, and blood. Both women made certain to stay well out of his arm's length.

He smirked. The older vampire had nothing to fear from him. At least not yet. As for Janet, it wasn't as though he hadn't already had her in nearly every way a vampire could take a donor. His fangs had been in nearly every one of her veins. Until she turned straight and went to work at Crimson Swan, she'd been his number one blood bunny, earning him an assload of cash. Only reason he'd let her stay gone was because he'd found Piper.

Piper. The bitch. He still couldn't believe she'd gotten away from him. If only that stupid-ass truck driver hadn't interfered.

Kirk lifted his shirt and checked the bandage covering the surprisingly deft stitches. No blood showed yet. That was good. He'd need to leave soon if he was going to make it out of town before Piper undoubtedly finished spilling her guts to the cops. But first . . .

Janet picked up the bowl that had once held warm water but now only contained a wad of sodden pink rags. As soon as she was close enough to him, he grabbed her around the waist and pulled her to him.

She screamed and dropped the bowl, trying to free herself from his grip.

Laughing, he fought for control of her arms, pulling

one behind her into an awkward angle and she stopped her struggles. His stomach rumbled as he brought her other wrist to his lips and inhaled. "I'd forgotten just how sweet you smell."

"Let her go," Emily said in a low, even tone.

He glared at her. "What's the matter? Afraid there won't be enough to share?"

"You said you wouldn't hurt her if I helped you."

"Fuck off, bitch. I lied." He bared his fangs, preparing to bite into Janet's tender flesh.

A hand came between his mouth and Janet's wrist. "I said, let her go."

"Don't *ever* tell me what to do!" Kirk grabbed a fistful of Janet's hair and used his free hand to backhand Emily across the face. She careened into a set of cabinets and then crashed to the floor.

Janet wailed as he forced her against the wall near the back door and sank his fangs into her neck. Blood—warm, thick, and sweet—pumped into his mouth. He greedily gulped down a mouthful, then another.

Memories that weren't his flooded his mind. Random images from Janet's life flashed before him. A vampire with blond curls and a wide grin talked with customers from behind a bar. The same vampire lay in a hospital bed, surrounded by flowers and balloons. Emily and a younger red-haired vampire stood nearby.

Kirk felt a stirring of recognition with the memories. The blood flow seemed to lessen even though he drew on the wound. Growling, he shook his head, ripping flesh, and was rewarded with more of the sweet liquid.

More of Janet's memories filled his mind. The image of the red-haired vampire stuck with him as recognition finally settled over him. He withdrew his fangs and staggered away.

Janet moaned and crumpled to the floor, unmoving.

He wiped the excess blood from his mouth and loomed over Emily, who had managed to push herself into a seated position. Squatting beside her, he cocked his head and grinned. "I know who you are now. You're that Enforcer bitch's mother."

The distant wail of a siren shot a flood of adrenaline into his system.

Emily smiled. "Time's up."

The first siren was joined by others and their cries grew louder. "You called them."

"Don't be stupid. You had Janet check me for phones. She didn't find any."

"Yeah, but she's also a fucking liar." He leveled the revolver with Emily's chest and used his other hand to quickly inspect her pockets. Somehow either she or Janet must have contacted the police. He was certain of it.

His search revealed nothing, just as Janet's had, until he shoved his hand down her shirt and felt the hard sleekness of a cell phone nestled between her breasts. Her defiant stare never wavered as he pulled the phone from its hiding place.

Kirk checked the display, saw the counter ticking away on an open call, and growled. He pressed the button to end the call and touched the barrel of the .22 revolver to her forehead. "Give me one reason why I shouldn't kill you right now."

She met his gaze with pure amber eyes. "Go ahead," she murmured. "Kill me. Kill Janet. You'll be dead before you can even set a toe outside this house."

Tires screeched and sirens and shouts erupted from outside. Cursing, Kirk pulled the revolver away, rose, and ran for the windows in the living room that overlooked the front of the house. He cautiously moved a section of the miniblinds and assessed the situation.

Uniformed human officers were busy setting up barricades in the street. Others were ushering neighbors across the street out of harm's way or telling curious gawkers to move back inside their homes. In the center of the action stood a tall, dark-haired vampire and even from a distance Kirk could see the burning gold of his eyes and the rigid set of his jaw.

Kirk let the blinds fall back into place and returned to the kitchen.

Emily now sat beside Janet with a towel pressed firmly against the unmoving girl's neck and shoulder. "She's badly hurt. She needs help."

"Sew her up like you did me."

"It won't work. She's lost a lot of blood and she's human. The wound is too deep. You have to let me take her out of here."

Kirk shook his head and checked the revolver's cylinder. Only five bullets remained. Not nearly enough to shoot his way out. "Move her to the living room and do what you can for her if you must, but you may as well settle in because this could take a while."

"She's going to die if you don't let them help her." Emily gestured to the front of the house with a bloodied hand.

He snapped the cylinder into place once more. "No one leaves." He strode toward the front windows again, throwing his final words over his shoulder. "Not without a tag on their toe."

seventeen

PETER HID IN A CORNER OF THE SHADOWLANDS ROOM he'd constructed to detain Alexandra's consciousness while he worked to sever her blood-bond with Varik. He remained motionless, watching, learning, and waiting.

She lay curled on the floor with her back to the video monitor. The chains binding her wrists and legs weren't true physical restraints but they were restraints nonetheless. Only he could release them, and he wouldn't until the bond was broken.

The monitor behind her continued to play scenes from both hers and Varik's pasts, with the attack that had forged the blood-bond repeated frequently. Reliving that moment was eating away at her willpower. Soon it would be easy to snap the bond and then she'd be wholly Peter's. That same memory was playing even now. Her pleas for Varik to stop turned to strangled gurgles followed by sharp snarls as Varik savaged her neck.

He watched as she fingered the scar that remained. It was time to show her something of what he could offer her, and he focused on the monitor.

One final soft plea to Varik played over the monitor before the sound of a heavy foot crashing into a door filled the room. Peter shouted his rival's name and his voice overlaid her brother's in the memory.

Alexandra rolled onto her back, staring up at the monitor.

On the screen, Peter stood in the place of Stephen.

She frowned and sat up, intensely watching the altered memory.

"Step away from her," Peter said, following the memory's dialogue like a script.

Varik glared at him with bright golden eyes over her motionless form and growled.

On the screen, Peter moved forward and Varik retreated, hissing like a cornered cat. He continued to move away as Peter confidently closed the distance. Once Peter reached Alexandra's side, Varik lunged. Instead of following the memory's script, Peter changed it. He grabbed Varik's throat and one arm, holding him in check as Varik's other—clawlike—hand ripped at Peter's arms and chest.

"You will *not* have her," he said, jerking Varik to one side. A sickening wet *pop* sounded and Varik ceased his attack.

"No!" Alexandra gasped and reached for the monitor as she watched Varik's lifeless body crumple at Peter's feet.

The picture paused, showing a frozen image of Varik's bloodied face.

"That's not the way it happened!"

"But it could have," Peter whispered, projecting his voice to appear as though he stood beside her. "It still could."

"You can't change the past."

"According to whom?"

She didn't answer.

"Who says the past cannot be changed?" he asked again. "Humans? Their gods? Your father?"

Color tinged her pale cheeks, and he felt the heat of her anger. "Don't talk about my father."

He chuckled, adding fuel to her anger.

"It's impossible to change the past, not without altering someone's memory."

"Nothing is impossible when you believe anything is possible," he quipped. He'd learned long ago that he was limited only by his imagination in the Shadowlands. The environment was different for each individual who found their way here, unless they knew how to manipulate its energies in such a way as to project their perception onto another individual. It was a skill he'd mastered, and one he would gladly teach Alexandra in time.

She searched the room, looking for him. "If you believe that, then show yourself."

"No."

"Are you afraid of me?"

"Far from it."

"Then why not reveal yourself?"

"In time." He projected a phantom version of his hand brushing her cheek and she flinched. "You aren't ready."

"Coward."

Peter ignored her attempts to provoke him into revealing himself. "He doesn't deserve you, not with the way he's treated you."

"Varik doesn't hold me prisoner, doesn't torture me."

"Torture isn't my intention. I merely want you to see the truth of what he's done to you. How he's corrupted you. You were pure and innocent until he seduced you and twisted you."

Alexandra laughed and it was sharp and derisive. "That's what you think? That *Varik* seduced *me*?"

"He corrupted you," Peter insisted.

"*I* seduced *him,* you jackass!" Her laughter took on the strained notes of one close to madness as tears rolled down her cheeks.

Peter shook his head, refusing to believe her. "No, you were pure, innocent, and he—"

"He resisted," she interrupted. "He tried to keep our relationship professional, but he eventually caved."

"Stop it! He twisted you with his perversions."

She flashed a cruel smile. "He didn't twist me. Hell, he wasn't even my first, but he's certainly proven himself to be the best."

Peter snarled and directed his attention to the monitor, shutting it off to reveal a flat black surface.

Alexandra glanced at her reflection. Her smile vanished, replaced with a look of horror.

In her reflection, a large gaping wound slashed across the left side of her neck from below the ear to her collarbone. Bruises, cuts, blisters, and bites covered her face, arms, and the upper portion of her chest visible above her shirt's V-neckline. However, when she raised her hands to her neck, confusion replaced horror and she looked down at herself and then back to her battered reflection.

"I've shown you every injury you've sustained as a result of *his* callousness," Peter said. "Will you continue this foolish assertion that he cares for you?"

Alexandra didn't respond. She covered her face with her hands, turned from the monitor, and lay down once more.

Peter turned the monitor on and her scream filled the small room. Soon she'd see the errors of her ways and renounce her blood-bond to Varik. Once she did, they would be free to start a new life.

Together.

Emily held the towel against Janet's neck, making sure to keep the pressure constant. She'd bandaged the wound as best she could but blood continued to weep through the dressing. The girl was pale and pasty and her skin was cooler now than it had been an hour ago. Janet was not only going into shock but was slowly dying in her arms. She had to convince Kirk to let her summon the Enforcers and get the girl the help she needed.

From where she sat in the middle of the living room, she could see the mass of cars and people milling in the street in front of the house. Kirk stood to one side of the windows, watching them through the slightly parted blinds. He'd remained there even while the phone rang for twenty minutes solid. Now both the phone and the house were silent, save for Janet's ragged breathing.

"They haven't moved," Kirk murmured. "No one's coming forward. It's like they aren't even trying to storm the house. Why?"

"They're probably waiting for you to make some sort of demands," Emily said and felt a rush of satisfaction when he jumped. "That's why they called. They want to know what you want."

He grunted. "What I want, I can't have. They'd never give her to me."

"Who?"

"It doesn't matter."

"They may, if you're willing to show some sort of goodwill in exchange."

"Like letting you go?" He chuckled. "Forget it. You're worth too damn much."

"Then let Janet go. Please. She needs medical attention."

His gaze dropped to Janet's pale face.

"If you release her, they may be willing to negotiate with you," Emily said. "But if she dies, you know the penalty for killing a human."

He looked out the window. "I'm already a walking dead man so what's one more human?"

"Let her go and I'll do my best to make sure you see your girlfriend."

Kirk was at her side before Emily could process that he'd moved. "You can do that?"

"I can try, but you have to let the Enforcers send in someone to help Janet."

He hesitated for a moment and then reached into his back pocket. He handed over her cell phone. "Keep it on speaker and make it quick. No tricks. If I think you're pulling a fast one, I'll put a bullet in both your brains."

She nodded and took the phone, dialing it with one hand while she kept pressure on Janet's wound. As soon as the first ring sounded, she switched to speaker mode.

"Emily!" Varik's voice sounded strained and tinny through the small speaker. "What's going on? Has that bastard hurt you?"

"No," she answered, watching Kirk. "I'm fine but Janet is badly hurt. She needs medical attention."

"What the hell happened?"

Kirk shrugged and smirked.

"She was bitten and has lost a lot of blood."

"Goddamn son of a bitch—"

Kirk frowned and pointed the revolver at Janet.

"Varik, I need you to listen to me very carefully," Emily interrupted his profane tirade. "He's agreed to let Janet go if he can see his girlfriend."

Caution crept into Varik's voice. "I'm not sure I can do that. We may have trouble finding her."

"Bullshit!" Kirk jerked the phone from her hand. "Her name is Piper Garver, and she's sitting her fat ass in the fucking Jefferson Police Department right now!"

He jumped to his feet, paced to the window, and peered outside. "You get her here—*now*—or a bitten human is going to be the least of your worries!"

"You listen to me, you little turdstain," Varik growled. "You so much as breathe on either of those women, and I'll hang your fangs from my rearview mirror."

"Try it, motherfucker, and you'll be mopping up the blood for days."

Kirk pressed the button to end the call, cutting off Varik's response.

From outside, Emily heard the Enforcer's roar of frustration followed by a loud *bang* and a siren's pitiful, short *whoop*. She glanced out the partially obscured front window and saw Varik walking away from a still-rocking patrol car, a large dent in its fender near the wheel well.

Janet moaned weakly as Emily peeled away the towel to check the bandage over the girl's neck. The blood flow had slowed to a trickle but Janet wasn't improving. Emily re-covered the wound and hoped help would arrive soon.

And that Varik would find a way to use the opening she'd created in Kirk's defenses. If he didn't, she would be left alone with an unstable young vampire. It wasn't the first time she'd faced someone like Kirk. However, the last was before Bernard was killed, and then, she'd been the one holding the gun.

Peter slowly opened his eyes, allowing himself time to reorient to being in the physical world. His body felt heavy and stiff as he swung his legs over the side of the narrow bed on which he lay and sat up.

Transitioning from the Shadowlands to reality seemed to become more difficult each time. The freedom he felt in the Shadowlands disappeared once he returned to his physical body with its limitations. When he parted the Veil, his consciousness was free to go anywhere, become anything or anyone, and the rush of power he felt there left him breathless. Here in the physical world he felt only barrenness and coldness so deep he sometimes wondered if he even still possessed a soul.

Perhaps that explained his collection.

He paused at the box on the floor beside the door. Inside were the remains of five of his dolls, destroyed and the souls contained within them lost. Their loss saddened him but in the end he'd gained his greatest possession—his most precious.

Gliding down the hallway to the largest bedroom, he carefully opened the door and slipped inside.

Alexandra lay motionless in the massive bed, her auburn hair a splash of color in the otherwise stark whiteness of the room.

Peter moved to the bed and stretched out beside her, keeping the thick comforter between them. He molded his body to mirror hers and draped an arm over her waist.

She whimpered and shifted in her sleep.

He only had a few more hours to work on severing the blood-bond before the drug he'd given her wore off and she awoke. He couldn't give her another dose without risking permanent injury to her.

Time was short and he needed to work quickly.

He stroked her hair and kissed her neck, inhaling her natural scent of jasmine and vanilla. His desire to make her his forever was almost more than he could bear but he forced himself to have patience. Soon she would forget about Varik and love him instead.

She mumbled something unintelligible and tried to pull away.

"Shh shh shh," he whispered. He flexed his arm and pressed closer, pinning her next to him.

She quieted and he nuzzled her neck once more. "It'll be over soon and then nothing will take you from me."

Peter closed his eyes and sighed, allowing himself to drift into the realm of her dreams.

Moonlight dappled the front lawn of 463 Alpine Way. Neatly trimmed grass, now brown and dormant in the November chill, played host to a collection of cement toads while colorful garden gnomes peeked out from behind evergreen hedges. Red siding and white trim gave the single-story bungalow homey warmth, but the large gathering of police cars with strobing blue and white lights kept visitors at bay.

Varik stood out of sight on one side of an awaiting ambulance, making final adjustments to the paramedic uniform he now wore, muttering, "I swear I'm going to use this son of a bitch's balls for target practice."

"You're not going to do shit until I give the order," Damian snapped from beside him.

Varik scoffed and carefully inserted a wireless receiver into his ear that would allow Damian to give him directions. A small radio transmitter was hidden in one of the ink pens stuck in a special pocket on the sleeve of his uniform.

He was taking a huge risk by attempting to sneak into the house disguised as one of the paramedics sent to retrieve Janet Klein. However, it was the best plan they'd devised, short of storming the house and putting Emily and Janet in even greater danger.

"I mean it, Baudelaire. We need this to be by the book with Dreyer in town."

"You let me worry about Morgan."

"Just because the two of you bumped uglies for a while doesn't give you a free pass with her."

"I'm aware of that."

"Then don't do anything stupid in there."

"Have you ever known me to do anything to jeopardize hostages?"

"Do you really want me to answer that? Because I *do* remember that incident in Munich."

Varik glanced at the taller vampire. "That wasn't my fault."

"The building blew up."

"The charge I used was small and was meant to be a diversion. The building collapsed due to shitty workmanship, and regardless, the hostages were recovered alive along with two of the kidnappers." He slipped a Jefferson Memorial Hospital baseball cap onto his head. "Let's check this transmitter," he said and called out a series of numbers.

A moment later a voice repeated the numbers in Varik's ear over the receiver. "It works. Now all we need is—"

"For JPD to bring the Garver girl over," Damian finished.

"Fuck. What the hell is taking so damn long?"

"The fact that Piper is scared out of her mind had something to do with it," Tasha Lockwood said from behind him.

He faced her and wasn't surprised to find Morgan standing with Tasha and the obviously frightened Piper Garver.

Damian motioned for Tasha and Piper to join him as he stepped a few feet away and began explaining the plan to them.

Morgan's eyes traveled to Varik's feet and back up. "I'd forgotten how good you look in a uniform."

"Save it, Morgan. Whatever you're after, I'm not interested."

She sidled closer and lowered her voice. "You may change your mind once you find out there's a formal complaint levied against you."

"For what?"

"Intimidation."

"By whom?"

Her gaze darted to Tasha and back.

"Goddamn it to Hell."

"You may even change your mind when I tell you I haven't actually filed her report with the Bureau." She traced the seam of his uniform along his shoulder with her finger. "*Yet.*"

He twisted away from her. "What do you want, Morgan? Don't give me that Tribunal bullshit either. You've been playing games ever since you came to Jefferson. Now, what do you really want?"

She hesitated and then whispered, "Enforcers have gone missing in Louisville."

"How many?"

"Eight as of a few days ago."

"Why haven't I heard anything about this?"

"The information is strictly on a need-to-know basis. So far none of the missing Enforcers have been located—no bodies, no demands. Chief Magistrate Phelps is calling in regional directors from all over the country under the guise of an internal audit but its real purpose is to covertly determine if more Enforcers are missing or if it's localized to Louisville."

"Does Damian know?"

"Not yet."

"What do you want from me?"

For a moment he thought he saw fear reflected in her hazel eyes. "When the time comes, I want—"

"We're ready," Damian called and Varik followed as

their group moved to the hastily erected barricade in front of the house.

He thought about what Morgan said. Eight missing Enforcers was certainly cause for alarm, but his primary concern at the moment was nailing the son of a bitch preventing him from finding his own missing Enforcer.

eighteen

KIRK CLOSELY WATCHED THE THREE PARAMEDICS CARRY-
ing equipment and a bright orange stretcher board into
the living room for signs of trickery. He kept a firm grip
on Emily's arm and the revolver pressed against the soft
tissue beneath her chin, using her as a precautionary
living shield.

"That's far enough," he said, stopping them short of
reaching Janet, who lay in the center of the room.
"Nobody touches the bitch until I see Piper."

The one holding the stretcher shifted his weight.

"You." Kirk gestured at him with the revolver. "Why
are there three of you?"

"Two to carry the board," he drawled in a thick accent. "One to carry equipment and hold an IV."

A cell phone trilled and Kirk tensed. "Answer it," he
ordered Emily. "Keep it on speaker."

She calmly pressed the button to answer the call.
"Hello?"

"This is Chief Enforcer Damian Alberez," a deep voice
rumbled through the speaker. "To whom am I speaking?"

Kirk nodded his approval when she glanced at him.

"Emily Sabian."

"Are you injured?"

"No, but Janet is."

"Are the paramedics helping her?"

Kirk draped his chin over her shoulder. "She gets help
when I see Piper. That was the fucking deal."

There was a brief pause. "And you are?"

"I'm the one with the gun pointed at Emily's pretty fucking face! If you want her to keep it, you send Piper in here *now*!"

"I can't do that, son," Alberez said evenly.

"You can and—"

"Kirk?"

Piper's voice slammed into him and stole his breath. They'd actually brought her to him.

"Kirk? Can you hear me?" An edge of desperation crept into her voice.

"Yeah," he muttered and then cleared his throat. "I can hear you."

"They won't let me come inside. They're telling me you need to let the paramedics help that girl and give yourself up."

"They can fucking go to Hell."

"Kirk, please, just do what the Enforcers say."

"Why should I? All I wanted was to see you and they won't even give me that. Why the hell should I do anything they want?"

There was a pause, and when she spoke again, her voice carried a tinge of hopefulness. "Why did you want to see me?"

Once again, he marveled at her gullibility. "You know why."

"You love me?"

He could no longer contain himself. He grabbed the phone, shoved Emily aside, and ripped open the blinds, searching the crowd for Piper. "So I could rip your fucking heart out and bathe in your blood, you lying bitch!"

A fist connected with his jaw, slamming him in the wall. He tried to raise the revolver, only to have it knocked from his hand. More blows struck his torso, leaving him breathless, and a final swipe of his legs sent him crashing to the floor. Stars strobed and burst before his eyes as he tried to focus on the snarling face above him.

One of the paramedics—the one who'd been holding the orange board—knelt beside Kirk and rolled him roughly onto his stomach. The familiar heft and click of handcuffs settled around his wrists. "Get up, turdstain," he growled with no trace of the heavy drawl he'd possessed earlier. "You're not so tough when you don't have a bunch of women to frighten, are you?"

"Fuck you," Kirk gasped and stumbled over his own feet as he was handed off to one of the other Enforcers now swarming throughout the house.

"What should we do with him, sir?" an Enforcer asked the paramedic.

"He killed a human," the Enforcer-paramedic said with a shrug. "Automatic death sentence. Take him out back and shoot his ass."

"No!" Kirk strained to free himself from the Enforcer's ironlike grip. "You can't do this! You have no evidence! This is fucking murder!"

"We have witnesses who saw you snap that truck driver's neck. That's all the evidence we need."

"I can give you names! Lots of names!"

The Enforcer dressed as a paramedic shook his head. "Not interested."

"Mindy Johnson!" Kirk screamed as the Enforcer holding him dragged him into the kitchen. "I can give you the last person to see Mindy Johnson alive!"

The Enforcer-paramedic held up his hand and the one holding Kirk stopped. "Say that again."

"I can give you the last person who saw Mindy Johnson alive," he repeated between ragged puffs.

The Enforcer-paramedic smirked. "Congratulations, kid. Now I'm interested."

* * *

"Princess."

Her father's soft voice called to her and Alex recoiled, closing her eyes and covering her ears with her hands. Wasn't it enough for Peter to dredge up the most painful memories of her and Varik's past? Was she now doomed to relive her father's death as well?

"Princess," he called again, more insistent.

"Go away," she mumbled. Chains clanked and rattled as she tightened her protective curl.

Gentle but firm hands wrapped around her arms, tugging her upright. She kicked and hurled curses at whoever held her.

"Alexandra!" The hands transitioned to the sides of her head, forcing her to meet a pair of emerald green eyes rimmed in gold. "It's me!"

Her struggles ceased, replaced with a wash of relief. "Daddy."

He smiled, showing perfect human teeth, and the corners of his eyes crinkled. The Irish lilt to his voice made his words almost musical. "There's my girl. I was beginning to worry that I might be too late."

"Too late?"

"To help you." He pulled her to her feet. "We have to hurry before he discovers I'm here."

Alex glanced at the video monitor, now playing a scene from her past in which she and Varik were working security for a high-profile vampire official. They'd been forced to hustle the official out of the building after someone in the crowd had opened fire.

She remembered the night well. It was the first night Varik had acknowledged he had feelings for her beyond teacher and student. Forcing down the rising sense of anguish, she watched as her father attempted to remove her chains. "Why is he doing this, Daddy?"

"Isn't it obvious, Princess?" He grunted as he tried to pry open the bands covering her wrists. "The Doll-maker has been obsessed with you for years. I think that much should be clear from the number of dolls resembling you that we saw."

"But why? What did I do to draw his attention?"

"I don't know, but if I'd known any of this when I was still alive . . ." He let the thought trail away, shaking his head. He gave her wristbands a final tug and sighed in frustration. "I'm sorry."

"Don't stop. Please, keep trying."

"No, I wasn't apologizing for the chains. I meant I'm sorry I haven't been there for you, Princess, to watch you grow up."

"It wasn't your fault you were murdered."

"Regardless, I just wanted you to know how proud I am—"

His declaration was cut short as a dark shadow rammed into his midsection, knocking Alex to the floor as it passed.

"Daddy!" She tugged at her chains, helpless as the specter and her father tumbled and struggled to gain the upper hand on the other.

Her father rolled backward, lifting his feet, and tossed the wraith aside but it was up and moving again before her father was able to rise to more than his knees.

"Too slow, old man," the shadow growled from where it crouched in the corner.

"I may be a little slow but at least I'm not a coward hiding behind smoke and mirrors." Her father gained his feet and slowly stood up. "But, then again, that's always been your specialty. Hasn't it, Peter?"

The dark mass rippled, solidified, and took on the appearance of the Dollmaker. "No fair trying to take what I rightfully stole, old man."

"Life isn't fair, Peter. That's one thing you never could accept."

A savage grin sliced across Peter's face. "Why should I when I hold the power to level the playing field?"

"You're a murderer."

"Who's the pot and who's the kettle here, old man? You took more than a few lives yourself."

"Liar!" Alex charged at Peter but was stopped short by the chains.

Peter stepped back and disappeared in a haze of gray mist.

"My father never hurt anyone!"

"Princess, don't—"

"Do you hear me, you sick fuck?" Alex shouted.

Gray mist surrounded her and materialized into Peter standing behind her, his fingers digging into the flesh of her arms. "Oh, I hear you, darling," he whispered in her ear. "And I weep at your ignorance."

"Let her go," her father ordered, reaching for her.

"Back off, old man." Peter held his hand up before them and a burst of blue energy smacked into her father's chest, sending him tumbling backward.

"Daddy!"

Peter jerked her against him roughly. "It's getting awfully crowded in here, darling. How about we go somewhere a little more private?"

"Fuck you!"

"Love to, but we have a few things to discuss first." He wrapped his arms around her, pinning her own arms to her sides. "Say good-bye to Daddy Dearest."

Her father and the surrounding room disappeared in a burst of gray mist, and then she was hurtling through the void, screaming Varik's name, with Peter's laughter ringing in her ears.

* * *

Varik entered the interview room, closed the door behind him, and leaned against it. He folded his arms across his chest and stared at Kirk Beljean seated at the lone table. Moments passed in silence before Kirk began to wiggle in his seat, eyes darting around the room, avoiding Varik's steady observation.

When Kirk finally looked at him, it was to explode in anger. "Stop staring at me, you fucking freak!"

Varik pushed away from the door. He took his time crossing the room to lean in close to Kirk. "You're eighty-three years old and hang out with girls old enough to be your granddaughters, and you think *I'm* a freak?"

"Go to Hell."

"Already there," he snapped. "The question is how soon will you be joining me?"

Kirk scooted his chair to the side. "Get away from me."

Varik retreated a few paces and studied the younger vampire—stringy brown hair, gray eyes, an unhealthy ashen complexion, too thin even for his small frame, and fingernails jagged and red from repeated biting. "Mindy Johnson. Where is she?"

"Dead, if she's lucky."

"What do you mean by that?"

"Because if I find out she turned on me, I'll kill the bitch myself."

Varik grabbed a fistful of Kirk's hair and slammed his head onto the table.

Kirk groaned.

"Where is she?"

"I think you broke my nose."

"I'll break more than that if you don't tell me where Mindy is."

"I don't know!"

"The vampire you sent her to—I want his name. Where does he live? Describe him."

"You don't understand. I never met him face-to-face, only dealt with him over the phone. He calls every six or eight weeks and orders a girl. He always has me send them to the Thrifty Pick parking lot at midnight because they don't have video cameras. I don't know what he does with the girls from that point on, and it's none of my business. But none of the girls come back, at least none come back to me."

"And you didn't think that was suspicious?"

Kirk laughed. "Man, some of these blood bunnies turn tricks for more than one broker. If they don't come back to me, I assume they're working for someone else or have moved on. Questions are unhealthy in my line of work."

"What's his name?"

"I want to see Piper first."

"No."

"Then I have nothing else to say."

Varik loomed over Kirk. "No, there *is* one word you can say."

He snorted. "And what would that be?"

"Mercy." He kicked the chair from underneath Kirk and as Kirk fell, Varik grabbed the back of his shirt, hauled him to his feet, and shoved him against the wall. He pressed his forearm against Kirk's throat, slowly choking off the younger vampire's air supply. "Give. Me. His. Name."

"No."

"Give me his fucking name," Varik snarled, increasing the pressure on Kirk's throat.

He gurgled his response.

"Tell me and you see Piper."

Kirk struggled to draw a breath. "P-Peter . . . That's all I know." He gasped. "I swear."

Varik released him and turned to face a camera in the corner near the door as Kirk tumbled to the floor behind him. "Did you get all that?"

Damian's voice filled the room from a hidden speaker. "We got it."

Varik nodded and headed for the door.

"Piper," Kirk rasped. "When can I—"

"Oh, yeah, about that." Varik half turned in the open doorway. "I lied."

Kirk's howl and shouted curses were muffled by the heavy door as Varik walked away and entered the nearby observation room. He joined Damian in front of a closed-circuit video monitor as they watched a live feed of Kirk using a chair in a futile attempt to break out of the interview room. "Persistent little fucker, I'll give him that."

"We'll keep the tape rolling for a while," Damian said. "In case he gives up any more names."

"What about this Peter?"

"It's not much to go on, but I've already called Freddy and Reyes says he has some new info on that doll left with the Johnson girl's car."

Varik nodded. "I'll be in the lab if you need anything."

He opened the door to leave when the blood-bond roared to life.

Varik!

Alex's call slammed into him with the psychic force of a small truck and bowled him over. Distorted memories mixed with flashes of conversation flooded his mind. Images of Alex chained and Bernard fighting shadows pushed to the forefront, only to be replaced by a dizzying sensation of free-falling through darkness.

Alex! He reached across the bond for her familiar warmth and felt the joy and hope that surged from her as she responded. Her mind brushed his, a gentle caress that was like a cooling salve to his tortured soul.

The bond trembled and Varik bellowed as Alex was ripped from his grasp.

A new presence filled with coldness and hatred tapped into the bond. *She's mine.*

Over my dead body.

That can be arranged.

Varik reached for the intruding mind as it retreated, but it slipped from his grasp. *Alex!*

Varik . . .

The connection faltered and collapsed, leaving the echoed memory of her touch and voice in his mind. He was unable to stop the hot tears that spilled from his eyes. On his knees, he voiced his anger, fear, and longing in a wordless scream.

nineteen

ALEX WAS SCREAMING AND FIGHTING. SHE TWISTED AND bucked, trying to dislodge the heavy weight that pinned her. "Get off me!"

"I don't think so," Peter said, laughing. "I'm rather enjoying myself."

Her fist connected with his jaw, leaving him momentarily stunned. She kicked him aside, scurried off the bed, and darted for the door.

Arms encircled her waist like iron bands and yanked her off her feet. "Gotcha!"

"No!" She clawed at the doorjamb, trying to find purchase for her fingers. Smooth wood offered no salvation. The world spun as Peter flung her onto the bed. She bounced over the mattress and tumbled to the floor on the opposite side. Something popped in her wrist as she tried to brace her fall and pain shot up her arm, making her cry out.

"We could've been so happy," Peter said as he stalked her from the foot of the bed. "But your father had to mess everything up."

Alex backpedaled across the floor. Her injured wrist refused to support her weight and gave way. Hissing with pain, she cradled it to her chest and continued her awkward retreat until her back hit a wall.

"And then you found a way to reach out to *him*."

"You're insane."

"Bernard thought the same thing. Even said as much when he refused to take me on as a Hunter-Talent."

As he spoke, Alex realized she could see again. At least somewhat. Instead of unending blackness, everything was now fuzzy gray with amorphous dark blobs. Imperfect vision was better than none at all. "What are you talking about? My father was a history professor."

"That's what he told you because you were too young to understand what he really was."

"You're lying."

"Your precious Varik"— he spat the name as if it tasted bad —"was Daddy Dearest's partner. Your father was the one who sent him to kill our kindred."

Alex dove for what she hoped was the bed, worming her way underneath. She shrieked as she felt a hand close over her ankle.

"Tricky tricky, chickie chickie," Peter chanted, pulling her out of her hiding place. "You're a quick little—oof!"

She used her free leg to kick him in the shin. As he collapsed, she scrambled to gain her feet.

He lunged and landed atop her.

"Let me go!" She raked his arms with her nails, leaving bloody welts.

He managed to grab her injured wrist and squeezed.

Alex gasped and wailed as fresh pain rushed up her arm.

Peter seized her other wrist and settled his weight over her, pinning her facedown to the floor. "You think I *like* hurting you? Huh? I don't, but you leave me no choice. We'll never be happy unless you stop fighting me!"

"Go to Hell, you lying sack of shit! There is *no fucking us*!"

He switched his hold on her wrists to one hand, used the other to flip her onto her back, and covered her with his body again before she could strike another kick. His breath beat against her face as he spoke. "That's your father and Varik talking. You'll see that you and I are meant to be together, that everything I've told you is true." He stroked her hair. "I'll *make* you see."

Alex grunted as he pulled her to her feet. He kept a firm grip on her injured wrist and tugged her along behind him, heading for a destination only he could see.

Tasha stood in the doorway of the employee break room, watching Varik as he sat on a low sofa in the separate lounge area, elbows on his knees and head in hands. She'd never seen anyone look so thoroughly dejected. The primal scream he'd sounded earlier turned her blood to ice, and the memory of it even now made her shiver.

"Good job today," Damian said from behind her within the break room.

"With what?"

He picked up the cup of coffee he'd poured. "Convincing the Garver girl to come to the scene and talk to Kirk. If she hadn't distracted him, we would've been forced to breach the house. The outcome probably wouldn't have been as tidy. As it stands now, docs at the hospital say Janet Klein will make a full recovery."

"What about him?" Tasha jerked her head toward Varik. "Will he make a full recovery?"

"He'll live," Damian said softly, joining her. "Once we find Alex."

"And if you don't?"

"I'll be looking for a new Director of Special Operations." He crossed the hall to the lounge and offered the coffee to Varik. When the offer passed unacknowledged, Damian sighed, lowered himself onto the sofa next to Varik, and began speaking in tones too low for her to hear.

She left the break room and entered the common area, where uniformed officers and the junior detectives crowded into small cubicle spaces. As she headed for her office, Tasha was surprised to see Morgan leaving it. "Can I help you, SI Dreyer?"

Morgan spun around, eyes wide and startled. "Lieutenant Lockwood," she stammered before composing herself. "I was just—I left some papers for you to sign on your desk."

"Step back in my office and we'll take care of it right now."

"No," Morgan barked. "What I mean is, I can't now. I have a meeting to attend."

"Okay, but it shouldn't—" Tasha stopped as Morgan walked away, clutching a thick stack of papers to her chest. "Fucking vamps," she muttered and entered her office, closing the door behind her.

The papers Morgan mentioned were for the complaint she'd filed against Varik. She skimmed the documents, verifying them for accuracy, and picked up a pen.

She hesitated. If she signed the papers, invisible wheels would be set in motion that would ultimately end with Varik standing before his own Tribunal inquiry. She'd been pissed off at him when she told Morgan she wanted to file the complaint. Now, seeing her harsh words outlined in black and white, she wondered if she could really go through with it.

"Ah, hell," she murmured and leaned back in her chair. Indecision clouded her mind. There would be no harm in waiting to sign the papers, at least until she had more time to think about the ramifications of charging a federal agent with inappropriate conduct.

Tasha picked up the papers and slipped them into her

desk drawer and discovered the evidence bag for Mindy Johnson's journal.

She frowned, staring at the bag. She'd removed it, taken it home with her, and promptly lost it, according to Rueben. Picking up the bag, she was gripped with confusion and suspicion as she felt its heaviness. She looked inside and discovered the journal, seemingly intact.

Tasha retrieved the pink leather-bound book and flipped it over in her hands. The pages slipped easily between her fingers as she scanned the looping handwriting she recognized as Mindy's. Halfway through the book, she stopped, staring at the jagged remains of several pages that had been removed.

Guilt stilled her breath. Had the pages been ripped out before or after she took the journal from the lab? Where had it disappeared and who'd returned it?

The most plausible explanation was that Rueben had stolen the book from her. But why? As for how it came to be in her desk, Morgan Dreyer had been in Tasha's office only moments prior. Could Morgan and Rueben be working together? If so, what was their connection to her mystery callers?

A commotion outside interrupted her thoughts. Shouts and curses drew her to the door and as she stepped into the common area, she saw two Enforcers dragging a still-ranting Kirk Beljean toward a rear exit of the Jefferson Police Department. The Bureau didn't waste time in cases where vampires were the direct cause of a human's death. Beljean would be flown to Louisville, evidence would be presented, and he'd be dead by morning.

One of the Enforcers reached for the exit and Kirk broke free, barreling up the hallway in a desperate attempt to escape.

Tasha went for her sidearm but was too slow. The

rampaging vampire slammed into her and her Beretta skittered across the floor. She shrieked as fangs pierced her clothing and sank into her forearm.

Hands grappled with Kirk, ripping his mouth from her arm. Tasha glimpsed Damian's massive silhouette before he scooped her up, carrying her to the safety of the deserted Municipal Center's lobby.

He set her down on the lower wall surrounding the silent water feature. "Give me your arm."

Breathing hard and fighting back hysterical tears, she obediently held her arm out for his inspection.

The big Enforcer ripped the sleeve from her blouse at the shoulder in one fluid movement. He glanced at her with golden eyes when she sucked in a breath and then turned his attention back to her arm. His oversized hands were gentle as he assessed the damage. "No apparent broken bones, but it's a nasty bite. You're going to want a doctor to check it out."

A high and long screech sounded from the JPD wing and suddenly fell silent, leaving an eerie quiet in its wake.

"Shouldn't you—" Tasha began and stopped as Varik pushed through the glass doors and into the lobby.

Crimson beads dotted his face and ran down the front of his shirt in dark splotches. He limped wearily to Damian and Tasha, extended his hand toward Damian, and dropped two bloody nuggets in the Chief Enforcer's palm. He then focused on Tasha. "Kirk won't bite you or anyone again," he said, deadpan.

Tasha cradled her injured arm to her, watched him head toward the exit and disappear down the front steps of the Center. Only after he'd melded with the night's shadows did she look at what he'd left behind.

Two bloody fangs lay in Damian's hand.

The world tilted violently and then she was surrounded by darkness.

* * *

Staring out Janet's hospital window, Emily wondered if she was fated to spend a majority of her life in hospitals. When she and Bernard married, she'd been the one to care for him and any wounds he suffered as a Hunter until he was tapped as a Talent and taken out of the field. Then Stephen was born and the usual boyhood scrapes and occasional broken bone had to be tended.

Her boys had been boys through and through, and Alex had been no slouch in the rough and tumble department either. Bernard may have called her "Princess" but the precocious child had been anything except a princess. Emily had lost count of the number of trips to the emergency room Alex had fostered during her teens. She smiled with the memories.

However, her smile soon faded, replaced by sorrow. Alex was missing and there'd been no word on the search. Varik offered no updates after he arrested Kirk and Janet was whisked away to the hospital. He'd simply said if he had any news he would call.

"Mom?" Stephen said softly from the room's doorway.

Emily motioned for him to enter and to be quiet. "She's sleeping," she whispered as he drew closer, glancing at the bed in which Janet lay. "The doctor says she'll be fine but they want to keep her overnight as a precaution."

Stephen nodded, his eyes locked on Janet. He suddenly turned to Emily and placed his head on her shoulder, wrapping her in a tight embrace. "I'm so sorry, Mom. I should've been there with you both."

Dampness spread over her shoulder and she realized he was crying. "Oh, honey," she murmured, hugging him in turn and gently stroking his back as she had when he was a child. "You can't blame yourself for any of this. You had to meet with your investors and discuss the plans to rebuild Crimson Swan. Janet and I both understand that. I'm sure the police tried to reach you."

Stephen pulled away, swiping angrily at his tears. "That's the problem." He flung himself onto the small couch beneath the window. "There was no meeting. I lied."

"You lied?" Emily frowned and perched on the edge beside him. "Why? Where were you?"

"At the library, in the archives." He sighed and avoided looking at her. "After Damian told us Alex was kidnapped and what happened to Varik and they suspected this Dollmaker guy of being the one who grabbed Alex, I felt so helpless, like I should be doing something—*anything*—to find Alex but I didn't know *what*."

"Stephen—"

"*She* didn't give up on *me* when those Midnighters kidnapped me and burned Crimson Swan. *She* knew what to do and didn't let anyone stand in her way. I'm not an Enforcer. If I tried to shoot a gun I'd probably blow off my foot."

"Alex knew what to do because she's been trained to do it." Emily draped her arm over his back and gave him a sideways hug. "No one expects you to go charging after her like a white knight on horseback."

"I know, but I couldn't just sit around waiting. That's why I lied about the meeting, and why I went to the archives and started looking into this Dollmaker." He reached inside his jacket and produced a stack of folded papers from an inner pocket. "Mom, what I found scares the hell out of me."

Emily took the pages from him, unfolded them, and began reading the fuzzy printed images of old newspaper articles. The oldest dated back to the early 1900s in

Chicago with the most recent from Louisville, dated 1968.

Each article detailed the gruesome murder of at least one young girl, but most often several. There seemed to be no pattern to the victims in age, ethnicity, or occupation. The only commonality Emily could see between any of them was the horrible manner in which they died—partially skinned and their throats slit.

"*This* is the psycho that the Enforcers suspect took Alex," Stephen whispered. "And that's not all." He handed her another page. "Look in the background of the photo."

She studied the grainy black-and-white photo. Stone-faced men carried what could only be a body wrapped in sheets down the front walk of a Colonial-style home. Holding the paper at an angle to increase the amount of light, she searched the equally grim bystanders who stood outside of the police barricade. One face stood out and she whispered, "Bernard."

"That photo was taken in Louisville in 1968, just a few months before he was killed. What was he doing at a crime scene in the middle of the day?"

Emily folded the paper, hiding the photo. "I don't know. Perhaps it was near the university and he stopped on his way to work."

Stephen shook his head and took back the paper, unfolding it. "The article listed the address. This house is close to the river, nowhere near the campus. So why was he there?"

"I said I don't know, but I'm sure he had a reason."

"I thought he might be in the area because of the affair, so I looked up Siobhan, which wasn't easy considering I only knew her first name."

Fear sliced through Emily, leaving her cold and robbing her of her voice.

"The only reference I found to a Siobhan in

Louisville, Kentucky, around the time that Dad was having the affair was a listing on the FBPI's Most Wanted list." He produced another page and read from it. "Siobhan Kelly, brown hair, blue eyes, age 184. Location unknown. Wanted for the murder of three Enforcers in January 1963. Considered armed and dangerous. Approach with extreme caution."

Emily looked away when he turned his focus to her.

"Is this the same woman Dad was sleeping with?"

She glanced at the small image provided along with the description. It was badly rendered and appeared to have been taken from an old snapshot, but the dark-haired smiling woman was undeniably Siobhan Kelly. Emily nodded. "Yes, that's her."

Stephen leapt to his feet, muttering curses, and paced in front of her. "How could Dad get involved with someone like this?" After the fifth circuit, he stopped. "What if she's the one who killed *him*?"

"Siobhan didn't kill your father—or anyone else, for that matter."

"They never caught the person responsible for Dad's murder. How can you be so certain it wasn't her?" He paused. "Unless you know who did it."

"Don't be silly. Of course I don't know who killed Bernard."

"You said Siobhan didn't kill Dad or anyone else." He held up the page in his hand. "If she didn't kill these Enforcers, who did and why is she being blamed for it?"

"It was your father," Emily said and continued in a rush before he could interrupt. "Your father killed those Enforcers in order to protect Siobhan and her newborn baby. Afterward, it was decided Siobhan would leave Louisville and take the blame for the killings so Bernard could stay behind and raise his family."

"Dad killed three Enforcers? What-what about the baby? What happened to him?"

"*She* stayed in Louisville with Bernard."

"She?" Stephen repeated. Realization crept into his eyes and he dropped his jaw. "It's Alex, isn't it? Alex is Siobhan's daughter."

Tears brimmed in Emily's eyes as she took a shuddering breath and nodded her confirmation.

Alex's memory haunted Varik. He stood in the center of her silent hotel room, and everywhere he turned his eye was drawn to a reminder of her: discarded clothing, a bottle of lotion, a book she'd been reading. The entire room smelled of her, and perhaps that was why he'd broken every speed limit in town and ran more than a few red lights to get here.

He stretched out on the bed, sending up a wave of jasmine and vanilla. Memories of their lovemaking flooded his mind, seizing on an image of her lying beneath him, the engagement ring he'd convinced her to wear for that night nestled between her breasts.

I love you, the memory whispered.

Varik shuddered as an overwhelming sense of loss crashed into him. How cruel was fate to give her back to him only to take her away?

Dweezil hopped up from the opposite side of the bed, sat down, wrapping his long fuzzy tail around his paws, and stared at Varik. The cat blinked and looked to the door and then back, as if asking where his mistress was.

"She's gone," Varik whispered, his voice breaking. "And I'm not sure I can get her back this time."

Dweezil stretched his long Maine coon body to its fullest before striding across the bed to rub his head under Varik's chin. His omnipresent purring was oddly quiet as he circled once before curling in a tight ball.

Varik stroked his hand over the cat's thick black-and-tan fur. He laid his head on the pillow last used by Alex. "I miss her," he said to no one in particular.

Dweezil began to softly purr next to him, as if voicing his agreement.

Peter secured the final strap around her waist and stepped back to admire his handiwork. Bands immobilized her arms, legs, and torso. He allowed her the freedom to move her head, a luxury he hoped would be a sign he intended her no harm.

It hadn't been easy to restrain Alexandra—she was much stronger than he anticipated—and she fought harder than the humans he normally had to control. Of course, the humans had all been drugged, but Alexandra needed to be awake and lucid if she was going to understand the level of betrayal perpetuated by those closest to her.

He gently stroked the developing dark bruise on her jaw. He'd had no choice in the end but to punch her, stunning her long enough for him to lock the bands in place. Hurting her was the last thing he wanted. He brushed his lips over the bruise, wanting to kiss away the pain.

His hands followed the line of her arms, her torso, her hips. His fingers found the hem of her shirt and slipped beneath, feeling the flat smoothness of her stomach. It would be so easy to claim her. So easy . . .

"No," he gasped and forced himself to back away. "I've come too far to risk losing her now."

He drew a ragged breath, calming his chaotic thoughts. She was his soul mate. He'd known that from the moment he first saw her in the Shadowlands when she was just a child. Forty years he'd waited for this moment. A few more hours at most wouldn't kill him.

She groaned and her eyes fluttered open. She tried to

move but the bands held her in place. Her attempts to escape became more frantic. "What the hell? Let me go!"

Peter moved to stand in front of her. "Not until you're willing to listen to reason, darling. After all, I'm only trying to help you."

"Help me?" She smirked. "How about you help me out of these things and let's see just how reasonable I can be?"

"Nice try." He picked up a folder from his workstation. "I'll give you an 'A' for effort but I don't believe you're ready to run free yet."

While she continued to struggle and hurl insults at him, he opened the file and withdrew a large black-and-white photo. He held it up for her to see.

She seemed to stare through him.

"Look at this photo, Alexandra."

"I can't fucking see, asshole."

Peter frowned and set the photo aside. He grabbed her jaw, forcing her to tilt her head back, despite her resistance. He carefully examined her eyes and then released her. "Temporary blindness most likely resulting from too rapid a transition through the Veil. It'll pass."

"Thank you for the enlightenment, Doctor Quackenstein."

He picked up the photo again, determined to proceed regardless of her limitations. "I got this photo from the FBPI archives. The Freedom of Information Act the humans cooked up has been incredibly useful." He examined the photo depicting a group of men and a handful of women—twenty-five in total. "It's interesting. Here are some of the most well-known Hunters turned Enforcers, and who should be standing among them but Daddy Dearest."

"That photo is a lie. My father was a history professor."

"No, Bernard was the big fucking liar." He picked up

a stack of papers from the worktable. "I checked the University of Louisville's faculty roster going all the way back to when the school was founded. It *says* Bernard Sabian taught history there from 1957 until his death in 1968."

"He did."

"No!" Peter slammed the stack onto the table. "His name was added *after* he died."

"That's insane! Who would—"

"The Bureau—or rather, the organization that would become the Bureau." He held up the photo again. "I believe you'll recognize the names Damian Alberez, Morgan Dreyer, Woody Phelps, who now sits on the Bureau Tribunal, as you know, and Gregor Wahl—oh, yes, and of course your father and Varik Baudelaire."

She clenched her jaw but said nothing.

"They were partners, your father and Varik," he explained, pointing to each individual as he named them. "You see, Daddy Dearest started life as a Hunter. Yes, underneath that lovable exterior, your sainted father was a cold-hearted, murdering bastard."

"You're lying," she whispered.

"Sadly, no." He sighed and continued his story. "Once Phelps discovered Bernard's ability to enter the Shadowlands and, more specifically, the Hall of Records, he was removed from active duty. He—along with the other Talents, as they were called—would routinely scan the vampire population using their psychic abilities, looking for rogues and violations of vampiric law. However, Bernard was given a very special assignment: he was told to scan only other Hunters, including the Talents, for signs of turning rogue."

He tapped his finger on Baudelaire's likeness. "Any Hunter or Talent found to be rogue was turned over to Lover Boy, who then dealt with them as quickly and quietly as possible. You see, while Bernard had psychic talents, Varik's talents lie in killing. He became one of the most feared Hunters of all times."

He shrugged. "Well, at least he *was* until he killed an innocent boy who was in the wrong place at the wrong time and swore never to kill again. He then moved on to training other Hunters, and eventually Enforcers, which is how the two of you met."

His gaze drifted to the dark-haired woman standing to the left of Bernard. "Siobhan Kelly." Peter smiled. "You recognize the name, don't you?"

She leaned her head back against the faux wall housing the restraint devices. "No."

"Now who's lying, darling?"

"I'm not your fucking *darling*, asshole!"

"Not yet."

"Not *ever*."

"We'll see about that." He set the folder and photo on the worktable. "I'll give you time to think about what I've said. Shall we continue in the morning?"

She rested her head against the faux wall once more, refusing to look in his direction.

He hopped down the attic stairs and opened the hidden door into the hallway. As he made his way to his bedroom, a sense of satisfaction enveloped him. Everything was going according to plan and once he finished showing her the extent of the lies that framed her life, she would willingly sever the bond to Varik and finally give herself over to him.

twenty

ALEX HAD BEEN MISSING FOR NEARLY NINETEEN HOURS, and Varik drifted in numbness.

The memory of Alex screaming his name over the blood-bond continued to haunt him. If he closed his eyes, he could still feel a specter of her touch, a spark of her mind's warmth. He wanted to reclaim them both and knew, as he sat in the mobile forensics lab, that it was possible with the help of the two analysts before him, if he could muster the energy to focus on their words.

Reyes Cott stood in front of him, gesturing to a porcelain doll encased in a large clear plastic evidence cylinder. "It's supercreepy," he said. His overly large eyes protruded farther than normal. "I've seen some weird shit but this doll beats it all."

"Spare me the melodrama, Reyes," Varik snapped. "Just tell me what you found."

"Human blood."

"On the doll?"

"*In* the doll." Reyes picked up the cylinder. "As you know, the body is made from human skin that's been turned into a type of leather, which is itself very high on the creep-o-meter, but the real show is in the porcelain head. At one time it was filled with human blood. A crack along the neck caused the blood to seep out."

"Why fill a doll's head with blood?"

"Good question. Why make the body out of human skin?" Reyes set the cylinder aside. "I think I have an answer to both." He jiggled the mouse connected to his laptop computer and the monitor flickered from a screen saver to a website. "I found this site—it's sort of like Wikipedia for occult practices—and there's a bunch of stuff on here about poppet magic, or using dolls as a stand-in for a real person."

"Voodoo dolls," Varik said, pushing to his feet to view the site over Reyes's shoulder.

"Not exactly. Voodoo's a religion, whereas a lot of what's detailed on this site is just straight-up magic. Really freaky magic." Reyes clicked on a series of links and an article featuring a lifelike doll with glowing red eyes appeared.

Varik leaned forward. "Soul transference?"

"According to the author of this article, a portion of the soul can be trapped in a vessel, in this case a doll, and used to boost the creator's *prana,* or psychic energy."

"Which is what vampires feed on when we consume human blood."

"Precisely." Reyes tapped the screen. "Now, going back to what we discussed yesterday, I'm thinking if this *is* possible, and you *could* perfect the storage devices and get enough of them, the need to consume blood would practically flatline, once you overcame the cravings for the taste."

"Alex said she heard hundreds of screams in the Dollmaker's house."

"If he does have hundreds of these and if he has any form of psychic ability, which you say he does, each one of these would act as a battery. The guy would be turbocharged."

Varik straightened up and sighed. "That would explain why the bond has been cold. He's blocking it somehow."

"But that has to be taxing, regardless of the number of spare batteries."

"Is there *anything* this doll can tell us about who he is?"

Reyes smiled, showing a crooked left fang. "I saved the best part for last. Because I'm such a thorough guy, I checked out this doll from stem to stern, so to speak. I found a partial print embedded in the porcelain underneath the doll's wig. I used a high-tech modeling compound to get a workable negative—"

"He stuck Silly Putty to the doll's head and then froze it," Freddy Haver chimed in from his station across the lab.

"Hey, it worked. You said it wouldn't, and you still owe me twenty bucks."

Varik seized the back of Reyes's neck and squeezed, earning a pained squeak from the analyst. "You could use your mother's face to get the print. I don't care how you got it. I want to know whom it belongs to. Understand?"

"Yes, sir."

"Did you get a hit from IAFIS or VIPER?"

"Freddy has it."

Varik released him and moved to Freddy's station. It was standard procedure to submit all prints to IAFIS—the Integrated Automated Fingerprint Identification System maintained by the human-run FBI—as well as its twin, the Vampire Identification Patterns and Enforcement Resource, or VIPER. The systems were maintained separately since vampire fingerprints weren't as pronounced as humans' and were often overlooked by them as smudges.

Freddy handed him two sheets of paper. "VIPER lists the print as belonging to Peter Strahan. I knew you wanted it so I put a rush on the request for a current address for Strahan—5726 Caspian Drive. It's in the southeastern part of Nassau County. The second page is a map showing—"

Varik didn't wait to hear more. He took the pages and in two paces had reached the lab's entrance. "Radio Damian and tell him where to meet me!"

Forgoing the steps, he jumped from the converted RV to the pavement, his feet already in motion as he hit the ground. "Hang on, baby," he muttered, running for his Corvette. "I'm coming."

Alex banged the back of her head against the wall in frustration. A lunatic laboring under the delusion that she was his soul mate held her captive, and all she could think of at that moment was her growling stomach.

She'd passed the night trying to get free of Peter's elaborate restraints to no avail. After she'd worn herself out she'd slept fitfully for a time since standing up wasn't the most comfortable of positions and her slumber was plagued by nightmares.

In her dreams, winged demons and skeletal monsters chased her through an endless stone labyrinth. Shadows brandishing fiery swords stood guard at the exits. She'd been driven deeper and deeper into the maze. She called to Varik as she ran but it only seemed to spur the things pursuing her to quicken their pace. She finally awoke, to find herself still tied to a wall in a windowless attic and at the mercy of the Dollmaker.

At least her eyesight had improved. Gone were the fuzzy grayness and amorphous dark blobs. Now she could see individual objects, although they were out of focus and blurry, and could discern different colors. So long as Peter believed she was still blind, perhaps she could use it to her advantage and find a way to escape.

Trying to distract herself from the increasing amount of noise coming from her gut, her attention centered on the photo Peter had left on a table a few feet away. Everything he told her about it was a lie. It had to be. Her father wasn't a Hunter. He'd taught history.

But how could she explain the photograph? If it was even a photograph at all. From this distance, until her eyes made another improvement, she couldn't even be sure it *was* a photo.

The simplest answer was to rule it a fabrication, a product of clever computer manipulation.

But then, where did Peter find source photos of her father, Varik, Damian, and all the others?

The more she tried to deny the authenticity of what he told her, the more questions she raised that had no simple answer.

What if Peter *was* telling the truth? What if her father had been a Hunter and had been partnered with Varik? It would mean everything she knew about her father was a lie. Her relationship with Varik, past and present, would also be a lie.

It would mean the blood-bond was a lie, and she was forever bound to a man she couldn't trust.

However, she couldn't allow herself to dwell on such matters. She needed to find a way to convince Peter to release her from the restraints so she could escape. The kernel of a plan formed in her mind and soon blossomed. But in order for it to work, she would have—

Singing from the floor below the attic intruded on her musings. Footsteps on the stairs and the smell of freshly cooked sausage, eggs, and coffee signaled Peter's approach. He bounded into the attic with a spring in his step, humming a ballad, and carrying a large wooden tray. "Did you miss me, darling?"

She bit back her sharp retort. She needed to do whatever she had to do to survive, to escape, and angering him wasn't a part of her plan.

Peter set the tray, complete with a glass bud vase containing a single long-stemmed red rose, on a corner of the worktable. "I cooked some of your favorites—scrambled eggs with cheese, spicy sausage patties, grits with extra butter, and of course, coffee."

Alex's stomach churned with the thought of eating anything he'd cooked. She swallowed her discomfort and offered a weak smile. "Thank you. It smells wonderful."

He beamed and picked up a fork. "Well, where shall we start? Eggs or grits? This could get a little messy, but . . ." He shrugged.

Alex laughed nervously. "Uh, darling . . ."

Peter hesitated, looking at her with suspicion.

"Before we start, I thought we could do without these restraints, and we could sit and eat together and talk."

He shook his head, still smiling, and picked up the plate of eggs. "You'll just try to run again, my tricky chickie."

"No, I won't. I've been thinking about what you said and want to know more."

He looked unconvinced but set down the eggs and fork.

She tried to shift her weight and winced. "Plus my wrist is hurting, really bad," she said, giving her words a slight whine. "Please, Peter."

He was in front of her before she realized he moved. His hands cupped the sides of her face, keeping her from looking away. "Say my name again."

"Peter."

His lips closed over hers and Alex forced herself to

remain still, to not succumb to the urge to bite him as he kissed her.

He stepped back and grinned. "I knew you would come around, darling. Now, let's get you out of these restraints."

Alex waited as he first unbound her torso and then her legs. Lastly he freed her arms, but kept a tight grip on her injured wrist so she had to grit her teeth to keep from whimpering.

"Just one last bit of business, darling," he said as he forced her into a chair at the worktable. He produced a set of plastic zip-tie cuffs and looped one end over her uninjured wrist.

"What are these for? I thought we were going to talk."

"We are." He looped the other end over the chair's ladder-style back. "There, that should do it." He gave her another quick kiss. "After you've cleaned your plate we'll discuss taking those off."

Alex tried to remain cheery while he placed the plate of eggs and sausage patties in front of her. She picked up the fork and thought for a moment of gouging out his eyes but dug into the eggs instead. She would need her strength for the next part of her plan to work.

She shoveled the first forkful of cheesy scrambled eggs into her mouth. The softness of the eggs combined with the slightly oily bite of the cheese made her mouth water and her stomach grumble.

Peter smiled. "You like it?"

She hated to admit it but she nodded, spearing a piece of sausage with her fork. It was tender inside and slightly crispy outside. Peppery spices exploded across her tongue and she had to stifle a satisfied groan.

"Now that we're together, darling, I'll make all your favorites—key lime pie, sweet-and-sour chicken, shrimp scampi." He poured a cup of steaming dark coffee and set it beside her. "I even have your favorite movies on DVD. We can pop popcorn and watch *To Kill a Mockingbird* anytime you want."

She swallowed the soft mass of eggs that had suddenly turned cold in her mouth. "How do you know so much about me?"

"We're soul mates, darling," he answered as if that explained everything.

"But I've only just met you. I've been blood-bound to Varik for years and—"

"Do not speak his name!" Peter's fist crashed onto the table with the force of a gunshot. "You will *never* speak of him again!"

Alex recoiled from his anger. "I don't understand. If you and I are soul mates, as you say, what harm can there be—"

"He is a deceiver," Peter hissed. "He tried to steal you from me. The sooner you forget about him the better."

Alex toyed with the coffee cup. "And if I don't want to forget about him?"

He grabbed her jaw, fingers digging into an already-tender bruise, and forced her to look at him. "You *will* forget about him. I'll see to that."

"I'd like to see you try," she spat and flung the scalding coffee into his face.

He shrieked and released her, trying to wipe the burning liquid from his eyes.

Alex jumped to her feet, grabbed the back of her wooden chair, and with a roar, smashed it across his back. The chair shattered, and Peter collapsed onto the table, groaning. The zip-tie looped around the chair's back slipped loose, and she dashed for the attic exit. She neared the top of the stairs when Peter's hand grabbed her hair and pulled her back.

His leg swiped hers and threw her to the floor. He covered her with his body, pinning her like a moth stuck to a specimen board. "That's the last time you're going to do that, tricky chickie," he snarled, inches from her face.

"Go to Hell," she growled.

He gently stroked her face and then entwined his fingers in her hair. A savage grin split his face. "You first."

Alex felt the floor drop away beneath them, and she screamed as he forced his way into her mind.

Hurtling down Interstate 55 at speeds nearing one hundred miles an hour, Tasha reconsidered the wisdom of agreeing to ride with Damian and his Enforcers as they raced to catch up with Varik. However, time had been a factor and she hadn't been afforded the luxury of rational thought. Damian had simply held open the rear door of the black Ford Expedition and told her to get in or get left the fuck behind. She'd gotten in. Now she was sandwiched between two Enforcers decked out in body armor and carrying more firepower than she'd seen short of the last open house day at the National Guard Armory.

"Talk to me, Reyes," Damian barked into the handheld radio from the front seat. "What can you tell me about Strahan?"

"Not much, unfortunately," Reyes Cott answered amid the static. "His record's surprisingly clean."

"I find it hard to believe one of the most prolific serial killers in history never had a run-in with the law somewhere."

"That's my point. I'm not finding *any* records for Peter Strahan before 2003."

"How is that possible?" Damian asked. "There has to be *something*—driver's license, tax records . . ."

"*Nada,*" Reyes said. "No credit cards, bank accounts, parking tickets—nothing. I can't even find a birth certificate. The guy's a fucking ghost, sir."

"How was he able to buy a house without even so much as a driver's license?" Damian asked.

Reyes issued a low whistle. "He didn't buy it. He inherited it."

"Inherited from whom?"

"Benjamin Corman."

"Wait a second." Tasha sat forward and grabbed the radio from Damian. "Is this the Cottonwood property?"

"Yes, ma'am," Reyes said. "Court documents refer to it by that name and they're all I've been able to dig up on Strahan."

"I was out there yesterday," Tasha said to Damian. "No one answered the door when I knocked. The place looked deserted."

Damian's fist slammed down onto the dash. "Goddamn it!" He took the radio back from Tasha. "Reyes, Strahan's a fucking vulture. He's been tailing Sabian for years, that much we know. Expand your search to include Louisville and surrounding areas. Look for properties like this plantation. Those will be his targeted marks."

"Yes, sir."

"What do you mean he's a vulture?" Tasha asked.

"The fucker lives off carrion," Damian explained. "He waits for someone to die and then uses a fabricated identification to swoop in and pick the estate clean. He'll hop from one to the other, changing identities each time. Peter Strahan is just a shell name. That's why we can't find information on him."

"How do you determine his real ID?"

"The only way is to keep him alive and question him."

"But he's killed hundreds of humans," Tasha exclaimed. "That gives him an automatic death sentence."

"We have a body for one, and we can't conclusively tie it to him yet."

"He has Alex. Surely kidnapping a federal agent is something you can pin on him."

"That we can make stick, but depending on what we find when we get there, he could be sentenced to prison instead of death."

"Which gives you plenty of time to question him."

Damian fixed his golden eyes on her. "Only if we catch Baudelaire in time, otherwise there may not be anything left of Strahan to question."

twenty-one

VARIK KILLED HIS CORVETTE'S ENGINE AND COASTED TO a stop outside the sprawling Caspian Drive farmhouse. The original house had been added onto in a haphazard fashion over the years with each addition featuring the dominant style of the period. Tying the disparate architectural elements to one another was the commonality of dingy and peeling white paint. The overall effect gave the house an appearance of a bloated toad lying in wait for its next meal.

He grabbed his Glock and badge and stepped from the car, leaving his cell phone behind. Gravel crunched beneath his boots as he cautiously approached the house. Experience tempered the instinct to rush inside and shout Alex's name. This was the Dollmaker's domain and as such it gave an advantage to his opponent. Varik would have to proceed carefully and hope he found Alex before—

He shook his head to clear it of negative thoughts. He couldn't afford to be distracted by the what-ifs.

Ancient cement steps crumbled in protest of his weight and porch boards creaked underfoot as he glided up the front stoop to the door. A screen door hung to the side but the weather-beaten main door swung open easily when he turned the knob.

Crouching to make for a smaller target, he entered the dark foyer and toed the door shut, pausing to allow his eyes time to adjust to the gloom. Blocky shadows slowly identified themselves as display cases and shelves clung to the walls, each holding an inventory of dolls whose eyes seemed to follow his movements.

He slipped through an archway and into what he assumed would've been a dining room if it held a table and chairs instead of floor-to-ceiling shelves. Hundreds of dolls watched him as he checked corners for hidden dangers. The room was thick with the stench of leather and old blood, and he was forced to sip the air to prevent himself from gagging.

Methodically, he checked each of the main rooms on the first floor and found nothing save more dolls. He eased into the foyer, passed a small fireplace, and headed for the stairs. Moving to their base, he glanced up quickly, holding his Glock at the ready, and saw only more darkness. The entire house was silent and void of any apparent signs of life.

As he mounted the first step, worry gnawed at him. What if he was too late? What if Alex had already been moved to another location, or worse, killed?

He thrust the thoughts aside. He would *not* succumb to his fears.

Hugging the wall, he slowly climbed the stairs to the second floor.

Peter crashed through the flimsy mental shields Alexandra tried to erect. Every barrier she placed before him, he knocked aside. He would not be denied. He would strip away all her memories of Varik Baudelaire and give her new memories—*his* memories.

He plunged into her mind, pressing against the last of her shields until it collapsed. He sensed her fleeing before him, trying to hide from him. He pursued and cornered her, enveloping her consciousness with his.

Get out of my head! Anger colored her thoughts a bright red.

Love me.

No!

It wasn't a request, my tricky chickie.

She screamed and lashed out, and he backed away. She lunged at him in an attempt to drive him out.

He deflected her assault, using the momentary opening to dive into her core. He burned a path through her subconscious. Thousands of memories flashed before him, but he was only interested in a select few. Images of Varik appeared and he delighted in reducing them to cinders. Some he replaced with those of his choosing and others he left to smolder, consigned to the realm of the forgotten.

A memory of her first kiss with Varik played before him. They were covered in mud and hiking up a steep riverbank. She stumbled and fell into his arms. They laughed and suddenly Varik kissed her.

Hatred fueled Peter's attack. The memory exploded before him and he felt her shudder as he ripped another hole in her mind. A new memory stitched itself into the fabric of her subconscious, one in which *he* caught her as she fell and *he* kissed her.

A flash of yellow passed through her mind and he paused. Something tickled the back of his brain. Following the sensation, he withdrew from her mind and returned to his own.

He groaned, weak from the effort of changing her past, and fell to the attic floor beside her unmoving form. His head pounded with a chorus of voices, shouting and screaming for help. The dolls were crying out, calling to—

Peter bolted to his feet, staring at the attic floor as if he could see through it.

He was here, in the house.

Peter growled and rushed to the attic stairs. Now was the time for him to take what he started in her memory and finish it in his reality.

Varik stopped his search of the second floor when he heard a faint *thump*. He waited, hoping to hear the sound again to determine its direction, but the house refused to give up its secrets.

He entered a bedroom and the familiar scent of jasmine and vanilla rocked him. His pulse tripled and his breath came in sharp, shallow gulps.

Alex had been in there, recently.

Circling the bed, he noted the signs of a struggle and knelt before a window. A few drops of blood stained the hardwood floor. He dipped his finger in one of the congealed puddles and rubbed together his finger and thumb. The warmth of his skin released a faint smell of leather and decay.

He stood, wiping the blood on the leg of his jeans. It was the Dollmaker's blood, not Alex's, and he suppressed a smile. If she was fighting hard enough to draw blood, his chances of locating her greatly increased.

Another *thump* sounded nearby and this time he was able to determine it came from the hallway. Sliding to the door, he peeked around the corner and saw only an empty corridor. He waited a moment in case someone appeared from one of the other rooms. The hall remained empty.

Varik left the bedroom to resume his search, passing an oversized print of Duchamp's *Nude Descending a Staircase*. A small draft ruffled his hair as he passed, and the scent of jasmine and vanilla combined with leather and old blood hit him once more. He turned back to the framed print as it swung outward and a body slammed into him, knocking him to the floor and sending his Glock tumbling down the stairs.

He used the momentum of his attacker and kicked upward with both feet, launching the assailant over his head. Varik completed the backward somersault motion to land in a kneeling position.

A tall blond vamp charged him, the flash of metal in his hands.

Varik blocked one blow but the other found its target. He grunted as a scalpel sliced open a gash along his left biceps. The blond vamp continued to slash at him. Varik gathered his legs beneath him and, with a roar, launched himself into the other's midsection.

They crashed into the wall beside the stairs, cracking plaster and sending plumes of dust into the air. Varik used his knee to dislodge one of the scalpels while he kept a grip on the Dollmaker's other arm.

Peter used his scalpel-free hand to punch Varik in the side of the throat. Varik gagged and stumbled back. He tried to clumsily dodge another swipe with the remaining scalpel but the thin blade connected with his chest, opening a wound diagonally from his right shoulder to his breastbone.

"She's mine," Peter snarled, dropping into a crouch. "She came to me!"

"You *took* her," Varik snapped as they circled.

"I *saved* her! I showed her the truth about you, about her father, and now she loves *me,* not you." He smiled. "She's already forgotten all about you."

The blood-bond opened and Varik cried out as pain seared his mind. He sank to his knees, helpless as Peter manipulated the bond to show him the hell in Alex's mind.

Memories—*their* memories—were nearly all gone, burned away and new ones erected in their place. Tears of agony tracked down his cheeks as he writhed on the floor at the Dollmaker's feet.

"You see now," Peter said calmly, kneeling beside Varik. "I've already touched her more deeply than you could ever dream of doing."

Varik groaned as another wave of fire burned his brain.

"I made her forget about you. Only a few memories to go and then she'll be completely mine." He grabbed the front of Varik's bloody shirt, pulled him to his feet, and walked him to the stairs. "And after I kill you, I'll finish what I started. I'll mindfuck her and when she no longer even remembers your name, I'll fuck her body until she cries out *my* name."

Teetering on the edge of the first step, Varik growled, "I'll kill you first."

"You can try."

Varik frantically grabbed for Peter and then the stair railing as he was shoved backward. He hung suspended in mid-air for a moment before crashing into the hard edges of the staircase. He felt something snap in his lower left leg as he tumbled head over heels to land in a battered heap at the bottom.

Laughter rang from above. "And he sticks the landing!"

Using the banisters and handrail, Varik maneuvered into sitting position. Footsteps banged on the stairs overhead. Groaning with the effort, he pushed to his feet and gritted his teeth, ignoring the sharp pain in his left leg as he hobbled to the fireplace. He found a set of rusted iron tools and grabbed the longest poker.

Peter skipped the last two steps, laughing as Varik haltingly turned to face him and hefted the poker like a bat. "You're going to beat me to death with a poker?" He snorted with laughter. "Oh, now *that's* original."

"Who said it was for you, asshole?" Varik rasped and swung the poker at the nearest display case.

"No!"

Glass shattered and porcelain doll heads disintegrated. The stench of decay intensified as the blood contained within the heads was exposed to the air for the first time since being sealed away.

Peter shrieked and clutched his head in pain.

Varik raked a line of dolls off a shelf, destroying them.

Peter howled.

He smashed another display case.

Peter roared and leapt forward.

Varik met his charge, thrusting the poker like a sword before him. The poker pierced Peter's flesh below the breastbone, impaling him on the hooked end.

The Dollmaker dropped to his knees, eyes wide. He clawed at Varik and blood bubbled from his mouth as he tried to speak, but no words came forth.

Varik released the poker and let him crumple to the floor. For the first time, he heard sirens wailing, growing louder as they approached. His eyes shot to the stairs. "Alex."

Using the wall for balance, he stepped over the struggling vampire and limped toward the stairs. He reached the steps and balanced himself between the wall and handrail. On one foot, he bunny-hopped up the first flight.

Sirens whooped outside as Damian and the others arrived. Varik gritted his teeth and repeated the process to hop up the remaining flight of stairs to the second floor.

Downstairs, the front door banged open and a cacophony of shouts filled the house.

Varik located the oversized Duchamp print in the hallway. He knew it concealed a door, if he could just find the opening trigger.

"Varik!" Damian's voice boomed downstairs.

He didn't answer. He ran a hand over the edges of the ornate frame and felt a hidden latch. When he flipped the trigger, the concealed door swung open to reveal another narrow set of stairs.

"Baudelaire!" Damian called. "Answer me, goddamn it!"

He tried to bunny-hop the new stairs but their narrowness prevented it. "Alex!" He listened for a response or any sign of movement. "If you can hear me, answer me, baby!"

Silence rang in his ears.

Fear spurred him into action. Grimacing with each step that scraped over his injured leg, he crawled on hands and knees up the stairs.

He reached the attic and saw Alex lying motionless a few feet from the stairs. "Alex?"

She didn't move.

"Baby," he called, crawling to her. "Baby, it's me. I'm here." Her face was turned away and he gently moved her head toward him.

Unseeing emerald eyes stared into his soul.

"Alex?" He shook her shoulders. "Alexandra!" He felt for a pulse at her throat and found none. "No, no, no! Don't do this to me! Alex!"

Stampeding footsteps rushed up the stairs. Damian and two Enforcers carrying medical kits entered the attic. One of the medics knelt beside Alex and began CPR while the other attempted to check Varik's wounds.

"I'm fine," he growled and pushed the medic away. "Help her."

The medic glanced at Alex and then Damian, who nodded, and the medic slid over to assist his partner.

Varik stayed beside her, holding her hand. "I can't lose her, Damian," he whispered as the big vampire squatted next to him. "Not like this."

Damian gave his shoulder a reassuring squeeze.

As the medics continued to work on Alex, tears fell from Varik's face to land on Alex's hand. Minutes ticked by with no change and it took Varik a moment to realize the medics had ceased their effort.

"Why did you stop? Don't stop! She's not—" His words ended in a strangled choke. "She's not . . ."

"Varik," Damian said softly. "They've done all they can. She's gone."

He shook his head. "No. I don't believe that. I would know. I would *feel* it!"

"You have to let her go."

"No!" Varik shoved Damian away. "She's not dead! We're bond-mates! I would know!" Pain ripped through him, tearing his soul in two. He brushed away the hair from her face. "I would know," he whispered.

He gently gathered her in his arms. As he looked into her unblinking eyes, anger burned away his grief and he lifted his head, shouting at the ceiling. "Bernard! You bring her back to me! Do you hear me? Bring her back like you brought me back!"

Fresh tears flowed in the tracks left by others as he looked down at Alex. "Bring her back," he whispered. He rocked in place with her. "Bring her back . . . bring her back . . . bring her back . . ."

twenty-two

ALEX OPENED HER EYES AND DISCOVERED A GRAY GRAN-
ite tombstone inches from her face. She sat up, looking
around at the rows of stone monuments and scattered
trees. It was a landscape she knew too well—St. Michael's
Cemetery in Louisville, the place where she'd discovered her father's body.

Resting her back against the grave marker, she tried
to remember what happened and how she'd gotten to
the Shadowlands. Her mind was a jumble of distorted
images and emotions. The more she tried to make sense
of it, the less sense the images actually made.

"Hello, Princess."

She wasn't surprised to see her father strolling
toward her. "Hi, Daddy."

He stopped in front of her. Worry knitted his brow as
he studied her.

His silence wore on her. "Is there something wrong?
Do I have something in my teeth?"

"How did you get here, Princess?"

She shrugged. "I don't know. I mean, I just sort of
woke up here. Why?"

"Look behind you."

Alex glanced over her shoulder at the tombstone and
gasped. She spun around in order to better see the name
carved in the stone. "Is this real?"

"It can be. It's for you to decide."

She traced the outline of each letter with her finger:

Alexandra Marie Sabian. "Am I dead?" she whispered, looking to him as he knelt beside her.

"Mostly. Your physical body has no heartbeat, no breath, no pulse, but you haven't fully crossed over into the spirit realm. Your soul's in limbo, for lack of a better term, which is how you came to be here in the Shadowlands."

Her head pounded in a staccato rhythm and she groaned, massaging her temples. Memories pressed forward, demanding her attention, only to be replaced by others in an overlapping and confusing tapestry. "How did it happen? I mean, how did I die?"

"You don't remember?"

"No. I remember being in an attic with someone." A recent memory presented itself and she shuddered. "Peter—it was Peter. He attacked me, entered my mind." A specter of pain rippled through her. "Oh, Daddy . . . he—" A choking sob replaced her words as the images playing in her mind fell into place and began to make sense.

Her father gathered her in his arms, holding her tightly while his own voice shook. "I'm sorry, Princess. I'm sorry I couldn't help you."

Alex clung to him as painful sobs racked her. "He stole them," she choked. "My memories. Destroyed them."

He held on to her and let her cry.

After several minutes, her sobbing turned to faltering gasps and loud sniffles. "Why? Why would he do that?"

"Peter is insane, Princess. You can't look for rhyme or reason with someone like him."

False memories of a life with Peter played in vivid color, but a few memories of Varik subverted the counterfeit ones, flowing beneath the surface in shades of gray and creating a confusing mess in her head. It was as though she'd experienced two separate, yet parallel, lives: one with Varik and one with Peter. "How can I still have some of these memories of Varik as well as the ones Peter planted in my head?"

"The more powerful the memory, the harder it is to destroy. Plus you share a blood-bond with Varik. The bond will preserve some shared memories. It's also why you haven't crossed over to the spirit realm. Varik's keeping you connected to the physical."

Alex pushed away from him, wiping her eyes. "Am I stuck here? A lost soul—like you?"

He gave her a half-smile. "No, Princess, but you do have to decide if you want to cross over or go back." He held up his hand to stop her from speaking. "Before you say anything, you should know if you cross over, the false memories Peter implanted will disappear. You'll retain all your memories of the life you lived and of Varik."

"If I choose to go back?"

"The memories Peter destroyed will be lost and those he gave to you will take their place."

"But you said the bond will retain some of the memories. Will I ever recover those?"

"In time, perhaps, and with Varik's help, but you should also know, Princess, the damage Peter caused was extensive. If you go back, you'll only have a partial memory of Varik."

"It'll be like I'm blood-bound to a virtual stranger."

He nodded.

She slumped against the headstone bearing her name. "I need time to think."

Her father stood and sighed. "Of course, but don't wait too long. The longer you're away from your body, the harder the transition will be if you decide to return."

Alex watched him walk away and disappear among a small stand of trees. She drew her knees up to her chest, wrapped her arms around her shins, and rested her head on her knees in an effort to hide from the predicament in which she found herself.

In order to retain her memories of Varik, she had to die. However, she could live out her life with him if she returned, but she would bear the false memories implanted by Peter. Regardless of her choice, she would lose Varik in some way, whether it was their past or their future.

Assuming they had a future. If she returned, she still faced a Tribunal inquiry. If they ruled against her and found her guilty of corruption, the verdict would carry an automatic death sentence. If she crossed over to the spirit realm now, there would be no inquiry.

But could she be so selfish? Wasn't it better to answer to the charges and spend any remaining time with Varik, even if that time was spent getting to know each other again?

She raised her head and was surprised to see a young boy dressed in wet clothes sitting on the headstone across from her.

"Hi," he said, a familiar smile lighting his pale face.

"Hi, Edward." She leaned back against her headstone and sighed. "What are you doing here?"

He shrugged. "I wanted to see you."

"How did you know I was here?"

"I heard Papa crying. I think he misses you."

She swallowed the painful lump that had formed in her throat. "I miss him, too."

"Are you dead?"

"Not exactly. I'm in limbo."

"I'm dead." He swung his legs back and forth, his heels scuffing along the back of the headstone on which he perched. "What does 'limbo' mean?"

"It means I have to decide if I want to go back or move on."

"You could stay here."

"I don't think that's an option for me."

"If you go back, Papa will be happy again. He's always happy when he's with you."

A smile tugged at Alex's lips. "Yeah, he makes me happy, too."

Edward grinned, reminding her so much of Varik, and Alex knew there could be only one choice for her.

Tasha paused to allow the medics exiting the attic to pass before she scurried up the steps. Word had spread quickly of Alex and she hadn't believed it.

Until now.

She hovered close to the stairs, watching in silence as Varik cradled Alex to his chest and slowly rocked in place with her. His hushed chant of "bring her back" was the only sound in the room.

Damian moved to stand beside her. "Any word on Strahan?"

Tasha shook her head. "They're still working to stabilize him."

He nodded grimly.

"What are you going to do about him?" Tasha whispered, nodding toward Varik. "And her family?"

"I'll deliver the news to her family personally. As for him, he needs medical attention. Some of those cuts are deep." Damian sighed. "There's only one thing to do."

Tasha watched as he stepped forward and knelt opposite Varik, speaking in low tones.

Varik remained unchanged, as if he hadn't heard.

Damian reached for Alex's body and Varik came to life. He grabbed the larger vampire's wrist and growled. When Damian laid his other hand on Varik's shoulder, Varik released the arm he held to bat away the other hand. The two began a war of hands that ultimately ended with Varik grabbing Damian's sidearm and shoving it in the Chief Enforcer's face.

"Get out," Varik commanded. "No one touches her. She's coming back. She can't be moved."

"Varik," Damian addressed him calmly. "Put the gun down."

"I said, get out."

"She's not coming back."

"Don't make me kill you, Damian."

Tasha held her breath as the two vampires faced off over Alex's body. Varik's reluctance to accept Alex's death was understandable. Even though she'd had her own issues with Alex, it didn't prevent her from feeling the loss.

Movement drew Tasha's attention to Alex and she frowned. Had her fingers twitched? She watched and jumped when she saw the fingers on Alex's left hand close. "Oh, my God," she said, pointing at the newly formed fist. "Look at her hand!"

Damian and Varik both glanced at her and then down.

Alex suddenly drew a deep breath and immediately coughed it out again.

Varik dropped the gun to help Alex as she fought to sit up.

Damian was already on his feet, running to the stairs and shouting for the medics.

Tasha stood frozen in place, watching as Alex greedily took in more breaths and coughed them up. Varik continued to speak to her, reassuring her, trying everything he could to help her breathe.

The medics bounded up the stairs, pushing Tasha into a corner in their haste to reach Alex. Everything that followed seemed to happen faster than her brain could interrupt.

One of the medics slipped a portable oxygen mask

over the struggling vampire's mouth and nose. The hiss of gas feeding into tubing filled the room. The medics began checking the revived vampire, asking questions, and receiving weak answers.

Another pair of Enforcers, carrying a bright orange stretcher board, clambered up the attic stairs. They moved with efficiency to transfer Alex to the stretcher, strap her down, and hoist the board.

Damian grabbed his sidearm and then wrapped his arm around Varik's waist. The injured vampire leaned against the other and the two made a rapid, albeit awkward, descent in the wake of the team in charge of transporting Alex.

Within minutes, Tasha was left standing alone in the attic. Not knowing what else to do, she turned toward the stairs and felt dampness on her face. She swiped a hand over her cheek, expecting the clear wetness of tears.

A crimson stain covered her hand and another drop fell from above to add to it.

Looking into the rafters, Tasha gasped and then screamed as the silvered eyes of Mindy Johnson stared back at her.

"Damian?" Emily asked upon answering her cell phone. "Did you—"

"We've got her," Damian interjected.

She exhaled the breath she felt she'd been holding since Damian first called hours prior to say they had a lead on Alex's location. Looking over to Stephen where he sat on the edge of Janet's hospital bed, she smiled and gave them a thumbs-up. Stephen whooped and Janet clapped.

"She and Varik are on their way to the hospital now."

Emily waved for Stephen and Janet to curb their celebration. "How badly are they hurt?"

"Varik's cut up pretty bad, possible broken leg."

"And Alex?"

"There's no easy way to say this . . ."

"Is she—" Emily choked back a sob. "Is she dead?"

"She *was* but we got her back."

Emily could no longer contain her tears. It didn't matter that she hadn't given birth to Alex. She'd raised her from infancy, had been there for every triumph and every setback. All that mattered now was her daughter was alive. "Thank you, Damian, for everything."

He muttered a response and Emily pressed the button to end the call.

Stephen was at her side before she was able to lay the phone aside. "Mom? Is Alex—"

Emily hugged him, cutting off his question. "She's alive," she cried. "She's alive!"

She wasn't certain how long the two of them embraced with their tears soaking each other's shoulder. She released Stephen when her cell phone rang again. While Stephen sought solace in Janet's arms, Emily checked the caller display on her phone:

INCOMING CALL—GREGOR WAHL.

Emily stood and left the room before answering. "Gregor, I was getting worried. Where—"

"Hello, Emily," a woman's voice said.

A chill started at the base of her brain and traced down her spine. "Who is this?"

The woman chuckled, a familiar sound that sent another shiver through Emily. "Come now, Emily. Surely you remember me."

Something in the laugh, in the musicality of the voice . . . "Siobhan?"

"So you *do* remember me. That's good. That's *very* good."

"Where's Gregor?"

"I'm afraid your dear Mr. Wahl is unavailable at the moment. You see, he found someone who didn't want to be found."

"Siobhan, what did you do to Gregor?"

"What did *I* do? No, Emily, *I* didn't do anything to Gregor, but because *you* broke your oath—"

"I didn't! I haven't told anyone, I swear!"

"*Someone* did, and since the only people who knew of our arrangement were Bernard, you, and me, that leaves two choices, Emily."

"No, there has to be someone else."

"There isn't anyone else. The pact is broken and now I'm coming to collect what is mine."

"Siobhan, please—"

The open line suddenly closed and she was gone.

Shaking, Emily pressed the button to power down her phone. Chaos reigned in her mind.

Where had Siobhan been all these years?

What had happened to Gregor?

Who else could know of the pact she and Bernard had made with Siobhan?

What was to become of Alex?

As she headed for the elevators to travel down to the emergency room and await the arrival of Alex and Varik, Emily couldn't shake the feeling that decisions made in the coming weeks would change many lives.

Forever.

twenty-three

"A LITTLE TO THE LEFT," ALEX DIRECTED AND GRUNTED in frustration as Stephen moved her new couch to the right. "I meant *my* left."

"Will you make up your mind?" Stephen grumbled. "This thing weighs a fucking ton."

"Don't curse," Emily said as she entered the open front door of Alex's newly renovated apartment carrying half a dozen sacks of groceries. She dropped them on the kitchen counter and brushed a stray silver curl out of her eyes. "Alexandra, are you sure you want to *cook* Thanksgiving dinner?"

"Yeah," Stephen groaned as he set down the couch and then sprawled across it. "Your previous culinary efforts usually ended with a broken smoke alarm and fifty bucks' worth of Chinese takeout."

"Shut up." Alex smacked the back of his head. She dodged his return slap, laughing. "Yes, Mom, I'm sure I want to cook."

Her mother glanced at Stephen and rolled her eyes before starting the process of putting away the groceries.

Alex ignored the gesture, picked up a stack of books, and arranged them on the shelves beside the fireplace. It'd been over a month since her apartment had sustained heavy smoke and water damage in a fire. Living in a hotel had been challenging, but now she was moving and trying to get her life back in order.

Part of putting her life back together centered on filling the holes in her memory.

When she'd woken up in the hospital two days after the attack, two people had been at her side. She'd instantly known her mother, but the dark-haired vampire was a virtual stranger to her. It was as if he was someone she'd met long ago and could no longer recall his name.

She'd since learned he was Varik Baudelaire, Director for the FBPI's Special Operations unit. Her mother had tried to explain everything to her—that she and Varik had been engaged and were blood-bound to each other. While Alex did sense a connection to him, any memory of sharing a life with him was gone, burned away by Peter Strahan when he held her down and mind-raped her.

Pain exploded in her head and she dropped the books she was stacking. "Damn it," she muttered, massaging her temples.

"Come here." Stephen's gentle voice and hands guided her to a chair. "Sit."

Alex sucked in a breath and waited for the pain to pass. She couldn't predict when the false memories planted by Peter would resurface, but when they did, or if she thought of him, her head felt as though it were imploding.

Peter had wanted her to love him. As she sat doubled over in a chair, fighting back tears of pain, she felt only hate.

"Honey," her mother whispered and knelt beside the chair, wrapping her arms around Alex. "It'll pass. Everything's going to be okay."

"Is it?" Alex asked, a hard edge to her voice. "Half of my life is gone, taken by a fucking psychopath. How is that okay, Mom?"

"I mean the pain will pass."

"And if it doesn't? What then? What if I can't reverse what he did?" Another stabbing pain pierced her skull and she flinched, closing her eyes.

"Look at me." Emily cupped Alex's hot face in her cool hands, encouraging her daughter to look into her clear blue eyes. "You're going to get through this. Stephen, Janet, and I will help you. So will Varik."

Stephen snorted at the mention of Varik's name, and Alex pulled away from her mother. "What can Director Baudelaire do?" she asked. "I don't know him."

"But *he* knows *you*," her mother insisted. "He may be able to help you recover your memories."

"By poking around in my head!" Alex pushed to her feet and stalked to the opposite side of the room. "I don't want another stranger in my head, thank you very much."

"Varik isn't a stranger. He loves you."

"Yeah," Stephen chimed in. "He loves her so much he—"

"Stephen," her mother hissed in warning. "This isn't the time."

"Why not?" He gestured to Alex. "It's her life, her memory."

"She's been through a lot. She doesn't need to be reminded of certain events just yet."

"Yeah, great idea, Mom. I'm sure that will win her a lot of points with the Tribunal."

"*She* also doesn't want to be talked about as if *she* isn't in the fucking room," Alex snarled.

"Oh, honey, I didn't mean—"

"I think it would be best if you both left now. I'd like to be alone for a while."

Hurt swam in her mother's eyes, but after a moment, she nodded. "If you're sure that's what you want."

Alex crossed her arms in front of her, eyes downcast. "It is."

"I need to pick Janet up from class anyway," Stephen said. He and Emily quietly gathered their things, and Stephen gave her a quick peck on the cheek and ruffled her hair as he passed.

Her mother wrapped her in a tight embrace. "I love you," she whispered.

Alex didn't return the embrace but nodded her silent acknowledgment against her mother's shoulder.

They filed out of the apartment, and Alex closed the door, locked it, and slumped against it before sliding down to sit on the freshly installed carpet.

Outside, kids played in piles of fallen leaves. She listened to the sounds of life carrying on around her, lives untouched by violence and with promising futures. Fingering the scar she no longer remembered obtaining, she envied them.

Hot tears slipped over her cheeks and she wept until nothing remained of her envy but a cold, numbing hatred for Peter Strahan.

Varik held the ID card up to the electronic card reader. He'd stolen it from the same hospital orderly whose green scrubs he now wore. The system registered the valid card, issued a soft *beep*, and the doors to Jefferson Memorial Hospital's intensive care unit swung open.

He entered the unit and confidently strode toward the nurse's station. He slipped behind the empty desk and checked the chart detailing which beds were occupied and by whom. Peter Strahan was assigned to bed nine at the end farthest from the entrance.

Shift change gave him the best opportunity to carry out his plan. It'd been a simple matter of obtaining an ID card and scrubs. Once he had those, he had the freedom to wander the hospital at will. It never ceased to amaze him how few people questioned a stranger if they appeared as though they belonged in their surroundings. It was a fault he'd learned to exploit long ago.

As he left the nurse's desk, he heard laughter from the nearby employee lounge, followed by an off-key choir wishing some unfortunate recipient a happy birthday. The party wasn't something he'd planned, but it certainly worked in his favor. He reached Strahan's room and slipped inside.

Monitors beeped softly and steadily as Strahan lay sleeping. The dim glow of the monitors cast strange patterns on his skin and bedding.

Varik ignored it all, focused on the vampire. He glided to the bedside and paused, listening for approaching footsteps or changes in Strahan's breathing. When he heard neither, he carefully covered Strahan's mouth while simultaneously using his finger and thumb to pinch his nose closed, cutting off his air supply.

Peter woke, wide-eyed and panicked. He attempted to grab Varik's hand but his own were restrained, tied to the bed rails, a precaution taken to prevent him from biting any of the human staff.

Using his other hand, Varik pressed against the still-healing wound below Peter's breastbone. Strahan's muffled scream was silenced by Varik's fist striking his throat.

He released Peter's nose long enough for him to draw a breath and then pinched off the flow again. He leaned close, whispering, "Remember what I told you, you son of a bitch? That I would kill you?"

Pale yellow eyes shot heated daggers at Varik, but beneath it was an intense fear.

"I'm going to kill you now. Before I do, I want you to know that Alex is *mine*—always has been, always will be—and I will do everything in my power to eradicate every memory you planted in her head. She won't even remember your name."

Peter strained to draw a breath, his face turning a bright red.

Varik struck him again in the throat and felt the soft tissue collapse. He quickly slipped his hand beneath Peter's head, grabbed a handful of hair, and sharply twisted his head to the side. A wet popping *crunch* was the only sound as his neck broke. Monitors immediately flatlined and Varik switched them off.

He had moments before the staff returned to their stations and realized something had gone wrong. He hurried to the door and checked the corridor beyond. It was empty and he heard another peal of laughter from the lounge.

He exited the ICU without anyone stopping him. No one spared him more than a quick glance, too frightened to question the golden-eyed vampire, trailing the scent of new death behind him, as he disappeared into the night.

Tasha sat behind her desk, taking in the sight of the office she'd called her second home for six years.

Now it was going to someone else.

Her resignation had been an easy decision. While she wasn't giving up police work—she would remain on as a detective—she was giving up her title of liaison officer. Someone else could have the job. She'd seen enough death.

Kirk Beljean's attack had planted the seed of leaving in her mind. However, the sight of Mindy Johnson's nude body hanging from the rafters of Peter Strahan's attic had been the final act for her. She woke up at night in a cold sweat with visions of the girl reaching for her, demanding to know why she'd died. Tasha had no answers.

It was the lack of answers that drove her to resign. That combined with the years of stonewalling she'd received from the vamps. She didn't like who she was becoming by working with them so the best solution—the *only* solution—was to step aside.

She also wanted to have more time to devote to her fight against Caleb. Seeing the grief the Johnsons experienced over losing their only child made her want to do whatever she could to keep Maya in her life.

She sighed and opened the final drawer she needed to clean out. Among the half-devoured rolls of antacids, energy bars, and unopened bags of herbal tea lay a simple brown paper bag.

Tasha frowned as she picked it up and was surprised by its weight. She opened the bag and gasped as it slipped from her hands to land in the drawer. It tipped on its side, partially spilling its contents.

Two bound ten-thousand-dollar bricks of cash peeked out from the bag's opening, along with a handwritten note.

With a trembling hand, she picked up the note and read:

THANK YOU FOR YOUR COOPERATION, LIEUTENANT. PAYMENT FOR YOUR RECENT SERVICES. WE'LL BE IN TOUCH.

Tasha stared at the money, her thoughts racing. If she accepted it, she could afford to hire a lawyer to fight Caleb, and she *might* even stand a chance of winning. It meant she could be the mother she wanted to be to Maya—to be the mother *she* never had.

It also meant that she was someone else's fucking pawn and nothing would change it.

She shoved the note and money into the bag and tucked it into her box of personal effects. If it kept her from losing her daughter, then she would play the part of a pawn.

Alex peered through the fish-eyed peephole in the front door and saw Director Baudelaire's distorted face. She swiped at the tears lingering on her cheeks, drew a deep breath in a futile attempt to calm her suddenly racing pulse, and opened the door.

The smile that had started on his face vanished when he saw her. "You've been crying. What's wrong?"

"It's nothing. I was—" Her words caught in her throat. "Is there something you wanted, Director?"

His spine stiffened at the use of his formal title. "I wanted to see you—to see if you needed anything."

Alex shook her head, avoided looking at him, and picked at a spot of peeling paint on the doorjamb.

"Right," he whispered, shuffling his feet. "Well, if there *is* anything I can do, let me know." He raked a hand through his hair and backed away. "I should probably go."

As he turned, sunlight flashed off the badge at his hip, bringing with it a half-formed memory: a glittering pink-diamond ring on a silver chain. Loss washed over her and fresh tears followed the tracks left by their kin.

Strong arms swept her into an embrace. "I'm here, baby," he whispered. A scent of sandalwood and cinnamon enveloped her. "I'm here."

Alex clung to a man she had no memory of, and for the first time since she'd learned of the Tribunal's inquiry or heard the name Peter Strahan, she felt completely safe.

She hoped the feeling would last.

epilogue

PETER STOOD BEFORE THE DOOR LEADING TO THE HALL of Records. Varik Baudelaire had no idea what kind of monster he'd unleashed when he killed Peter.

He grinned. He would make Baudelaire pay for what he'd done, and he would pay dearly.

He turned the knob to open the door but it didn't move. Confused, he tried turning it the other way but met with the same result. "What the fuck is going on here?"

"Hello, Peter."

He whirled around to find Bernard Sabian standing a few yards away with his hands in the pockets of his dark suit. "What did you do, old man?"

"Having trouble with the door?"

Peter pounded on the door. "What did you do!"

Bernard shrugged. "I didn't do anything. When you died—"

"I was murdered, old man! Don't play games with me!"

"Fair enough. When Varik rightly killed your pathetic ass," Bernard sneered, "all that stored soul energy you used to boost your abilities went *poof*."

Cold realization began to sink into Peter's mind.

"The magic you used to create all those dolls, so long as they remained intact, required a beating heart to contain them, and yours doesn't anymore."

A wind kicked up, whipping around them and carrying the wail of a thousand souls.

Peter scanned the horizon for its source until he spotted the dark roiling mass heading toward them.

"And here they come now," Bernard said. "I'd start running if I were you."

Peter spun and fled, running across the field as fast as his legs would carry him.

The roiling mass gained on him. The shrieks and screams of all the souls he'd trapped spurred his flight.

The mass overtook him and he felt hands grabbing at him. He cried for them to stop, begged them to release him.

The once-trapped souls lifted him from the ground, tossed him about, ripping and tearing his flesh from the bone, and Peter knew his screams would continue as they tormented him.

Forever.